Love Can Be Murder

Praise for *Headaches Can Be Murder*

"A fast-paced mystery/thriller with an innovative plot that will keep readers guessing until the exciting climax."
Christopher Valen, award winning author of *Bad Weeds Never Die*

"For their debut, the writing duo of Rausch and Donlon deliver an interesting story within a story that flirts with high tech science in a small town."
Julie Kramer, author of the highly-awarded Riley Spartz series

Comments from readers of *Headaches Can Be Murder*, the first book in the Can Be Murder Series:

"A roller coaster ride with some murders, some romance, some mystery, some heartache and lots of humor throughout.
Loved it!"

"A great read . . . funny, clever and oh so entertaining."

A romp that leads from intense to bucolic and back again."

"Definitely a must read by two sharp up-and-coming authors."

"The two story structure is fresh and beautifully done."

"I can't wait for the sequel."

Love Can Be Murder

Marilyn Rausch
and
Mary Donlon

North Star Press of St. Cloud, Inc.
Saint Cloud, Minnesota

Dedication

For my dad, who told the best stories, and for my mom, who taught me to cherish my family and friends. MJD

For my children, Edward and Ela, who keep me grounded and make me very proud. MJR

First Edition, June 2013

Printed in the United States of America

Published by
North Star Press of St. Cloud, Inc.
P.O. Box 451
St. Cloud, Minnesota 56302

www.northstarpress.com   Facebook - North Star Press   Twitter - North Star Press

Acknowledgements

Once again, we'd like to sing the praises of our two amazing writers groups, who offered terrific guidance and cheered us along the way. We send our thanks to Kathy, Lesley, Linda, Nico, Deb, Jane and Maureen.

Our sincere appreciation goes to our editor, Cathy Pate, who jumped into the fray just when we needed the her most.

Our gratitude goes out to the Bureau of Criminal Apprehension for taking us on a fascinating tour, along with a special thanks to Eldon, who so patiently answered all our weapons questions.

To our fearless leaders at North Star Press, thanks for making our bucket-list wishes come true!

And, last but not least, we want to send our love to all our family and friends who have made this journey such a joy. Thank you from the bottom of our hearts.

"They say it's the number of people I killed. I say it's the principle."
-Aileen Wuornos, Florida killer executed in 2002

"She isn't missing. She's at the farm right now."
-Edward Gein, Wisconsin murderer and body snatcher

CHAPTER ONE

Turners Bend, Iowa
Population 932
Mid-July

So, Chip, I hear Jane turned you down. Sorry, pal."

Chip Collingsworth removed his wire-rimmed glasses and rubbed his eyes with the palms of his hands. His head began to throb at the temples, and his stomach churned. "Who told you, Iver? I hope for our sake not too many people know."

"Too late. You've been in Turners Bend for almost a year now. You should know better. Oh, there may be a few bachelor farmers who haven't heard yet, but they'll know after the VFW fish fry on Friday night. But don't worry, the people in this town won't spread it around or make you or Jane uncomfortable."

Chip was astounded at the irony of Iver's comment. Apparently there was no one left in town *to tell*. The whole town now knew that he had proposed to Jane Swanson, the town's veterinarian, on the Fourth of July, and she'd said "No." In addition to saying "No" she said, "I can't marry you or anyone else right now. I hope we can just be friends. Your past, my past, my children. They're all problematic. I need time." Chip knew the cruelest words in a relationship were "just friends." It was a blow to his ego and an arrow to his lovesick heart. No woman had refused his proposal before, and he'd been married and divorced three times. He had a perfect proposal record, although admittedly, a poor marriage record. *Does the whole town know that, too?*

He thought he had left that all behind in Baltimore, but now he wasn't sure. Last year he had wiped his slate clean and started a new life in Iowa. A life completely and utterly unlike his former existence. But vestiges of it kept rearing their ugly heads like the stupid arcade game, Whac-A-Mole, where you bop a mole on the head and it pops up in another hole.

He and Iver sat in silence at the counter of the Bun, Turners Bend's café extraordinaire, the home of Iowa's best and biggest cinnamon rolls. Their rear ends warmed the red Naugahyde-covered stools that had been softened by the behinds of thousands of patrons . . . town folks who had sipped coffee and eaten homemade pie at the counter since the early 1950s.

Iver was Turners Bend's Incredible Hulk, a man of tremendous proportions. "Burly" was the best word Chip could think of to describe Iver. He was gentle and unassuming, and above all, generous beyond words. Not only would he give you the shirt off his back; he might give you three million dollars, as he had done recently to bail out the town's largest industry—a wind turbine company now named after him. Chip had learned you can't judge a book by the blurbs on the cover, and it was just as true when it came to Iver Ingebretson.

At five-ten and 190 pounds, Chip felt like a featherweight contender next to Iver. When he first met him, Chip was intimidated by Iver's size alone. Now, much to Chip's amazement, they were best buds. Sometimes it amused him to imagine Iver in his own past life— Iver at his exclusive prep school, Iver clubbing with him in New York, Iver sailing on the Chesapeake with his father, a noted neurosurgeon.

Bernice put two white mugs down on the counter and filled them with strong, black coffee. It was the kind of coffee that left dark sludge at the bottom of the cup, a brew many patrons doctored with lots of cream and sugar. No trendy coffee drinks, no artificial sweeteners, no non-dairy creamer in little disposable cups at the Bun, "Only the real stuff," according to Bernice, the Bun's only waitress.

Pinned to Bernice's uniform was a button that read: BEST BUNS IN IOWA. "What will it be this morning, boys?" she asked as she ran a well-worn rag over the gray Formica counter in front of them. Bernice never wrote down an order. She usually knew what her customers wanted, sometimes before they opened their mouth.

"Just a cinnamon roll for me, Bernice."

"Sorry, we're out of rolls, Chip. You know Thursdays are BOGO days. When customers buy one and get one free, we sell out by 8:30 in the morning. By the way, what did you do with the ring?"

So much for being discreet and not making me uncomfortable.

"I'd rather not discuss it, Bernice. Just give me an order of wheat toast."

"Well, if you ask me, I'd hang on to that ring. Jane will come around. You two are a match made in heaven . . . just like Romeo and Juliet."

Chip was fairly confident Bernice and Shakespeare were not well-acquainted, but nonetheless, it further dampened his spirits. He was a successful crime writer, but a failure at love. And a writer is only as good as his next novel, or so said Lucinda Patterson, his literary agent. Book three of his Dr. John Goodman series was not going well. To be truthful, it wasn't going at all. Writer's block had taken up residence in his head.

Soon Lucinda would start her relentless pressure tactics. He had struggled to finish book two, *Brain Freeze*, and missed his deadline. Then Lucinda turned around and put a tighter timetable on *Mind Games*. The woman would be waterboarding him soon if he didn't produce the first chapter or two. To say his agent was aggressive and pushy was an understatement. She was attractive and classy. Her designer clothes reeked of sophistication and success. But, deep down she was a clawing hellcat, and he had wounds to prove it. Yet, he couldn't deny a great deal of his success was due to Lucinda.

From the corner of his eye he saw Flora Fredrickson, city clerk and wife of the police chief, move across the café with her coffee mug in hand. Winding her way among the tables, her ample hips bumped into chairs and her black knit pants were stretched to the max. She plopped on the stool next to Chip and placed her pudgy hand with hot pink, lacquered fingernails on his arm. He braced himself.

"You rushed it, dear. After I worked so hard on my matchmaking, too. Fools rush, I suppose. Your track record isn't stellar, of course, but not to worry; Flora will work her magic again. It will just take more time. Flowers are in order, don't you think?" she said, as she patted his arm.

To divert Flora's babbling, Chip ignored her question and brought up her favorite topic—politics. "What do you think about the two women candidates for president, Flora?"

"I tell you, it just fries my bacon! We finally have women candidates for president and they turn out to be idiots. It's a fact that women are a hell of a lot smarter than men. There are more women than men in this country, and we would be much better off if one of them was president . . . except not one of those morons."

"You know what I think you should do, Flora? You should run for Congress," Iver piped in.

"Well, I very well might do just that. I think I would make a very good congresswoman. I'm a lot like Hillary, and we all know what a smart cookie she is."

"On second thought, I don't know. What with all those extra-marital affairs going on, like in the legislature up in Minnesota, you might get yourself into a pickle," Iver said.

He began to laugh and Flora punched him in the arm, which only made him laugh harder. She turned her attention back to Chip.

"You need a haircut . . . you're looking a little shaggy. Now as I was saying about Jane . . ."

"I know you're well-meaning, Flora, but Jane apparently needs some time and space. Plus, I'm preoccupied right now. The movie version of *The Cranium Killer*, my first book, premieres next spring and the publication date for *Brain Freeze* is this December. So I've got a lot on my plate."

"Well, far be it from me to meddle," Flora said as she slid off the stool and sashayed back to her table of cronies, which included several local business owners and her husband, Police Chief Walter Frederickson.

Iver chuckled. "I've never known a woman to meddle more than Flora Fredrickson. My Mabel would never do that, although she did say something about inviting that 'poor boy' to dinner along with Jane," he said with a sly smile on this face.

Chip stared into the glass pie case as Bernice loaded the day's special, strawberry rhubarb. The mirror behind the counter reflected the café's tables and booths. He studied the morning's clientele.

"Out front I saw lots of pick-ups with mounted shotguns and dogs. Those guys look like hunters," said Chip, nodding to a table of men wearing hunting caps and khaki shirts with patches on the pocket. "What season is it?" he asked Iver.

"I take it you're not a hunter. Can't hunt anything in July. Water fowl season doesn't start until the end of September. Those guys are on their way to the Outdoorsman Hunting Club in Webb. Probably going there to work with their retrievers." Iver lifted his cup and signaled Bernice for a refill.

"Maybe what you need, Chip, is a hobby to take your mind off Jane. That Runt of yours is a born retriever. You could whistle-train him. He'd make a fine bird dog."

"Not sure hunting is for me. Although, I must admit Runt could use some obedience training. You have a hobby, Iver?"

"Well, I guess you could say my collection of Escher lithographs is a hobby."

"You never cease to amaze me," said Chip shaking his head. "You collect Escher prints?"

"Yup, got a few. Only they're not prints, they're originals."

Just when Chip thought he had Iver figured out, the guy would hit him with a stun gun. Escher originals no less. *I'd like to own a few, even one.*

Iver drained his cup and put some change on the counter. "Well, I better get to my road maintenance duties. Some fool teenager took out the stop sign on County Road 25. Second time I've had to replace it this summer. See you around, Chip."

Chip's toast arrived and he took a few bites. He looked at his hair in the mirror behind the counter. He didn't mind the curls on the back of his neck. What he was less pleased about were the gray hairs which had started to crop up among the dark blond.

Between Jane's rejection and the mounting pressure to write, he had lost his appetite. He finished his coffee, and headed home to his yellow farmhouse. It was the only yellow farmhouse in Boone County, and his color choice had sparked lots of comments around town. He didn't care. Every time he drove up to his house, it made him smile.

As he sped along the gravel road, a cloud of dust swirled behind his Volvo. So far July had been hot and dry, much to the corn farmers' liking. He opened the sunroof and windows and stuck his elbow out the side. He was ready for the wave that seemed to be the peculiar custom along this stretch. When passing a vehicle or a person on the road or at their mailbox, a wave was considered good manners. There were several wave styles. He especially enjoyed the finger wave . . . just one finger lifted off of the steering wheel—it made him feel like a true Iowan. He stared at the cloudless, china-blue sky and watched a solitary hawk swoop and soar like a glider plane. It dove into a field after its prey . . . both majestic and savage at the same time.

Chip's dark mood suddenly returned, and he began to percolate and brew evil thoughts about the fate of his hero, Dr. John Goodman. He was sick of the hero in his crime novels, and sick of John's perfect life as a famous neurosurgeon and crime solver. He had grown to hate John's handsome face and six-pack abs, and he was envious of his romance with Jo, the fetching FBI agent.

* * *

July 25, 10:30 a.m.
Lucinda,
Working away on Mind Games. Thinking of ending this trilogy with having John murdered. First chapter to follow soon.
Chip

July 25, 10:32 a.m.
ARE YOU NUTS?! You cannot kill off the hero. That would be like John Sandford offing Lucas Davenport or William Kent Krueger fatally wounding Cork O'Connor. He's your money ticket. You can put him in danger or even maim him, but he must survive for more novels to come. Get your head on straight and send me a copy. SOON.
Lucinda

Chip read Lucinda's reply, which was as acerbic as usual, and then sat down at his computer determined to make Dr. John Goodman suffer as much as he himself was suffering. Living vicariously through his alter ego was not working for him anymore. He re-read the epilogue of *Brain Freeze* and got an idea of where he could begin. His conversation with Iver about hunting popped into his head as he wrote the opening scene of the novel he had entitled *Mind Games*.

CHAPTER TWO

Mind Games, by Charles Edward Collingsworth III
East Central, Minnesota
Late July

T HIS WAS HIS FAVORITE PART OF HUNTING. The pre-dawn anticipation. Perfect stillness, completely unobserved by his prey. Attuned to every nuance of movement.

He had already scoped out the location, watching for behavioral patterns. It took him less than a week to figure out the habits of his prey. Enough preparation to come closer and blend in. Patiently waiting in the small copse of trees on the edge of the clearing, he emptied his head of all things but his intended target.

A light, welcome breeze lifted the hair that peeked out from his dark green baseball hat. It was already humid, although the sun had yet to make its appearance. Minnesota was in the middle of a heat wave, with temperatures averaging in the upper nineties for the past week. The Hunter removed his hat to wipe the band of sweat which had gathered on his forehead and pulled his shirt away from his body. Cupping his hand around the face of his watch, he shielded the glow. 5:15 a.m. *Not much longer.* He felt calm and in control.

No movement around the perimeter.

He had concluded his reconnaissance yesterday. It was a good feeling—a job well done. There was no better feeling than the one right before the kill.

No hurry, though. The hunt was to be savored. His mother used to say that life was about the journey, not the destination. His lips curled up into a smile. *What would Ma say if she could see my journey now?*

It had been an ebony night, with heavy clouds obscuring the thin slice of moon overhead. Darkness had always been his friend, but now the light outside had turned to a gray-blue hue and he was beginning to make out more distinct shapes through the trees. He raised his rifle, and peered down the sights, looking for any sign of his prey. Still too early.

A crow cawed behind him and he heard the distant buzz of a car on the road. He lowered his rifle and crouched down. It was still dark enough to obscure his movements, but he was taking no chances. He was a careful man.

7

As he pushed aside a small branch to have a better view, it snapped back and grazed his cheek. He let out a quiet curse, and reached up to touch the scrape. He pulled his finger away with a stripe of blood smeared across it. He licked it off with the tip of his tongue, savoring the saltiness.

Out of the corner of his eye, he detected a flash of color. He raised his gun once again and searched the trail. His heart pounded in his chest. *There!* He removed the safety and peered down the scope. The rising sun blazed on its head, reflecting strands of copper. His target was moving rapidly toward him. He took a deep breath and released it slowly as he began to squeeze the trigger.

Agent Jo Schwann looked beautiful in his crosshairs.

CHAPTER THREE

Turners Bend
August

C HIP BOUGHT A DOG WHISTLE and the book, *How to Train Your Retriever*. He quickly learned that he would not be able to break Honey, his golden retriever, and Runt, her son, from their bad habits of sleeping on the furniture and begging at the table. Runt, however, loved the whistle-training sessions with his master. He raced to the side yard whenever he saw the whistle in Chip's hand. In no time he learned to come, sit, heel, stay and retrieve. Honey found a spot in the shade of the red maple and watched like a soccer mom in the bleachers. The training sessions were not only diversions for Chip, but also his excuse for slacking off on his real work . . . writing *Mind Games*.

Chip was putting Runt through his paces when he heard the rumble of a pickup in the distance. Soon he saw Jane's rusty red truck turn off the main road and head down the long drive to his farmhouse. Their "friendship" had been somewhat tense and awkward the past month. Chip cautioned himself not to be too hopeful as he watched the truck come to a stop by the shed.

He was disappointed to see it was not Jane, but her son, Sven, who jumped out of the cab and strode toward him and the dogs. During the past year Chip had seen Sven mature from a gawky, misdirected teenager into a self-confident young man. He was tall and lanky and wore his reddish brown hair styled like the pop singer whose name always escaped Chip. His jeans were tight and his muscle shirt revealed a few chest hairs. Chip liked the boy, and Sven had seemed to grow closer to him since the absence of the boy's father.

"Hey Chip. I'm just stoppin' in to say 'bye' before mom takes me up to Minneapolis for orientation week at MCAD."

"I've heard good things about the Minneapolis College of Art and Design. I'm sure you'll do well. You have time for a Coke?"

"Sure." Sven sat on the back steps waiting for Chip, who entered the house and returned with two cans.

"What about your friend Leif? What's he up to?" asked Chip.

"He dropped out of school the month before graduation, and I haven't seen much of him this summer. We've been friends for so long, but it's hard to hang on to friends who are going down a different path."

"I, for one, am happy about the path you've chosen. You're going to do great things, make great films. I just know it."

"Thanks, Chip. I won't forget how much you've helped me." Sven took a sip from his pop can, as he watched the dogs. "Hey, looks like Runt's turning into a fine bird dog. Dad and I would've loved a dog like him for duck hunting. We had old Archie, but he died before I got my first shotgun."

The two sat, drinking their Cokes and watching Runt nose around the yard. A wasp buzzed around Chip's can, and he shooed it away. The heat of the sun made their cans sweat. Sven finished his pop and crushed the can with one hand. He tossed it into a nearby garbage bin and said, "No rim . . . two points," pumping his arm.

Chip debated whether or not to broach the issue of Sven's missing father and Jane's ex-husband, Hal Swanson, who had skipped the country with several federal agencies on his trail. Since Sven had brought up the subject, he decided the time might be right. "I'm sorry about your father, Sven. It must be hard for you. Have you heard from him?"

Sven stared off into the distance, taking a few moments to respond. "No. I know he's done some bad things, but that doesn't mean that I don't miss him. Ingrid and Mom refuse to talk about him. Why did he do it, Chip?"

"Honestly, I don't know. Sometimes it's just a slippery slope. One thing leads to another. And, his drinking probably clouded his judgment."

"I didn't tell Mom or Ingrid this, but two undercover DEA agents came to the house right after the Fourth of July and questioned me about Dad. They asked if I knew where he was and if I knew anything about drug money. I told them I didn't know anything and didn't believe Dad was involved in buying or selling drugs. They kind of creeped me out. They were dressed like migrant workers, but I could tell they were packing heat."

Chip chuckled and shook his head. "Packing heat . . . I think you have been watching too many TV crime shows."

"Or reading too many crime novels." They both laughed.

"The FBI said several federal agencies would be involved, so I wouldn't worry about it," said Chip. "In fact, I remember those two guys and wondered who they were. Undercover DEA agents, huh? I never would have guessed."

Sven hesitated, and then said, "I'm sort of worried about Mom. Don't mean to pry, but what's with you two? I thought you had like a romance going on."

"So did I, but maybe she just needs some time to work through things. I don't have the best track record with women. Piece of advice for you . . . stay away from those pretty girls at MCAD."

Sven laughed. "That's one piece of advice I probably won't follow." He reached into his back pocket. "Oh, I brought something to show you. I found it this summer when I was working with the Historical Society on that documentary."

Sven pulled an old, sepia-colored photograph from his jeans pocket and handed it to Chip. "Seems Turners Bend had a theater for movies and stage shows back in the 1930s. It was named the Bijou. It was in the empty building next to Harriet's House of Hair. Sylvia Johnson told me she remembers it from when she was a girl, and that it was a grand place with gilt fixtures and a crystal chandelier and red velvet curtains. She said the owner died some years ago, and she heard the marquee that was taken down is stored inside."

Sven returned the photo to his pocket. "Wouldn't it be cool if it was restored and *The Cranium Killer* movie was shown at its grand re-opening? Maybe the director or some of the stars would even come to town. If I weren't going off to school, I'd get the town to do it."

Chip could sense the boy's excitement, and it was catching. "That's a great idea. Maybe I can help."

Just then Runt began to bark and chase something across the yard. He stopped at the woodpile and stuck his nose between the logs. Sven ran to the pile and pulled a baby kitten out of the gap.

Chip grabbed his whistle and blew the commands for 'sit' and 'stay' and Runt complied. Sven returned to the steps with the kitten clinging to his shirt by its claws. "Aaw, look at her, Chip. She can't be more than six weeks old."

"How do you know it's a female and how old she is?"

11

"First of all, she's a calico. See the three colors, white, black and orange? All calicos are females. Second, you're forgetting that my grandfather was a vet and my mother is a vet. I've been around animals my whole life. She's pretty scrawny and matted. I bet she's really hungry. We better feed her. Here, hold her. It looks like you have another pet."

Chip held the kitten in his lap. She began to purr and knead his legs, her sharp claws snagging his shorts. When she began to lick his hand with her sandpaper tongue, he had the sinking feeling he would be adding to his household menagerie. "But, I don't know anything about cats," he said.

"No problem, you know a good vet who can teach you." Sven's face lit up with a wide grin. He stood, unfolding his long limbs and waved at Chip as he ambled to the pick-up. He backed down the road too fast and gunned the motor as he sped away, spewing gravel from the rear tires.

Both dogs came to sniff at their new housemate. "Meet your new friend. What should I name her? How about Callie, since she's a calico?"

He and his pets went into the kitchen, and Chip dialed the animal clinic. "Mabel, this is Chip. I need to know what to feed a kitten, and I guess I better schedule an appointment to have her checked over by Jane."

He was happier than he'd been for weeks. His emotional state influenced his motivation to write. Happiness made him feel good about his new story, and he was eager to continue to build suspense by putting Jo in peril. He recalled a brief time in his past when he had tried to be a runner, mainly to impress a woman who was a fitness freak. Certainly an FBI agent would have to be fit . . . Jo would be a disciplined runner, he thought, as he opened his laptop.

CHAPTER FOUR

Mind Games
Minneapolis, Minnesota
Late July

SPECIAL AGENT JO SCHWANN FELT the exhaustion fall away as her feet pounded out a cadence on the asphalt of the Minnehaha Trail. For once, she didn't pay attention to the elegant homes lining the parkway—her thoughts were elsewhere.

She had run two miles before she realized she hadn't turned on her running playlist on the smartphone strapped to her upper arm. She smiled wryly to herself. It was a good thing the endorphins released in her brain were relieving some of the stress.

It was 3:00 a.m. before Jo had climbed into bed last night. She had been finishing up paperwork and getting everything in order for her staff before leaving on a long weekend away.

But I still have to deal with those damn depositions this morning before I can hop on the plane. Candleworth's widow had filed a wrongful death lawsuit against Jo and the Bureau. Her husband had created a multi-billion dollar corporation around mind-controlling microchips, and she blamed them when one of his employees shot him.

Jo felt the muscles in her neck bunch up again, so she lengthened her stride as she passed the bronze statue of a bunny near Portland Avenue. Normally, she took a water break at the whimsical statue of the reclining rabbit, but today she had no time.

The case had been officially closed for months now, and Jo felt like she was still treading water in a lake of red tape and Bureau CYA memos. Not to mention meeting after meeting with the lawyers. *All due to this bullshit lawsuit.*

And, of course, there was the last test subject. His disappearance nagged at her. Almost everyone at the Bureau, including her boss, assumed he was dead, like all the other NeuroDynamics victims. She shook her head. She couldn't let it go until they found the body.

Jo blew out a puff of air. At least she met John on the case. Dr. John Goodman, the FBI expert called in to assist had not only broken the case wide open, but he had saved her life.

And she had fallen in love with him.

Maybe we'll wrap up the depositions early and I can swing by the Victoria's Secret store in Mall of America on my way to the airport. Jo smiled at the thought of John's expression when he saw her in something new and barely there.

Just then, the smartphone buzzed on her arm. She came to an abrupt stop, and pulled it from the armband.

"Special Agent Schwann."

"Jo, where are you? Sounds like you're out of breath." It was the rich baritone of her boss, Tom Gunderson.

"Just on my way back to the house. What's up?" Jo tried to make her voice sound normal. "Never a good sign when you call me before I make it into the office."

"Yeah, well. I hate to do this to you, but . . ."

Jo's heart thudded harder, as if she was still running down the path. "Oh, no, don't tell me. Tom, I've been planning this trip for weeks. You get to have a wife and kids. At least let me have a boyfriend."

She heard him sigh across the miles. "Can't help it this time, Schwann. I need you on this one. I'm assuming you heard State Representative Freemont was missing."

"He's the one running for governor, right?" Jo paused, and then said, "Wait, did you say 'was missing'? Does that mean they found him?"

"Uh-huh. Just received a call a few minutes ago. He's dead, Jo."

Jo felt the bands of tension strapping themselves across her shoulders again. "What was the cause of death?"

"Single gunshot to the head. A construction worker found him in one of the wings of the Capitol undergoing renovation."

"Any idea how long he's been there?" Jo asked, as she wiped a trickle of sweat from her temple with the back of her hand.

"Medical examiner's trying to figure that out right now, but it could have been as early as Tuesday afternoon, the last time he was seen alive. Body wasn't discovered until this morning, because the construction crew has been on strike for the past two weeks. "

"Shit." She blew out a breath and wondered how she was going to cancel on John again.

"Yeah. You could say that. I need you to head over to the Capitol right away."

"Tom, what about the NeuroDynamics depositions?"

"I'll reschedule for you. Just get your butt over to St. Paul."

Jo clicked off the call and strapped the phone to her arm once again. She took off running down the trail, endorphins no longer helping her mood.

She was about a mile from home when Jo felt a sudden pain in her side. She didn't realize how agitated she had become until she developed a side-stitch from the irregular rhythm of her breathing. She stopped, and raised her right arm high above her head, inhaling deeply to relieve the ache.

"Damn it." She walked around in a circle, impatient to be on her way again. "There are times when I'm ready to chuck this whole job into Lake Calhoun." She spoke to no one in particular. "John, don't give up on me." She decided to call him on the way to St. Paul. She wasn't looking forward to breaking the news to him.

When the pain eased a fraction, she caught a flicker of movement in the grouping of trees to her far left, close to the creek. Rubbing the back of her neck where she felt the hair rise, she shook her head. Probably some squirrel jumping in the branches. *God, I'm getting paranoid. Too much wool-gathering in dark corners.* She broke into a run again, concentrating on her breathing.

* * *

THE HUNTER RELEASED PRESSURE on the trigger when Jo looked his way. He couldn't say what kept him from shooting her. Shock, perhaps. He had been picturing this exact moment in his head for months and now he had blown the perfect opportunity.

He almost fell backwards when he felt her eyes upon him as she ran past his hiding spot. He ducked down, but not before he realized she had stared right into his soul. That is, what was left of it.

She hadn't really seen him. He was sure of it. The Hunter had studied her long enough to know she would have marched right over to where he stood to investigate if she had detected him there.

His hands that brought the rifle upward again were slick with sweat. He watched her run toward her home through his scope, her copper-colored ponytail bouncing in time with her steps. He watched her shapely ass move in her tight running pants and felt himself growing aroused. *I could still shoot her. Even from this distance, I wouldn't miss.*

15

But he wouldn't do it. Not now.

She fascinated him. In the beginning, it was all about revenge. And relieving the rage. She and Goodman were responsible for the death of Dr. Candleworth, the genius who had saved him from a lifetime of unbearable pain. As if that weren't enough, the doctor had also provided him with a lucrative new career, one that suited his particular skill sets.

The anger and sorrow that had overwhelmed him when he learned of Candleworth's death had been replaced by a cold, weighty resolve. Which is why he now found himself standing in a small stand of trees, twenty yards from a running path in south Minneapolis.

He had never stopped at this critical juncture of a kill before. Murder didn't bother him; it was just a job.

Maybe that was the problem. This wasn't an assignment. It was personal. It was about to get too personal. For the first time in his life, he was in love.

He shivered in spite of the trickle of sweat that rolled down his back.

CHAPTER FIVE

Turners Bend
September

CHIP READ THE CHAPTER he had just finished. He wrote organically and was still amazed at the source of his ideas, the events from his life that tended to pop up in his stories. The political conversation with Flora Frederickson had obviously influenced his victim choice. And Jo's conflicted feelings about her relationship with John…that part was so close to his real life that he did not want to think about it.

He saved his file, emailed it to Lucinda and shut down his laptop for the day.

* * *

A NEW KITTEN WAS A GOOD EXCUSE to see Jane. As Chip entered the clinic he saw Jane standing at Mabel's desk. He grinned at her. *God, that woman is more attractive every time I see her.* Today her red hair was tied into a ponytail at the back of her neck, and she was wearing blue scrubs which hid her small frame. No make-up, no jewelry, and yet she was stunning. How could a guy not fall hopelessly in love with such a creature?

"Ah, I see you two have bonded already. Bring her in, Chip."

Jane examined Callie by checking her ears for mites and slipping a thermometer into her bottom to take her temperature.

"Today we'll start her immunizations, and I'm sending home an antibiotic to treat her ear mites. You can bring her back to be spayed in six weeks. Don't make the mistake you made with Honey. You were lucky to be able to find homes for all those puppies, but responsible pet owners should spay or neuter their animals. I recommend you make her an indoor-only cat. There are too many wild animals around your place for her safety."

She handed the kitten back to Chip. "How is she getting along with the dogs?"

"Callie can hold her own. Both dogs have scratches on their noses. She has already staked out her territory. I think we all can co-exist peacefully."

Damn. Jane was using her professional persona with him, when all he wanted to do was pull her into his arms and cover her with kisses. If this was going to be the new normal for them, he was going to be one very frustrated, unhappy guy.

Jane's demeanor began to change as she watched Chip cuddle Callie and stroke the kitten's back. "What's with you and stray animals? They seem to find their way to your door, and you fall head-over-heels for them."

"You know, I never cared one way or the other about animals until I came to Turners Bend. It's one of the things I've learned about myself in the past year, among other things."

The admission seemed to make Jane soften a little. She moved in to pet Callie, and Chip gave her a brief kiss. He stepped back, sighed audibly and waited for his heart rate to settle. The expression on Jane's face was puzzling. Was it pleasure or indecision? He waited for a response, but a response never came. He changed the subject quickly. "Will I see you tonight at the kick-off meeting?"

"Yes, after all it was my son's idea. I got a text from Sven today. He's so excited that you're pursuing the theater renovation. I know he would be here if his class schedule didn't have to come first. You helped him with his film career and now this. It seems I am always indebted to you for making my child's dreams come true. I hope you know that."

* * *

CHIP'S MOOD TOOK A 180-degree turn. He was buoyed by his hopes of rekindling his affair with Jane, and he was excited about the theater renovation. He loved his life in Turners Bend—he owned a farmhouse and three pets. *Life is good.*

He had caught Sven's enthusiasm for the Bijou and took it upon himself to spearhead a committee to bring it back to life. He had been in Turners Bend long enough to identify who had the money, who had the influence, who had the energy and who had the passion for such a project. They had all agreed to meet at First Lutheran that night. He had put up posters around town with an invitation to all parties interested, and the *Ames Tribune* had run a notice in the Arts section of the Sunday paper hinting at a possible Hollywood premiere.

He researched theater restorations and found that many Iowa towns had restored their old movie houses. He contacted the citizen group responsible for restoring the Castle Theatre in Manchester. Its chairman cautioned him by saying, "It will take a lot more time and money than you think, but it's worth it. We love our theater, and it's been a good money-maker to boot."

Pastor Henderson's wife, Christine, made coffee and lemon bars for the meeting. Chip had been raised a Christmas-and-Easter Episcopalian. He was just starting to catch on to Lutheran traditions, one of which was, for any and all occasions, coffee and bars are just one step below wine and bread in sacredness.

Chip arranged the fellowship hall chairs in a circle and put up an easel to display the old photos, newspaper articles, and playbills he had found at the Historical Society. He also posted photos of the restorations done in Harlan, Vinton and Marshalltown, as well as before and after pictures of the Castle.

Chip did not recognize the first person to arrive. He was a tall, good-looking guy in his late thirties or early forties by Chip's estimation. He was dressed in jeans, a t-shirt and work boots, but something about his too-perfect haircut and the way he carried himself did not fit with Turners Bend.

"Hello, I'm Lance Williams." His handshake was firm and his gaze direct. He smiled and revealed a set of perfect teeth—straight, white, and gleaming. "I'm new in Turners Bend. I just bought Oscar Nelson's place to try my hand at organic vegetable farming. I'm interested in your project. I was an architect in my not-too-distant former life."

"Welcome, Lance, I'm glad to meet you and equally glad I'm not the 'new guy' in town anymore. An architect no less, what a stroke of good luck for us."

Jane joined them and Chip introduced her to Lance. "We don't get many new residents in Turners Bend," said Jane. "I heard someone bought Oscar's place. Welcome, Lance."

Jane pointed out two men coming in the door. "Chip, it looks like we are drawing quite a crowd. There's Hjalmer Gustafson, bless his heart, and there's Ingrid's basketball coach, Stan Whittler. He usually doesn't get involved in community events."

Chip watched Gustafson, one of his favorite farmers, and Whittler, a tall, thin man dressed in a warm-up suit, seat themselves at the back of the room.

The room filled up, the ideas took form, and the energy of the small group grew. Fundraisers were proposed. "Let's do an old-fashioned cake walk," offered Christine. "Maybe with an old movie theme. I could bake a *Top Hat* cake with Fred and Ginger dancing on top."

"The VFW could host a casino night," suggested the president of the local wind turbine company. "Each table could be sponsored by a different local business."

Flora's t-shirt idea got a good laugh. She offered to have them printed with the words BIJOU or BUST strategically placed on the front. A work schedule was developed and a volunteer list passed around.

After the meeting was adjourned, Jane stayed to help Christine clean the kitchen, while Chip put away the chairs and easel.

Chip felt like he was on a winning streak. Maybe tonight was the night to move back to his previous relationship with Jane, the one where they were madly in love and couldn't keep their hands off each other. "How about a glass of wine at my place to celebrate our successful kick-off meeting?" He was trying to sound casual but feared his ulterior motive was transparent to Jane.

"Friends, Chip, remember? Nothing more. I have to get home to help Ingrid with her calculus homework, and I promised I would email Sven all the details about the meeting. He'll be thrilled. So, maybe some other time."

As Chip drove home, his mind was on Jane, not the Bijou project. The woman was always sending him mixed messages. *What is "maybe some other time" supposed to mean?*

* * *

IT WAS ALMOST MIDNIGHT WHEN CHIP heard a vehicle driving into his yard. He waited for the engine to stop, for the sound of a door slamming shut, but when he didn't hear either, he turned on the yard light. He saw Jane's truck and walked up to the driver's side.

Jane rolled down the window. "I don't want to talk, okay? I don't want to have it mean anything, but what it is. I don't want you to get your hopes up. I want you to get something else up. Are we understood?"

Chip opened the door of the truck, took her hand and guided her wordlessly into the house, through the kitchen and directly into the bedroom. They undressed each other slowly, one article of clothing at a time. He stepped back and let his eyes roam over her body. She reached for him and eased him onto the bed.

Later when Jane began to untangle herself from the damp sheets, he started to speak, but she put her finger over his lips to hush him and shook her head. He remained in bed, watching her dress. She left without saying a word and without a smile.

Chip was bewildered. *Was that make-up sex? Or maybe break-up sex?* Jane was a mystery to him, but surely a mystery he wanted to solve.

* * *

THE NEXT MORNING WHILE IN BED, Chip heard an all-too-familiar buzzing . . . a mosquito. He hadn't gotten around to fixing the tear in the screen on his bedroom window. He opened his eyes and watched the insect land on his left arm. He slapped it with his right hand, but it was too late and a splotch of blood appeared under the mosquito's squished body. He could feel the bite starting to swell.

The room was flooded with sunlight and already too hot for comfort. For three days the temperatures had been unseasonably warm. Regardless of the heat, Chip knew he would have to put in a few hours of writing. He thought about Jo and Jane, so much alike in looks and professional commitment. He was as conflicted about Jo's feelings for Dr. John Goodman as Jane seemed conflicted about her feelings for him. After last night, she was more puzzling than ever.

Surely his readers would expect Jo and John's relationship to grow and blossom and culminate in mad passion, but Chip wasn't all too sure it was headed in that direction.

CHAPTER SIX

Mind Games
St. Paul
Late July

Wɪᴛʜ ᴅᴏᴡɴᴛᴏᴡɴ Mɪɴɴᴇᴀᴘᴏʟɪs ɪɴ ʜᴇʀ rear-view mirror, Jo drove east on I-94 headed toward St. Paul. She tucked a damp strand of hair behind her ear, evidence of the four-minute shower after her run. She put thoughts of the case out of her mind as she mapped out what she was going to say to John about their abandoned weekend plans.

As if on cue, her cell phone buzzed. She glanced at the caller ID, her stomach doing a flip. She took a deep breath and accepted the call on her Bluetooth. "Morning, John. I was . . . just about to give you a call."

"Good morning, beautiful. Glad to hear you were thinking about me, since I can't seem to get you out of my mind. I've got some ideas of what we can do, although, most of them involve not leaving my bedroom the entire weekend." She loved the slight teasing, husky quality of his voice and her heart pounded faster.

Stupid case.

"There's been a slight, um, change of plans," she said. Silence followed. "John. Are you still there?"

She could hear his exhaled breath. His voice, when he finally responded, was quiet. "Yes. I'm still here. And you're still there. Am I right?"

Her stomach no longer flipped, but she felt the beginning of a dull ache. "John, I'm really sorry. The body of a missing state representative has been found. Tom put me on the case. I didn't have a choice . . ."

"And you're the only one qualified to handle it, I suppose."

Jo felt her face flush, and she gripped the steering wheel a bit harder than necessary when she maneuvered around a slow-moving delivery van. "No, I'm not the only one qualified, but I'm the one Tom chose. It's not like I'm happy about this. You have no idea how much I was looking forward to getting away this weekend. Seeing you."

John's tone softened when he spoke again. "Look, I'm sorry. I've seen first-hand how great you are at your job. Tom is smart to put you on the toughest cases. It's just . . . it's just that we never see each other anymore.

You had to cancel coming for the Cherry Blossom festival because of depositions and I had to cancel the trip in June because an emergency surgery came up. Those are only the most recent examples."

"I know."

"It never seems to end. There's always something coming between us. Hell, this is probably the longest conversation we've had in a long time without one of us getting an emergency phone call. We can't base a relationship on two-minute phone calls and twenty-word text messages."

She sighed. "You're right, John. But, I don't know what else to do except to keep making plans and hope one of these times the plans will actually work out."

There was silence at the other end, and Jo could imagine him standing in his condo, rubbing his hand up the back of his head, as she'd seen him do so many times during the NeuroDynamics case. He was just as frustrated as she.

"Jo, I don't think I can do this anymore. I love you, but this isn't working."

She jerked the wheel of the car and heard an angry bleat of a horn from the black sedan in the adjoining lane. She quickly corrected her path, her heart pounding. It felt like someone had punched her in the stomach, and she couldn't breathe for a moment.

"Jo, say something. What was that noise . . . are you driving?"

"Give me a second. I'm okay. Just . . . I just need a minute." *Why does this have to be so damn difficult?*

"John, look. I need to get to this case. Can I call you tonight and we can discuss this then? I can't focus right now."

"Yeah. Sure. Call me at home. Don't worry about the time." He paused, and then continued. "I do love you, you know."

"I do know that. And, I'm sorry."

"Me, too." He said, ending the call.

Jo stared at the traffic in front of her that had slowed to a snail's pace. She slapped both of her palms on the steering wheel, relishing the sting. "Damn this job!"

* * *

JO PULLED HER CAR into the parking lot at the south side of the Capitol building in St. Paul. A guard stopped her and was about to turn her away when she

23

showed him her credentials. He waved her into the lot. Emergency vehicles and official cars and trucks of all types filled every available spot. Finally, she nabbed a spot at the far right corner, just before a news van pulled into the lot. *Great. Here come the vultures,* Jo thought.

She pulled the rear-view mirror down to look at her puffy eyes. "Get yourself together, Jo. I'll never hear the end of it from the guys if I go in looking like I've been crying." Yanking a tissue out of the glove box, she wiped away the black smudges of mascara from under her lashes. She dug in her purse for a hair band and twisted her damp hair up into a bun, tucking the stray hairs behind her ears. After checking the mirror one last time, she put it back in place and climbed out of the car.

Jo's heels clicked on the stone of the massive staircase leading up to the entrance. The early morning sun glinted off a space above her head, and she glanced up toward the dome to see the gilded statue of the four horses pulling a chariot with a man and woman. Jo recalled from a field trip to the Capitol in sixth grade that the horses represented the four powers of nature: earth, wind, fire and water.

The Capitol was one of her favorite buildings in the Twin Cities. She turned around and her eyes briefly followed the wide boulevard all the way to the Cathedral of Saint Paul, which boasted the best view in the city.

Just as she faced back toward the Capitol, a reporter called out to her. "Ma'am. Excuse me, ma'am. We've had reports that the body of State Rep. Lee Freemont has been found in the Capitol. Are you involved in the investigation?"

Jo looked at the impeccably dressed blonde woman racing toward her, with her cameraman struggling up the steps behind her. Jo rolled her eyes as she recognized Marjorie Payne, the news reporter from the local NBC affiliate, KSMN-TV. Everyone in Jo's office referred to her as "Major Payne." "No comment," Jo said to her.

The reporter's eyes narrowed and she tilted her head to one side. "You're Special Agent Jo Schwann, aren't you?"

Jo put her hand on the handle of the large bronze door and repeated, "No comment." She yanked the door open with more force than necessary and entered the lobby area. Another guard stepped toward her and she flashed her badge.

After the gaurd stepped aside, Jo tucked away her badge and said to the man, "Do me a favor. There's a reporter behind me . . ."

The guard held up a hand, "Say no more. I've already received orders to keep the media out until further notice."

"Good man. Now, tell me where I can find the crime scene."

He pointed straight ahead. "Go through the Rotunda area and make a left at the first entrance. Head up the stairway and then just listen for the ruckus."

As she walked past him, she heard him murmur, "Hope you skipped breakfast. Pretty gruesome."

* * *

JO WOUND HER WAY DOWN the marble corridors, following the trail of various law officials and crime lab specialists. She ducked under yellow crime scene tape and entered what appeared to be a large meeting room. The furniture was draped in plastic tarps, and a table saw sat silently in a corner.

Sorting through all the officials in the room, she recognized a few familiar faces. She finally located the salt-and-pepper hair of Carole Miller, the lead Ramsey County Medical Examiner, who was now kneeling next to the body. Jo had worked with Carole on a few cases in the past and admired her professional, politics-be-damned manner.

Carole looked over her leopard-print reading glasses as Jo approached. "Not a pretty sight, Jo. When I heard the Bureau was called in, I hoped they would send you."

"And I'm glad we'll get a chance to work together again. Although, I'm surprised to see you here. I thought they usually don't let the lead ME escape the office."

Carole smirked and said, "Well, when it comes to high-profile cases like this one, they like to pull in the big guns. I have to say, feels kinda good to be back in the field."

Jo smiled. She snapped on a pair of latex gloves and crouched down next to Carole. She looked down at the body of State Representative Lee Freemont.

While Jo wasn't always in agreement with the man's political views, she only felt pity for him now. Although his much derided $300 haircut was still perfectly in place, his once handsome face had been destroyed. The eyes were wide open in a permanent frieze of horror and agony. The shotgun blast had been to his mouth and his jaw hung at a grotesque angle.

"What a horrible way to go," Jo said.

Carole looked into her eyes. Jo had rarely seen such a naked reaction on the normally placid face of the coroner. "You're right about that. It would have taken quite a while to exsanguinate. Must have been excruciating." She shook her head. "Poor man. I never liked the guy's public policies, but you wouldn't wish this on your worst enemy."

Jo looked around. "This wasn't the original crime scene; there's hardly any blood. How the hell does a killer just waltz in here with a dead body without anyone noticing?"

Carole nodded. "Complicates your investigation quite a bit, doesn't it?"

"Sure does." Jo tilted her head to get a better look at the entrance wound. "What do you think about the location of the shot? Bad aim or was the mouth the target?"

"I might know more once I get him on the autopsy table, but my guess is that it was intentional." She pointed to a black splotch on the victim's chin. "See that? Gun-powder marks. Must have been at close range. We'll have the lab techs at the Bureau of Criminal Apprehension run a proximity test to determine the actual distance of the shot."

Jo crouched down next to the ME and leaned in for a closer look. She had to resist an urge to gag at the musky scent of the dead man's cologne co-mingled with the stench of blood and gore. She swallowed back the bile, and then said, "You're right. Looks like someone was making a statement."

"Got an estimate on time of death yet?"

Carole said, "I would say last night, maybe early evening. Since this isn't the original crime scene, my timing could be off if that location was either extremely hot or cold. Again, I'll know more after I examine him back at the lab."

Jo was silent for a moment, thinking. Finally she said, "I hate these shotgun cases because there isn't a bullet to run ballistics. And since this isn't the original crime scene, we don't even have a cartridge to compare the firing pin marks."

Jo tilted her head and continued, "Wonder why he was put here. Someone was obviously making a point. But what? We'll have to run down everyone who has access to this part of the building."

She leaned in closer to the body again. "Do you see that? There, on his shirt, right below the spread of blood?"

Carole peered through her glasses. "Smudge of dirt, maybe?"

"Looks like it could be a partial boot print. Could we have gotten that lucky?"

Carole said, "Not going to be easy to track someone down from a fraction of a print."

"No, but it's a start. Any defensive wounds?"

Carole lifted up the sturdy hands of Lee Freemont. "Nothing obvious. I'll scrape under his nails for trace. We'll bag them before we transport the body."

Just then, Jo heard a familiar voice behind her, "Special Agent Schwann! I heard you were assigned to the case. Good to see you again."

Jo whirled around and looked up into the smiling face of Detective Mike Frisco. She stood up and clapped him on the shoulder. "Frisco! What the hell are you doing here? Duluth not exciting enough for you anymore?"

"Nah. Family issues pulled us down to the Cities. My boss put in a good word for me with the St. Paul Police force. Worked out well. They had a guy retiring about the same time I was looking for a place down here."

Jo was delighted. She had worked with the detective on her last major assignment, and she had been impressed with both his compassion and keen eye. Not to mention Frisco was like a bull dog when it came to working a case. Not even a beating could keep him down for long.

She shook his hand and said, "So, how long have you been here?"

"Not long. A couple of months or so."

"Only a few months on the job and they've already assigned you to a high-profile case like this one?"

A sheepish grin crept across Frisco's face. "Got some mileage out of working the NeuroDynamics job with you. Amazing what a major-league case can do for a career." He shrugged his shoulders. "Although I'm not convinced it's always a good thing."

His smile disappeared as he looked back down at the body of the state representative. "Looks like being a high-profile personality didn't help him any."

CHAPTER SEVEN

Turners Bend
Late September

Chip HASTILY FED HIS PETS and hopped in his Volvo for the drive to
the Bun where the renovation steering committee had agreed to gather
on Saturday morning. Despite the heat and humidity, he drove with the
AC off and the windows down. In the spring he had been intoxicated
with the smell of freshly turned soil, and now the air was filled with
the ripeness of glorious green vegetation—corn, soybeans, sweet potatoes and beans. He drank it in through his nose as if it were a fine perfume . . . Eau de Iowa.

The Bun was already bustling with volunteers partaking in the
café's strong coffee and calorie-laden cinnamon rolls. Mayor Johnson
stood and clinked a spoon on his coffee mug. He held up a ring of rusty
old skeleton keys.

"Well folks, this is an exciting day for Turners Bend. Flora
hunted up the keys to the Bijou, and I had Boone Power turn on the
electricity. Now I'd like to introduce Alice Hedstrom, a building inspector from Ames."

A short, rotund woman with thick glasses, that gave her the look
of an owl, stood and nodded to the assembled group. She held a clip-
board in her hand. "Let's move on over to the Bijou and see what surprises are in store for us," she said. "No telling what we might find in
a building that has been abandoned for so long, so please be careful."

The small group, which also included Jane, Flora and Chief
Fredrickson, Sylvia Johnson, Stan Whittler and Lance Williams,
marched down the street to the deserted building. As Mayor Johnson
opened the door, it creaked and then one of the hinges broke. The committee entered and stood in what was once the lobby. They slowly wandered around, looking at the broken glass on the ticket booth and the
mold growing on the popcorn popper. They gingerly inspected the
poster boxes that had once been out front and the sections of the marquee that had been dumped in the lobby. Thick dust and cobwebs cov-

ered everything, and the air was dank and musty. A few people started to cough and cover their noses.

"Would someone please hold this door open?" Marion Schultz requested, as she pushed Doc Schultz in his wheelchair.

"I had to come," said the town's long-time physician to Chip. "I have many fond memories of this place. The first time I stole a kiss from Marion was in the back row. It was 1935, and we were watching *The Bride of Frankenstein.*"

"No, dear, it was 1936, and it was *Mr. Deeds Goes to Town* with that handsome Gary Cooper." Marion gazed around the lobby. "It was such a beautiful, magical place, but look at it now."

"Don't fret, we're going to restore it to its original glory and maybe Doc will steal another kiss," said Chip. "Let's have a look inside the theater and projection room." He took over pushing Doc's wheelchair.

The Mayor switched on the lights and an orange glow emanated from the sconces along the walls of the theater. The seats and stage looked like the set for a B-Grade horror show.

Jane said, "Oh Lord, Chip! This place is covered with mouse droppings. And the mice have built nests in the stuffing of the seats. We'll have to get an exterminator. Let's just hope we don't see any evidence of bats."

Lance hopped up on the stage and parted the velvet curtains, which were hanging in shreds. "It looks like there are some rooms behind the movie screen."

"I bet they were dressing rooms and prop closets," offered Sylvia. "The Historical Society has clippings from vaudeville troops who performed here in the early days. Take a look, Mr. Williams."

"No, you better let me inspect the stage first," said Alice, testing floorboards as she walked towards the doors and opened one. "Sure enough, it looks like a dressing room, and there's a rack of costumes hanging in here." She carefully traversed the stage, continuing to test the floor boards with each step. She opened a door on the opposite side of the stage. "Looks like a prop room." She walked in.

"What's inside?" yelled Flora.

Everyone stopped and stood, waiting for Alice's reply. When she emerged, the lighting gave her face an ashen glow. "Chief, I think you better come and have a look at this."

Police Chief Fredrickson climbed up on the stage and joined the inspector in the prop room. Then he, too, stuck out his head. "Someone help Doc up here."

Chip and Lance lifted the wheelchair up to the stage, and the chief pushed the doctor into the room. All the volunteers gathered expectantly at the foot of the stage. It was perfectly quiet, except for the sound of scurrying mice.

"This place is giving me the creeps," said Flora, as the three came out, grim-faced.

"Sorry folks, everyone will have to leave. There is a human skeleton in here. Doc says it's probably the body of a woman who has been dead for a long time. This is now an official crime scene. Don't touch anything." He placed a call to the station with his cell phone. "Sharon, have Deputy Anderson bring some yellow crime tape to the Bijou and place a call to the county coroner. We need him out here ASAP."

"Who is it, Walter?" asked Flora.

"Damned if I know. Christ, Turners Bend has never had a murder."

***

MOST OF THE GROUP RECONVENED at the Bun. The excitement continued, but now it was of a completely different nature. Speculations took flame and spread like wildfire.

"Doc, how do you know it is the body of a woman who has been dead a long time?" asked Iver.

"Well, I can tell by the pelvis. In a woman, the pelvis is wider and flatter and more rounded than a man's. All the flesh is gone. Most of the clothing has deteriorated, but I see remnants of women's undergarments. There's not much left for identification purposes except teeth. The coroner would need dental records, of course, for comparison."

"Please spare us the details," said Flora. "Never heard of any woman missing from around here. A few have taken off and haven't returned, like the tart who ran off with Hal Swanson." She grimaced and turned toward Jane. "Oh sorry, didn't mean to bring up your ex. That was indelicate of me."

"Some outsider must have come through town years ago and hid the body here," said Stan Whittler. "I'm sure of it."

Iver chimed in, "Maybe it's the radio announcer from Iowa City who's been missing for years. You know, the one that was on *America's Most Wanted*. Her abductor could have stashed the body here."

The Bun's patrons began to disperse, but Jane and Chip remained and ordered hot roast beef sandwiches for lunch.

"You're looking a little spooked, Chip. Does the thought of a dead body make you squeamish?" asked Jane.

"I just wrote a chapter in which a dead body is found."

"Isn't that how most crime stories start . . . with the discovery of a corpse?"

"Yes, but the eerie thing is my corpse was a man found in the construction site of a renovation. Life is imitating art, instead of the other way around, just like Oscar Wilde proposed. He thought it happened more often than art imitating life."

Jane laughed. "Don't be silly. It's just a coincidence."

"Well, it still seems a little déjà vu to me, and there are those who don't believe in coincidences."

"Who killed the man in your story?"

"I don't know. I'm waiting to find out, just like my readers."

***

SPECULATION TURNED TO GOSSIP and gossip turned to certainty as the news spread through town and around the countryside. The good citizens of Turners Bend were convinced the woman's body was that of the Iowa City radio announcer, Tracy Trent. An anonymous call was placed to the *Ames Tribune*, and all hell broke loose.

CHAPTER EIGHT

Mind Games
Minneapolis & Saint Paul, MN
Late July

THE HUNTER STRETCHED OUT on Jo's bed. He watched the lazy ceiling fan blades slice through the air, creating a downdraft that flowed over his body. Closing his eyes, he imagined himself living here with her. Their life together would be perfect. Not like the life he lived before, drenched in pain and loneliness. Now his life would be full, maybe even include a couple of kids. He smiled as he pictured the children they would create together—a boy with his eyes and a girl with Jo's red curly hair.

Mostly though, he envisioned their children living a normal childhood, nothing like his own. Crippling migraines from the age of ten onward stole his youth. He transformed from a carefree boy with many friends to a hermit unable to leave his room. He missed so many days of school in the eighth grade that his mother had to quit work and try her best at home-schooling. At his request, his father painted his only son's bedroom pitch black, including the windows. Any reflection of light pierced his brain and caused intense agony. At an age when most boys were discovering girls, he was curled in a tight ball on his bed, begging to be released from his misery.

Of course, all that changed when Dr. Charles Candleworth came into his life. Since then, he had reclaimed the life he was meant to live. No more headaches, no more isolation. He was confident again, charming even, when he wanted to be. On top of everything else, the Hunter now had a new, lucrative career. One that rewarded him handsomely.

He was still angry about Candleworth's murder, but he had decided to forgive Jo. The neurosurgeon, Dr. Goodman, was another matter. Not only was he the reason the healer was killed, but Goodman stood in the way of the Hunter's future with Jo. And that simply wouldn't do.

He turned his head into Jo's pillow, inhaling deeply to take in her scent. Vanilla and a hint of something more filled his nostrils. Of course, she would have to quit her job. Someone had to stay home and care for their children, to make sure nothing happened to them.

The Hunter snickered and spoke out loud, "I guess being married to an assassin might create a conflict of interest for a Special Agent of the FBI."

He flipped over on his side and flicked his forefinger across the screen of his iPad. It had been easy enough to install a Ghost Rider, a tracking device no larger than a pack of cigarettes inside the bumper of each of her vehicles. Finding Jo at any time was as simple as turning on his tablet. His screen showed that Jo's vehicle remained at the State Capitol, but at this point, he was probably pushing his luck if he stayed in her house any longer.

The Hunter stood up and dressed quickly. He ran his palms across Jo's comforter, to smooth out the wrinkles from lying on her bed. Pulling a lint roller out of his bag, he carefully picked up any stray hair or fibers he had left behind. Finally, he checked his iPad screen to make sure the surveillance cameras he had planted around the house earlier in the day were all up and running.

The Hunter was good to go. Now he had to find a way to insinuate himself into her life.

He was going to make her love him. One way or another.

$$****$$

IT WAS MID-AFTERNOON by the time Jo and Frisco wrapped up their work at the Capitol in St. Paul. They walked toward the front entrance, but Jo hesitated when she saw the parking lot was still filled with television vans, reporters, and camera crews. *No need to be part of the ten o'clock news. The brass can handle the news conferences.* She turned to the guard next to the door. "Any chance this place has a back door?"

He looked out to the scene in the parking lot, and said, "Sure does. Hang on a minute. I'll radio for Al, and he can show you to the loading dock area. It's where they deliver food for the Rathskeller, the café in the basement."

As they waited for their escort, Frisco said, "So, now we'll head to interview the widow, right?"

"Yes, she's already been notified about her husband's death, so at least we don't have to deliver the bad news. I'm sure she's going to be surrounded by people who aren't going to be happy we're questioning her."

Frisco frowned. "And that would be a problem because . . ."

"Tanya Freemont comes from an old-money family. One of the oldest. Her great-great-great grandfather was Cornelius Reynolds, a crony of James

J. Hill, the railroad baron. Reynolds started out in lumber, moved into flour mills, and then expanded from there. Today, the family's net worth is in the billions. Tanya lives in the family mansion on Summit Avenue in St. Paul."

"A lot of money and power behind the widow, then."

"Yes. And they aren't going to appreciate that we are questioning one of their own about her husband's murder, especially if we treat her like a suspect."

"What about Lee Freemont? Was he old-money, too?"

"Not at all. State Rep. Freemont went to college on a scholarship, where he met Tanya. He certainly married up."

Their escort appeared just then and showed them the back service entrance. "This way, folks."

As they followed Al through the various corridors of the building, Frisco said, "Why don't we just go in my car? I'm parked in the back lot. I can drop you off after our interview."

"Perfect."

They got into Frisco's police-issued Chevy Caprice and drove down John Ireland Boulevard from the Capitol toward the Cathedral of Saint Paul. They veered left onto Summit Avenue, a wide boulevard strewn with Victorian mansions built by railroad and lumber barons. After checking the address, Jo directed him to the wrought-iron gate of the Reynolds mansion. A private guard sat on a stool just outside the fence. They flashed their credentials to the guard and he waved them in.

Frisco whistled when they drove up to the carriage house in the back. "This reminds me of the mansions on the North Shore in Duluth. Can you imagine having the kind of money it took to build this place back in the day?"

Jo smiled. "Not a chance."

They were greeted at the door by a tall, bony woman who said, "This is not a good day for visitors. Might I suggest you come back next week?"

Frisco cocked his eyebrow as if to say, "Guess you were right about the cold reception."

Jo pulled out her badge and showed it to the woman. "I'm afraid this can't wait. We are investigating the murder of State Representative Freemont, and we need to speak to his wife."

The woman's lips curved downward, as if she had tasted something sour. She said, "Very well, please follow me."

Jo and Frisco trailed behind the tall woman to a double door. She turned to them and said, "I will let Mrs. Freemont know that you wish to speak with her. Please wait here."

Frisco's eyes wandered around the sumptuous hallway while they waited for the woman to return. He ran his hand along the polished woodwork of the doorframe, clearly admiring the workmanship of the previous century.

A few minutes later, the thin woman stood aside while they entered the massive library, and closed the doors behind them.

Tanya Reynolds Freemont stood at one end of the room, in front of a large mahogany desk. She was more petite than Jo expected. Having seen her in various campaign ads for the state representative, Jo expected her to be youthful and commanding. In person, Mrs. Freemont looked frail and depleted. *Of course, intense sorrow will diminish anyone.* Jo felt a surge of compassion for her and wondered if anyone could fake this look of utter grief.

Flanking the widow were two men, both dressed in expensive suits. *Looks like she's already lawyered up.* That made it easier for Jo to begin her questions.

Mrs. Freemont stepped forward to greet them, holding out a well-manicured hand. A diamond-encrusted tennis bracelet slid down her thin arm and glistened in the sunlight coming through the high windows. "I'm Mrs. Freemont." She waved a hand toward the two men on either side of her and said, "These are my attorneys, Theo Stanford and George Wilcox. They've been most kind in assisting me since I received the news. Thank you for your attention to my husband's murder . . ."

The widow swallowed hard and tears began filling her eyes. Theo Stanford offered her a tissue and patted her on the shoulder.

Jo squared her shoulders and said, "Mrs. Freemont, please let me begin by offering our sincere condolences."

"Thank you so much," Tanya Freemont said as she delicately dabbed her eyes.

Wilcox stepped forward and said, "Can't all this wait? This is a very bad time for the family. There are a lot of details to take care of."

Ignoring the attorney, Jo looked pointedly at the widow and said, "Mrs. Freemont, please. Why don't we have a seat on the sofa, where you'll be more comfortable. We have several items to cover with you and I promise we'll be as brief as possible."

Stanford puffed up his chest and said, "What kind of items?"

Frisco jutted out his jaw and said, "Investigation items."

Mrs. Freemont put a restraining hand on Stanford's arm and shook her head. She turned to Jo and said, "Of course. Agent Schwann, is it? Anything to help you discover what happened to my husband." She briefly faced each of her attorneys and said, "It's all right, I can handle this myself. I will speak with the two of you in the morning."

Both men blinked a few times. Wilcox finally sputtered, "Mrs. Freemont. I must insist we stay. Someone needs to protect your rights. As your attorneys, it's imperative we be present during this interrogation."

Tanya Freemont smirked and said, "I highly doubt I am going to be put under a hot spotlight. I have nothing to hide."

Inside, Jo cheered. It was always easier to ask questions when a witness or potential suspect was alone.

After a few more protests, Wilcox sighed and said, "As you wish. However, we will adjourn to the next room, in case you should change your mind."

"Thank you, George. You've been most kind in all of this."

After the attorneys departed, Mrs. Freemont motioned to the couch and said, "Please be seated."

Once they were settled, Jo began. "Do you know if your husband had any enemies? Recent threats, perhaps?"

Tanya frowned. "I'd be hard-pressed to find any person holding a political office who hasn't acquired some opposition along the way. Public office isn't all about doing what's popular. It's about doing what's right."

Frisco shifted a few times, looking uncomfortable in the stiff-backed chair across from the sofa and said, "Are you saying your husband had received threats?"

"Yes, Detective. He did. Although, I'm sure he kept me in the dark about most of them so I wouldn't worry. However, I'm not naïve."

"Who would have detailed knowledge of these threats?" Frisco asked.

"His head of staff, Kim Clark. I can provide you with her phone number."

Jo was curious about Tanya Freemont's composure. She knew bereavement appeared in different forms and this woman was probably trained at an early age to be unflappable. But Jo wanted to throw her off her game a bit, so she said, "Can you tell us about your personal lives?"

"What would you like to know?" Tanya said flashing her brilliant blue eyes at Jo.

"For starters, how long have you been married?"

"It would have been thirty-eight years next month." She clasped her hands in her lap and said, "Look, let's just get through these uncomfortable questions, shall we? My husband and I have not always enjoyed the smoothest relationship. Early on in our marriage, Lee worked for my father. They rarely saw eye to eye, and Lee traveled away on business a fair amount while I stayed home raising the children."

She grimaced and then continued. "And yes, I know what you are thinking. There were times when Lee wasn't the best husband."

Mrs. Freemont stopped and dabbed her eyes again, but it seemed to Jo that the woman was using her tissue as a prop to collect her thoughts. Jo looked over at Frisco, who watched the widow very closely, his face betraying nothing.

Tanya continued, "We went to a marriage counselor. This was, let me see, I guess about twenty-five years ago, around the same time Lee entered politics. Ever since then, we've had a marriage that's been the envy of our friends. Lee is . . ."

Her chin quivered and she took a deep, shuddering breath before continuing, "*was* a good father and a good husband. I don't know how we will go on without him. But that's what he would have wanted."

Frisco scribbled down some notes and said, "Mrs. Freemont, could you please tell us where you were the last several days?"

The widow directed her gaze to the detective and raised an eyebrow. "Am I under suspicion?"

"Just covering all bases, ma'am."

"Very well. Up until my husband's disappearance, I was traveling extensively throughout the state, campaigning on his behalf. I came home immediately when I received word that he was missing. You can corroborate my story with our pilot and the rest of my staff."

Jo stood up. "Mrs. Freemont, thank you for your time. I will follow-up with Mr. Freemont's head of staff, as you suggested. We will let you know if we discover anything new. Again, you have our sincere condolences." Frisco followed her lead.

Tanya Freemont rose. "Let me know if there is anything else you need, Agent Schwann. Please find my husband's killer. "

* * *

As soon as they were back out on the driveway, Frisco said, "Wanna grab a pizza at Red's Savoy? Wife's out of town with the kids visiting her sister up north."

Jo pulled back the sleeve of her jacket and peeked at her watch. She thought about her promise to call John, but really was in no hurry to have that conversation. Besides, she realized she hadn't eaten since grabbing a banana and yogurt on the way out the door that morning. "Yeah, sounds good. I'm starving."

Frisco drove through the downtown area, and pulled into the chain-link enclosed parking lot of Red's. Once inside, it took a minute for Jo's eyes to adjust to the dimly lit restaurant and the stale scent of old cigarette smoke which clung to the upholstery of the booths.

Jo said, "Only been in town a few months and you've already found one of St. Paul's institutions. I'm impressed."

Frisco loosened his tie and replied, "Doesn't take long to discover the cops' favorite hangouts."

A waitress who looked like she had been with Red's since the day it opened in 1965 came to their table. She was tall and wiry, with frizzy hair teased within an inch of its life. Evidently not much on small talk, she dove right in. "What'll ya have?"

After they gave their order, they enjoyed a pitcher of beer while they waited for the food.

"So, Frisco, how do you like the Cities so far?"

"Not bad. Can't say I like all the friggin' traffic and the house prices compared to Duluth, but I gotta say, it's working out okay so far. The guys on the force know their stuff. I mostly just keep my head down and do my thing. I am still getting used to the flow here. Never was one for that political BS at the station."

Frisco took a swig of beer and then fidgeted with the drink coaster. After a few moments, he continued, "Anyway, we're all getting used to life in a big city. And my wife loves her new job."

Jo heard a melancholy note in his voice. "So, you relocated here for her work. What does she do?" Jo questioned.

"Katie's the head ER nurse at United Hospital. It was an offer she couldn't turn down."

Jo watched Frisco, who continued to study his beer glass. She thought about the problems she and John were having because their careers were located in different parts of the country. "Must've been a tough decision, just the same," she said.

"Yeah, well. Whatcha gonna do? She got a big bump in salary and was fed up with her old boss. It was the right decision for her."

Jo tilted her head, staring into Frisco's eyes. "But maybe not for you?" she quietly said.

Frisco looked away. He drained his glass and reached for the pitcher. "Oh, I don't know. Plenty of crimes in the big cities, as you know." After re-filling his glass, he set the pitcher down and said, "It is what it is."

She helped herself to a refill and changed the subject. "So, what did you think of the widow?"

"Seems like the type of woman who never forgets her public face . . . you know? Always making sure she says and does the right thing at the right time. I'm sure it was the way she was raised in that big, fancy house." he said with a shrug and continued. "But, my gut tells me she didn't do it."

"I agree. Obviously, we'll check out her alibi. Still, she doesn't strike me as a vengeful wife. If he was cheating on her, she could have easily divorced him, and cut the purse strings. I'll bet those attorneys made sure the family money was well protected with an iron-clad pre-nup. What are your other impressions about the case so far?"

"Well, the state representative damn sure wasn't murdered in the spot where we found him. Tomorrow, I'll run through the backgrounds of all the people with access to the Capitol."

"Including the construction workers, right?"

Frisco took a swig of beer and said, "Yup. Actually thought I'd start with them. After all, they come and go at odd times. And the guards wouldn't think much about seeing them around. Anyone with a hardhat, work boots, and a rolled up set of blueprints could probably just stroll on in there . . ."

"Certainly plausible. Any thoughts on the building security?"

"I took the kids on a tour of the Capitol back when we first moved to town. Practically no security at the front doors, just a guard at the desk, along with the tour guides. No metal detectors or anything. I remembered thinking at the time how easy it would be for a terrorist to stroll in and start shooting."

Jo raised her eyebrow and said, "You mean they don't have armed security guards patrolling the building?"

"I'm told they beef up the Capitol safety measures when legislature is in session or any big shot is in town. And of course, they have security cameras all over the place, but if someone looked like they belonged, who would look at them twice?"

"And we didn't get lucky enough to have security footage of the conference room where the body was found?"

"Nah. The conference room itself is not monitored, and the cameras outside the door were disconnected during the renovations."

Jo played with her glass, thinking about their next steps. "So, we'll need to check into anyone with motive. The usual suspects, such as his wife, and any business associates who might have a grudge. But with Freemont's politics, we will need to cast a wider net."

The detective nodded and said, "Yeah, you mean like political opponents and anyone else who had beef with his opinions. The guy was anti-global warming, anti-gay marriage, anti-tax hikes for the wealthy . . . yikes, we're going to need a really big net to land this fish."

Just then, the waitress returned to their table. "Here ya go, nice and cheesy, just the way you ordered it." She plunked the heavy tray down on the table between them, and the tantalizing scent of sausage and peppers made Jo's mouth water. She slid a couple of squares onto Frisco's plate, and then helped herself.

Frisco spoke between bites, "Dripping with grease. Now, I ask you, is there any other way to enjoy pizza?"

Jo bit down on a corner piece and felt the hot cheese singe the roof of her mouth. Just the way she liked it; her taste buds were in heaven. "Not to my knowledge," she said taking another bite.

They munched in silence for a while, pausing only to add another couple of slices to their plates before they resumed talking about the case.

Jo took another drink of beer to wash down the pizza and then wiped her lips clean on a napkin. "You have to wonder why he was shot in the mouth, though. Think something he said pissed off the wrong person?"

"Oh yeah. That was the message, all right. Of course, there are a lot of people who wish the politicians would all just shut up. Our boy just chose an extreme way to do it."

"So, you think it was a male perp?"

Frisco reached over to top off her beer glass, and then poured some into his own. "Just going with the stats; most shotgun homicides are committed by men."

"True, but then again, did you take a look at the smudge mark on the victim's shirt? If that was a footprint, it was awfully small for a guy."

Frisco shrugged. "Maybe the autopsy will give us some additional direction."

"Let's hope."

They finished their pizza in companionable silence. Frisco pushed back from the table. "Man, I'm stuffed. Probably won't sleep a wink tonight with such a heavy gut, but it was so worth it."

"You've got that right," Jo said thinking how she probably wouldn't sleep well and it had nothing to do with eating too much pizza.

As if reading her mind, Frisco tilted his head and said, "So, have you heard from Dr. Goodman lately?"

Jo could feel the heat rise up in her face. "No, I haven't. Our, um, schedules haven't exactly meshed lately."

Frisco's voice was gentle. "Gotta be tough, with you running after the bad guys here and him taking care of patients back East. Good man though."

"Yes, yes he is." Jo glanced down at her watch. "Frisco, do you mind if we head back to my car? I've got a call to make."

"Let me grab the check and I'll have you back in no time."

CHAPTER NINE

Turners Bend
September

WHEN WRITING HIS LAST CHAPTER, Chip had surfed the Internet looking for a St. Paul pizza place. One link led to another until he came upon a write-up about the Savoy. It seemed like the perfect place for Frisco and Jo to eat. Writing about pizza dripping with melted cheese made him hungry. He checked his freezer . . . no pizza, only a tray of shriveled up ice cubes and a gallon of crystalized chocolate ice cream. He looked in his cupboard and was trying to decide between Spaghettios and Spam, wondering what had ever possessed him to buy either of them. The phone rang. It was Sharon, the police dispatcher, speaking in a hushed voice.

"Chip, you might want to come into town to see the media circus and your old FBI friend, Agent Masterson. The shit is going to hit the fan as far as I can tell."

* * *

WHEN CHIP ARRIVED AT THE POLICE STATION, Chief Fredrickson was seated at his desk across from FBI Agent Angela Masterson, who was in the process of berating him. The chief's uniform shirt, straining at the buttons, was wet under the arms. He ran his hand across his face and over the stubble of his five o'clock shadow. Still apparently shaken by the discovery of a body and frazzled by the national and state media, who had rolled into town with satellite dishes on top of their vans, Chip thought the chief looked like a damp dishrag. Agent Masterson, on the other hand, was as cool and icy as an outhouse in January.

Chip hesitated to remain in the office, but since Masterson did not acknowledge his presence, he quietly took a seat near the door.

Few people intimidated Chip as much as Angela Masterson. She was a trim, black woman who, despite her petite size, exuded power. She packed a gun, and he was sure she had no qualms about using it.

He had first encountered her earlier in the year when the FBI came to Turners Bend, along with half a dozen other federal agencies, to investigate a criminal case.

"Chief, it's beyond my imagination how a quiet little burg in the middle of Iowa can be such a hub for crime," said Masterson. "Again, you have totally mismanaged this case. Now I am going to clean up your mess and leave you to your own devices. I would not be here at all if the Tracy Trent case had not been mentioned. Whatever led you to that conclusion?"

She did not wait for a response nor did she seem to expect one. "I can tell you this, I've looked at the coroner's preliminary report and your corpse is not Tracy Trent. Due to a previous injury not publicly known, we can easily tell when a victim is not the Trent woman."

Masterson stood and paced back and forth in front of the chief. "This is no longer a federal case and it's back in your jurisdiction" she said. "Now you and I are going out to inform the press, and I am getting out of this place faster than a speeding bullet, and believe me, I know my ballistics."

The chief stood, put on his jacket and cap and followed the FBI agent to the steps of the City Hall, where a bank of microphones had been set up for the press conference. Chip followed and joined the group of reporters as Masterson approached the microphones to address the eager crowd.

"I am FBI Special Agent Masterson. I can tell you, based on firm evidence from the coroner's report, that the remains uncovered three days ago in the Bijou Theater here in Turners Bend, Iowa, are not that of Tracy Trent, the missing radio announcer from Iowa City. We will continue to investigate her disappearance, as we have for the past five years, but the local authorities are now handling this case. Police Chief Fredrickson will brief you further. Thank you."

Fredrickson looked startled, as if he had not expected to speak. He stepped to the microphones with stage fright written all over his face and cleared his throat.

A reporter shouted, "Chief, Chet Roper, from the CBS affiliate in Chicago. Why did you think the remains were those of Tracy Trent?"

"I never did. Someone around here just jumped to the conclusion, I'm afraid."

Another reporter jumped in. "If it isn't Tracy Trent, Chief, who is it?"

"When I know, I'll let you know. Until then, I hope you'll clear out of town and leave us alone to do our job. I have no more comments," he concluded and pushed his way through the crowd.

* * *

THE BELL JINGLED as Chip opened the café's door, but no one noticed it above the din of gossipmongers. He heard a familiar laugh and glanced in the direction of the small table he and Jane had at one time selected as their own. Jane was there and not alone. Lance Williams seemed to be entertaining her, and Chip winced as Jane put her hand on his arm.

He did all he could do to stop himself from rushing over, pulling Lance out of his chair and decking him in the jaw. Chip knew he should be cool and just saunter over and join them, but he was in no mood to do so and feared he might make an ass of himself. He turned on his heels and exited before they noticed him.

He fussed and fumed all the way back to the farmhouse. Sure, he himself had been a newcomer who wooed the local vet, but that was different, wasn't it? He loved her and asked her to marry him. And anyway, how lame was this character . . . an architect who wanted to be an organic farmer? Who was Lance kidding? The guy didn't know the first thing about farming. Then again, he thought, he hadn't known the first thing about writing crime stories, and look at him now. *Relax, Jane would never be interested in Lance, she's too smart, too sensible. Oh God, maybe she's too smart and sensible to marry a two-bit crime writer, one who's been divorced three times!*

He clipped a neighbor's mailbox and the side mirror of his Volvo snapped off. *Damn.*

He arrived home to two barking dogs and a kitten who was taunting them from her perch on top of the refrigerator. He let the dogs out into the yard, snatched down Callie, and then headed to his laptop to check emails.

September 23, 4:00 p.m.
Chip,
Good news, bad news. The good news is that Amy Chang from Good
Day USA wants to interview both of us for a segment about crime nov-
els that are being made into movies. The bad news is that she wants to
do the interview in Turners Bend, which means I will have to make an-
other trip to that odious little town. Amy and I plan to arrive next Tues-
day to film. Try to look and act like a noted author for once.
Lucinda

His life was a roller coaster ride. Just a few days ago he had
been excited about the Bijou renovation and the positive signs from
Jane. Now the theater project was on hold, Jane had a potential new
suitor and worst of all, Lucinda was coming to town.

His only comfort was the purring kitty in his lap.

CHAPTER TEN

Mind Games
St. Paul & Brooklyn Center, Minnesota
Late July

THE MEDIA VEHICLES HAD CLEARED out of the parking lot in front of the Capitol by the time Frisco pulled alongside Jo's black SUV. The Capitol and St. Paul's Cathedral across the way were brightly lit by spotlights—two jewels lit against a velvety black sky.

"Looks like the media packed up their circus wagons and left for the night," Frisco said.

Jo laughed. "Glad the head muckity-mucks get to deal with them, not me." She grasped the door handle. "Thanks for the company at dinner, Frisco. I hope you like living here."

In the glow of the lights in front of the Capitol, Jo saw a shadow pass across the detective's features. "As long as my family is all together, that's the important thing." As Jo stepped out of the car, he leaned over and said, "I'll give you a call tomorrow when the autopsy is set up."

"Sounds good. Night, Frisco."

Jo started up her SUV and headed north out of St. Paul, working her way to the highway. Dinner with Frisco had been a welcome respite, but now she was itching to get back to work. Even though it was past normal working hours, she knew a case this big would fill many of the FBI headquarter offices until late into the evening.

As she entered the west-bound lanes of I-694, she said to herself, "I really should call John now, while I've got a moment." But dread and, if she were being honest, fear kept her from plugging in her Bluetooth. *What do I say to him? I can't tell him to drop everything and move here, and I would have a hard time starting over there.*

She kept thinking about Frisco and his move to St. Paul. She sensed he wasn't thrilled with the relocation, but was making the best of it.

On the other hand, as difficult as her job could be and as much as she hated all the bureaucracy, she genuinely loved what she did for a living. It gave her an energy that went way beyond anything else she'd ever known. Except John.

I need to stop thinking about how I was supposed to be in Baltimore right now. She spoke out loud, "I'm making myself crazy." Jo clicked on the radio.

Adele's "Rolling in the Deep" filled the interior with powerful, bluesy notes and her mind eased back into thinking about the case. Even as a child, Jo loved solving riddles and puzzles. She thrived on following leads, even if they sometimes led to dead-ends. There was a method to it all; a systematical search for the truth.

Maybe that's the frustrating thing about relationships. Romantic connections with other human beings usually didn't have a right or wrong answer. There was nothing methodical about them. They were messy.

The highway miles drifted by as she plotted out what she'd like to accomplish tonight in the office. Tomorrow would be a crazy day, and if she planned ahead tonight, she could hit the ground running.

Jo passed through the high palisade fence surrounding the newly built FBI building in Brooklyn Center, a northern suburb of Minneapolis. She pulled out her identification card to show the security guard on duty and then proceeded up the ramp into the parking structure.

From the outside, the headquarters looked like the other sleek, modern office buildings in the Twin Cities area. However, a closer look revealed a state-of-the art building, including a screening area for visitors, blast-proof glass, a reinforced structure, and a closed-circuit television security system.

She pulled out her gun and placed it in the basket before she walked through the metal detectors. Jo smiled at Dan, one of the night guards.

"Late night, Agent Schwann?"

"Yeah, well. All in a day's work. I hear your retirement party is scheduled for next Thursday. I'm looking forward to it."

"Me, too. Gonna be hard adjusting to sleeping at night again after all these years. Don't work too hard," he said as Jo retrieved her weapon.

"Thanks, Dan, you too." She took the stairs two at a time to the third level and stepped onto her floor, gaining entry by waving her ID card over the panel to the right of the door. The new carpet muted her footsteps as she walked across the large room to her cubicle. Just as she removed her suit jacket and hung it on the back of her chair, she heard Tom Gunderson, her supervisor, call out to her.

"Schwann. What have you got so far?"

Jo stepped into his office and settled into the chair across the desk from her boss. "Good evening to you, too, Tom."

He had the decency to look abashed at his lack of social niceties. "Sorry, Jo. This case has stirred up a shitstorm. Been getting calls from everyone . . . the media, the mayor, the speaker of the house. Hell, even the governor is screaming in my ear, demanding to know what's going on."

Tom leaned back into his chair. "Given our honorable governor and the deceased were on opposite sides of the political spectrum, I suspect he's not too heartbroken. However, I think it scares the crap out of him that he might be the next target. He very loudly reminded me that his office is right down the hall from where the body was discovered."

"But Capitol Security is on high alert and he has his own bodyguards."

"I reminded him of that, but it didn't seem to make him any less jumpy. I'm telling you, Jo, people are riled up." He took a swig of coffee from the Caribou mug on his desk. "So, where are we?"

Jo quickly launched into what they knew so far. Tom listened carefully, taking notes here and there. When she had finished, he asked, "What are your next steps?"

Jo sorted through all of the plans in her head and said, "Frisco and I are headed to the ME's office in the morning. Trace evidence on the body should help narrow down the search for the original crime scene.

"We're winnowing down the list of people who had access to the building, especially those who could have slipped a body into the Capitol without drawing suspicion. We're following up on any threats that State Rep. Freemont may have received. With Freemont's political views, he probably pissed off quite a few people."

"Sounds like you are off to a good start. Keep me informed. This is going to be a media monster. There's a meeting scheduled at noon tomorrow in the Emergency Operations Center upstairs. I'll expect you to join us."

"Yes, sir."

Jo headed back to her desk and clicked on the lamp. Just as she was about to turn on her laptop, she was interrupted by Agent Mark Daniels. He leaned against her cubicle wall and said, "Hey, Schwann. I heard Tom put you on the Freemont job. Guess all you have to do around here is bat your eyes to get the best cases."

She turned her chair around to face him. "Don't be an ass, Daniels. I didn't ask to be put on this case. As a matter of fact, it put a major kink in my plans. Just because you had some high-profile cases in your last assignment in Omaha doesn't mean you're more qualified."

Agent Daniels sneered. "This case should have been mine."

"I suggest you take it up with Tom, if that's the way you feel."

He spun on his heel and marched off.

She fired up her laptop and quickly forgot her encounter with Daniels as she spent the next several hours deeply entrenched in cyberspace, searching for cases with a similar MO.

She revised her search criteria, limiting results to deaths with shotgun blasts to the face. As she waited for the search results, she closed her eyes. Her head throbbed and she rubbed her temples. Jo mumbled to herself, "Guess those beers with Frisco weren't such a great idea after all." Opening her center drawer, she pulled out a couple of ibuprofen and popped them in her mouth.

Looking back at her laptop screen, she was startled to see a crime scene photo which looked eerily similar to Freemont's, except this victim had been female. Same close-up and personal blast to the jaw line.

Jo's heart pounded as she leaned forward to read the details of the nine year-old cold case. UNKNOWN FEMALE, APPROXIMATE AGE: 22 YEARS. CASE STATUS: OPEN. SUSPECT QUESTIONED AND RELEASED. ORIGINAL CRIME SCENE UN-DETERMINED. Jo's eyes tracked to the bottom of the screen. The body had been discovered in an alley in Baltimore, Maryland.

"Baltimore! Damn it." She looked at the clock in the lower right hand corner of her laptop screen. "I should have called John sooner." She snatched her cell phone out of her pocket and headed to the small conference room on her floor. Jo quietly closed the door behind her. The smell of new carpet and fresh paint assailed her nostrils as she walked over to the windows. The lights from the parking structure cast a dim, yellow light into the room. In the distance, she could see the storm clouds rolling in.

An invisible band tightened across her chest as she dialed John's number. A voice in her head insisted, *Don't answer. Please don't answer.*

The phone rang two times before she heard his drowsy voice. "Hello, beautiful. Wasn't sure you'd call."

Jo's heart raced, but the tension in her chest eased a little. It had been a while since she'd heard that sleepy voice of his in her ear. It reminded her of waking up next to him, and she felt a weight in her stomach when she realized she might never wake up next to him again. "Sorry to call so late."

"That's okay. I know you're working a big case. I'm sure it's hard to break away. How is it going?"

"Ugly. Brutal. The only bright spot is that Detective Frisco is now a part of the St. Paul PD. It's good to work with him again." She gripped the phone tighter. "I . . . miss you, John."

She heard a heavy sigh on the other end of the phone. "I miss you, too. You have no idea how much I miss you." In the intervening silence, Jo watched the first rain drops hit the window, blurring her reflection in the glass. The wind whipped the trees back and forth. *It's going to be a wicked night.*

She finally got up the nerve to speak again. "So, what are we going to do?" Jo held her breath, afraid of his response. Jo traced the trail of a lone raindrop gliding down the glass with her fingertip.

"I don't know. All I know is that this can't go on. It's tearing me up inside. I can't see my life without you in it. But this half-life of broken plans, abbreviated calls . . . it doesn't work for me."

"Me either." A thunderclap outside startled her.

She heard him blow out a puff of frustrated air. "Maybe we should take a break."

Jo sucked in a sharp breath. Her mind screamed, *No!*

John quickly continued, "Just until you sort out this case. You can't focus on your job when you're thinking about us."

A crooked stitch of lightning appeared in the distance above the Minneapolis skyline and lit up the conference room. She knew John was still talking on the other end of the phone, but all she heard was a buzzing in her ears, as if she was underwater.

Finally, his voice came through, "Jo? Are you still there?"

She pushed the words over the lump that had formed in her throat. "Yes, I'm still here. You're probably right. Maybe it's for the best."

"Is this crazy? I don't know. If I wasn't so damned worried about you all the time . . . when I can't see you, my mind naturally wanders to a worst-case scenario."

"No, you're right. I get it. We'll give it some time then." She felt as if the floor was shifting beneath her. She just wanted to end this call and bury herself in the case. Anything not to feel this sharp pain in her chest. Even for a moment.

"I'm sorry, Jo. You have no idea how sorry I am."

"Me, too. Goodbye, John."

After she clicked off her phone, she stumbled back to her cubicle. She sat there for several minutes, her whole body numb. She tried to get back into the rhythm of the case, but the momentum was gone. All she could think about was John. He said it was just a break, until the case was done. But it felt like the end of a play, not intermission. When this case was done, there would be another to take its place. What was going to really change?

She looked around the office and was startled to discover she was the only one left. Everyone else had called it a night. *Forget it. I'm not getting anything else done tonight.* She printed off the information on the case in Baltimore and swept up her notes, shoving them in her briefcase. If inspiration struck at home, she could pick up where she left off. Jo knew she would not get any sleep tonight. Even a sleeping pill would not provide refuge from the turmoil in her heart.

Jo walked out into the parking structure and was about to unlock the door to her SUV, when she was startled by a mewling sound. She looked around, trying to detect the source of the odd noise. "Hello? Anyone there?" Jo unlatched the strap on her gun holster, her heart beating rapidly.

She stood stock still, waiting. A moment later, a bawling sound greeted her ears once again.

Jo turned back toward her SUV. She walked over to the passenger side of the vehicle and reached under the wheel well. She was startled to feel soft fur. Just as she closed her grip around the little bundle, she felt sharp claws dig into her hand and she let go.

"Ow! Damn it. Didn't have to scratch me." She sucked on the back of her hand, soothing the stinging pain. She bent down and gingerly tried again, this time speaking softly. "Don't worry. I'm not going to hurt you." Carefully, she pulled out the creature. She chuckled when she saw the black and white kitten in her hands. "Well, well. Looks like I've got a little stowaway. How on earth did you get up there?"

She held the kitten close in her arms and stroked its ears, eliciting an immediate thrum from the little body. "Probably looking for a warm spot on a stormy night." Jo held the cat up to the light for closer inspection. "A girl, then."

Jo stroked the midnight-black fur. It was warm and soft beneath her fingertips. "I don't see a collar. Don't you have a home?" The purring increased to a loud rumble.

"You sure are a sweet little thing. The shelters are all closed by now. Guess you'll have to come home with me."

Jo unlocked her vehicle and gently placed the kitten on the front seat. "Just so we're clear. Don't get too comfy. It's only until I can find you a permanent home, okay?"

The kitten sat up straight, watching Jo buckle her seatbelt. Jo said, "You sit like a queen. Makes me think of Cleopatra. How 'bout I call you Cleo for now?"

The kitten climbed into her lap, curled into a ball and fell asleep almost immediately. Jo sighed. "What have I gotten into?" She started the car and drove out into the rain. For one brief, peaceful moment, she forgot about her conversation with John.

CHAPTER ELEVEN

Turners Bend
October

Chip read through the chapter he had written the day before. He liked the details about the new FBI building, which had been covered extensively in Minnesota online newspapers. He began to realize a trip to the Twin Cities was in order. He made a list of places he should visit: Savoy Pizza, FBI Building, State Capitol, Lake Harriet. He jotted down a reminder to take his camera and placed the yellow Post-it-Note on his refrigerator—his make-shift bulletin board. *Maybe I should take Lucinda's advice and start acting like a real author. Have an office and do actual research, not just find information on the Internet.*

Thinking more about the chapter, he could see his own relationship frustrations coming out in Jo. *Boy, my character sure doesn't know if she should love John or leave him.* Another call from Sharon interrupted his musings and summoned him to the police station.

* * *

Chip sat across from Chief Fredrickson in the chief's cramped office. The desk top was cluttered with papers, empty coffee cups and an ash tray full of half smoked Camel cigarettes. "I didn't know you smoked, Chief."

"For the official record, I don't. And this is a non-smoking building. Understand?"

The chief yelled to the dispatcher in the outer office. "Sharon, get us a couple cups of coffee, will you?"

"Decaf or regular?" she shouted back.

"Better make it regular."

Fredrickson briefly closed his eyes and rubbed his temples. "Lord, Chip, I've lost complete control of this department. My deputy is driving me crazy."

"What's Deputy Anderson up to?"

"The usual. He watches all those CSI shows and acts like he's a big city cop. He's over at the Bijou now, dusting for prints and taking digital photos and collecting evidence in little plastic bags. The place is coated in dust. How in the hell can he dust for prints? Truth is neither of us has been directly involved in a murder investigation. We could use an extra set of eyes on this one. How about helping us out?"

"Walter, I'm a crime writer, not a detective. I just make up crimes and make up solutions, and half the time I don't know what I'm doing. I did a little sleuthing about that business with Hal and his company, but it was really the FBI who uncovered the criminal acts and identified the felons."

"I know, but I read your book. You seem to know how criminals think. I just need you to consult on this one. Kind of like the crime writer on that TV show." He laughed and shook his head. "Hell, I should be so lucky as to have a detective like that gal on *Castle*. Instead of Kate Beckett, I have Jim Anderson . . . cripes."

Chip smiled. *Now who's watching too much TV?* He was rather intrigued by the chief's request and decided to play along.

"Okay, what does the coroner's report tell us?"

"She was between eighteen and twenty-five, about five-ten, with blonde hair. He can't determine exactly how long she's been dead, but it's probably been years. She had a fractured skull, so that could be the cause of death, but he can't be sure. Looks like the body was dumped there after she was killed, no blood or signs of a struggle at the theater. That's about it." The chief took a Camel from his almost empty pack, lit up and offered one to Chip.

"No thanks. I have lots of bad habits, but smoking isn't one of them. Did you check on missing women?"

"Yes, I checked on the national database. It's scary to find out how many missing females there are in the Midwest alone. Darn near thirty percent could be our victim. I sent inquiries to all the police departments involved, but no hits yet."

"Who do you think made the anonymous call to the newspaper?"

"Boy, it could have been anyone in town. I just assumed it was a misguided person, not a troublemaker." The chief blew a smoke ring and watched it rise and then slowly vanish into the befouled air of his office. "Why?"

"It could have been the killer or someone who knows who the killer is. You might want to contact the *Ames Tribune* and see if they can trace the call."

"Thanks for the suggestion. I'll let you know what I find out and keep you in the loop. In the meantime, keep mum on the details. You can resume the renovation of the theater; just keep out of the prop room for now."

As Chip left the office, he heard the chief ask Sharon to get him the number for the *Ames Tribune.*

* * *

LUCINDA, AMY CHANG, and the film crew were due to arrive that evening. Chip did not have time to think about trips to the Twin Cities, solving crimes or renovating theaters—his mind was on the upcoming interview. He admired Amy Chang and was looking forward to meeting her. It was Lucinda he dreaded seeing. He supposed she was a good literary agent, but she was also a burr under his saddle and just about as prickly. He was scheduled to meet them at the Bend, the only bar in town.

Chip arrived early to fortify himself before the meeting. The Bend was decorated for Halloween. Paper bats and witches were suspended from the ceiling, fake cobwebs festooned the mirror behind the bar, and a plastic pumpkin sat on each table. He went up to the bar and greeted Joe, the owner.

"I'll have a scotch on the rocks, Joe."

"Coming up. You hitting the hard stuff tonight, buddy?"

Joe delivered the drink with a smirk on his face. Chip looked down into the tumbler and gasped. Joe chuckled.

"Gets 'em every time. I make those eyeball ice cubes every Halloween. Put a black olive and some strands of red thread in the middle. Been doing it for years; it cracks me up."

Chip was about to comment when the door opened and Lucinda made her entrance. Every head in the bar turned almost in unison to watch her. She was dressed in thigh-high leather boots and a short fur jacket. In her ears were hoop earrings as large as hub caps. The bar's stale air was overpowered by her perfume, a musky exotic scent. She air-kissed Chip.

"Be a dear, Chip, and order me a Cosmo. Amy and her crew will be here in a few minutes. God, the last time I was in this establishment I met that vile man who turned out to be a crook, as well as an asshole."

Ignoring her comments, Chip ordered her drink and another one for himself. Lucinda Patterson was more than a sober man could handle.

In contrast, Amy Chang, who arrived shortly after Lucinda, was charming and professional. Her long, straight black hair was tied back and her dark eyes made direct contact with him, urging him to be open and relaxed.

As Amy sipped a white wine, she went over her program notes. Vince Minnelli, the cameraman who accompanied her, gave Lucinda and Chip a copy of the shooting schedule.

"We'll start with a promo on the street," said Amy. "Where would you suggest we film, Charles?"

"Either outside the theater or the Cinnamon Bun Café."

"We'll be doing the interview in the theater, so let's shoot outside the café."

Vince jotted a note on his pad. "That will be at eight a.m. sharp," he said.

"No need to prepare anything for the interview," continued Amy. "I'll keep it a folksy, Charles Kuralt-style interview. Anything in particular that you want me to include, Lucinda?"

"The movie, of course, and Chip's next book, *Brain Freeze*, which will be released in December."

Amy nodded. "That's all for this evening. See you early tomorrow morning. Thanks for your time," she said, as she and Vince gathered their belongings and left the bar.

Chip caught Joe's eye and signaled for another round for himself and Lucinda.

"Well, I think that went very well, don't you?" Lucinda said. "Just think, national PR for your books and *The Cranium Killer* movie, and it won't cost you a cent. That is except for my expenses, of course."

A cold draft of air blew into the room as the door opened. Lance Williams entered looking in Chip's estimation like a European playboy. He wore a short leather jacket and a light blue cashmere scarf casually draped around his neck. He smiled his Crest White-bleached smile, waved to Chip, and moved to a barstool.

Great, this makes my day just perfect . . . first Lucinda and now my archrival. He glanced over to see Lucinda's reaction, and he was stunned. She looked as though she was in rapture. Her eyes were sparkling, and she sounded breathless as she whispered to him. "Who is that hunk of delicious manhood?"

"He's an organic vegetable farmer," Chip said taking a swig of his scotch, savoring its woody aroma and letting its heat work its way down his throat.

"I don't care if he is a ditch digger, invite him to join us. Please."

Chip had never before heard Lucinda say "please." He beckoned Lance over to the table. "Lance, meet Lucinda Patterson, my agent and the woman who is the bane of my existence. Lucinda, Lance Williams, our town's wannabe organic farmer. If you two will excuse me, I have to get home to walk and feed my dogs. Why don't you buy this lovely lady another drink, Lance?"

"My pleasure, Chip. Your loss is certainly my gain. What are you drinking, Lucinda?"

As Chip left the table he could swear he heard Lucinda purring. He left the bar without paying his tab.

* * *

LATER THAT NIGHT CHIP SAT with Callie on his lap. To stem his fantasy about Jane driving up to his house unannounced again, he began the next chapter of *Mind Games*. He had planned for Jo to fall for her stray kitten, which was a given. Cats are such a comfort to a person with a troubled love life, as he well knew.

He also thought it might be time to heighten the risk and raise the stakes.

CHAPTER TWELVE

Mind Games
Minneapolis, Minnesota
Late July

Jo Schwann had a hard time getting up when her alarm went off at 5:45 a.m. Tempted to roll over and go back to sleep another hour or so, she was in no mood for a run. "Exactly the reason I should get out there." She had dozed more than slept last night, thoughts of John and their future together– or lack thereof–rolling around in her head like loose marbles. Cleo stretched in her spot at Jo's feet and walked across Jo's body, coming to stand on her chest. She sniffed at Jo's chin and then meowed, rather pitifully.

"Okay, okay. I'm getting up. Jeez, don't you know guests are supposed to be on their best behavior?" Jo pushed the covers aside and sat up. The morning sun was already streaming through the edges of the blinds as she walked across the rug-scattered, hard wood floor. Her eyes felt puffy and gritty, as if she had cried in a dream.

She staggered into the bathroom to wash her face and brush her teeth, not bothering to check her reflection in the mirror. Cleo wound her way in and out of Jo's legs, meowing impatiently. "Okay, already. There has got to be something in this house a kitten would like to eat."

She found a can of tuna in the pantry and put it out for Cleo. As she watched the kitten gulp down her breakfast, Jo sighed. "Guess I'll have to contact the Humane Society today. You need a home and I don't have time for a permanent guest." Jo's voice broke on her last words, and she forced herself to turn around and head into the bedroom, where she threw on her running clothes.

* * *

Jo walked down her front steps, checking her smartphone for messages. One text was from Frisco, letting her know the ME would be ready for them at 10:00 a.m. She was disappointed and relieved at the same time to see there were no messages from John. "Guess I'd better get used to it." She could feel a lump forming in her throat and she swallowed hard a couple of times.

She flicked the screen on the phone to pull up her running playlist and started down the street. Jo looked up in time to see a man walking toward her. He was tall and fit, with dark hair. She was surprised to see he was wearing slippers with a bathrobe billowing out behind him. Underneath, he wore a white t-shirt and tartan plaid pajama bottoms.

He blushed as she approached. When she saw he wanted to speak to her, she came to an abrupt halt.

"Excuse, me," he said. "So sorry to bother you. I'm afraid I made a rather stupid mistake this morning. You see, I just moved into the house over there." He pointed at the stucco and stone house two doors down from her own. "And I, well, I locked myself out when I took out the garbage. Would you mind terribly if I borrowed your phone? I need to call a locksmith."

"Oh, you bought Mrs. Matthew's house." Jo hadn't known the house had even been for sale, but then again, she'd been out of the loop of neighborhood gossip lately. And it was hard to be suspicious of a man in his pajamas. "You know, I think I might have an extra key at my house. She asked me to keep a copy several years ago, just in case. If you haven't changed your locks since you moved in, I'm sure it'll work."

The man looked immensely relieved. He had kind, pale gray eyes and a dimple in his right cheek when he smiled at her. Jo guessed he was somewhere near her age. He said, "Really? That would be terrific! I'm so sorry to screw up your run."

"Not a problem at all."

He followed her to her house and reached out his hand when they arrived at her front door. "I'm Stephen, by the way. Stephen Paulson."

She shook his hand, "I'm Jo Schwann. Nice to have some new blood in the neighborhood. Mrs. Matthews was a dear, but I was afraid the house was becoming too much for her to handle."

"That's what her son said. He moved her into an assisted-living home close to his house. He said she's settling in very well," Stephen replied.

"I'm so glad to hear it. I worried about her, being by herself so much. I'm sure the house needs a bit of work."

Jo stuck her key in the back door lock and let them into her kitchen. "If you'll wait here a minute, I'll go and see if I can find that key."

He called out to her as she moved into her den. "Yes, looking forward to making some changes to the place. I love your house. Did you and your husband do all this yourselves?"

Jo had noticed Stephen didn't wear a wedding ring, and she wondered if his question was an attempt to determine her marital status. She sidestepped the part about her husband – or lack thereof – and said, "Some of it, but I've got the numbers of a great plumber and electrician. I'll get them for you."

Jo walked back into the kitchen, and handed him the key, along with a list of handymen. "They're sometimes hard to reach, but be persistent. I think you'll be happy with the results."

"Thanks, I owe you one. Would you be free for a cup of coffee some morning?"

"Actually, that might be a bit tough to swing. I . . ." She was interrupted by the ring of her cell phone. She looked at the screen and saw it was Frisco calling. She held up a finger to Stephen. "Excuse me a moment, I have to take this call."

"No worries, I'll just let myself out. It was very nice to meet you." He held up the key, "And thanks again. You're a lifesaver." With that, Jo heard the front door shut.

She answered her phone. "Good morning, Frisco. What's got you up this early? I didn't think we were due at the ME's office until ten."

"Jo, there's been another murder."

"One that involves the FBI? Who this time?"

"You're not going to believe this, but it's that woman who writes all those columns in the editorial section of the *St. Paul Pioneer Press*."

Jo was shocked. "You mean Annie McDonald?"

"Yeah, that's her. She was found at the newspaper offices this morning. Wouldn't have called you, except there are a lot of similarities between her case and our recently deceased state representative."

"Such as?"

"Well, for starters, they are both well-known and ultra-conservative. Both were shot in the face by a shotgun, and they were both moved from the original crime scene."

"Wow."

"Yeah, wow is right. Can you join me at the crime scene?"

Jo looked down at her running shorts. "Sure, Frisco. Be right there."

CHAPTER THIRTEEN

Turners Bend
End of October

THE WEEK BEFORE HALLOWEEN turned cold and blustery. Most of the leaves had fallen, but a few stragglers hung on, fluttering in the wind. Amy Chang, bundled in a camel coat and red muffler, was filming the teaser for the segment from the middle of the street outside the Bun. Chip stood on the sidewalk, out of earshot, shivering in the dark gray suit he had not worn since Iver and Mabel's wedding on Valentine's Day.

"This is Amy Chang reporting from Turners Bend, Iowa, the home of crime author Charles Collingsworth. In our next entertainment segment, I'll be talking with Charles and his literary agent, Lucinda Patterson, about the upcoming movie version of his first book, *The Cranium Killer*, and about the next book in his Dr. Goodman series. You won't want to miss the startling discovery about a real-life crime in this charming little town in the middle of the country's heartland. What's Collingsworth's connection to the crime? Stay tuned in the nine o'clock hour for the surprising details."

Chip glanced into the window of the Bun and saw a collage of faces above the café curtains. Like children pressing their noses against a toy store window, many had turned out to see the famous TV personality. Two of the smiling faces, side-by-side, were Lance and Jane. The sight un-nerved him.

"That should do it here, Amy," said Vince. "Let's move over to the theater and get out of this ball-busting weather. Lucinda is going to meet us there for the interview."

Amy, Chip and the film crew walked down to the Bijou with shoulders hunched and hands in their pockets. Lucinda was waiting inside the theater. She removed her fur coat to reveal a skintight black dress. On her shoulder was a huge ruby- encrusted brooch, the color of her cherry-red lipstick. To Chip she looked oddly overdressed for a morning show, especially in comparison to Amy, who had removed her coat to reveal a pale blue sweater set and navy skirt.

While the crew quickly set up the equipment, Amy explained, "First Vince is going to film the lobby and theater while I describe the renovation and the crime recently discovered here in a voice-over. Then the three of us will sit in the theater seats, and I'll conduct the interview. Remember we'll be editing down the shoot to a four-minute segment to be aired on Friday's show."

The filming got underway, and Chip was pleased Amy had done her research on the theater, giving him a nice shout-out for his work on the renovation and also mentioning Sven as the initiator of the project. When she was finished they moved to the theater's seating section and arranged themselves for the interview.

"Today I'm here in Turners Bend, Iowa, with crime writer Charles Collingsworth and his New York literary agent, Lucinda Patterson. Charles, can you tell us about your next Dr. Goodman book?"

"*Brain Freeze* takes place in Two Harbors, Minnesota. Dr. Goodman teams up with Jo Schwann, a beautiful FBI agent, to solve a crime. It's due to be released in December. Actually Jo, rather than Dr. Goodman, is the main character. I found I like writing from her point of view. I'm now working on the third book in the series."

"I understand your grandfather, father, and brother are all neurosurgeons. How did you end up becoming a writer instead of a physician?"

Chip had not anticipated this question and hesitated before stammering his response. "Well, it's kind of a long story. Let me just say I am happy where I am and with what I'm doing. Medicine just wasn't in the cards for me."

The reporter raised an eyebrow and said, "I see . . . touchy subject it seems." She turned her attention to Lucinda.

"Ms. Patterson, you were instrumental in selling *The Cranium Killer* to the famous movie producer, Howard Glasser. How did you persuade him to buy the copyrights, and what do you think about the casting?"

"Glasser is a brilliant producer and a risk-taker. It wasn't difficult to convince him of the book's cinematic potential. I suggested several actors for the role of Dr. Goodman, and he did the rest. I think movie-goers will be thrilled with the results."

Amy switched back to Chip. "I've heard suggestions the body found in this theater last month was a hoax, just a PR stunt to promote your books. What do you have to say about that? Is there any validity to the claim, Charles?"

Chip was stunned and angered by the question. "Absolutely not! I can't imagine where you heard that. I'd never stoop to anything so foolish or outrageous. The death of that young woman is a real crime, not a fictional one."

"But isn't it true you started the rumor that it was the remains of Tracy Trent, a rumor that was subsequently denounced by the FBI?"

Lucinda jumped into the fray. "Certainly not. I can assure you we would never be involved in such sleazy tactics. This is an outrage."

Amy turned to look directly into Vince's camera. "Unfortunately we're running short on time, but *Good Day USA* will be following the outcome of this criminal investigation and also reviewing *The Cranium Killer* when the movie is released in March. Until then, this is Amy Chang, reporting from Turners Bend, Iowa."

Vince stopped filming and the crew began to pack up their equipment. Chip was at a loss for words. The congenial Amy Chang of the previous evening had turned into a viper in the grass, complete with venom. He felt violated and deeply regretted the consent form he had signed prior to filming.

"Sorry about that," said Amy. "TV journalism is a pulverize or perish business. If I don't report something sensational or badger an interviewee, our ratings fall. I hope you understand."

"I'd call it cut-throat, but I understand it's all part of the game, and two can play this game," said Lucinda. "You can watch for my rebuttal on your rival networks soon." She put on her sable coat, lifted her head and walked out of the theater with a malicious smile on her face.

As the *Good Day USA* van pulled out of Turners Bend, Chip watched it move down Main Street and wished he had poured molasses into the gas tank.

"I need a cup of coffee and a word with you, Lucinda. You can expense it like you do everything else."

He took hold of her arm and swiftly moved her along to the Bun. They took the remaining clean table. The crowd had dissipated, leaving Bernice to clean up the mess. She approached the table to take their order. "Sorry, Chip, we're wiped out of every pastry in the place, but I can brew a fresh pot of coffee. This has been a bumper day. Who would have thought we'd have Amy Chang reporting right outside of the café?"

"I'll have a Skinny Vanilla Latte," said Lucinda.

"Then I'll give you driving directions to the Starbucks in Ames," replied Bernice. "We've got regular or decaf, and the cream and sugar are on the table."

"Ah, just the kind of service I would expect in this place," snapped Lucinda.

"Give us two regulars, Bernice," said Chip. *Christ, first a cat-fight with Amy Chang; now one with Bernice.*

Bernice returned with two mugs of coffee and plopped one down in front of Lucinda, not bothering to apologize for spilling some on the table.

"I thought the interview went quite well, didn't you, Chip?" asked Lucinda.

"Are you kidding me? It was practically slanderous. Where did she come up with that hoax stuff? I certainly didn't expect a tabloid-style interview. And you, you turned it into a pissing match."

"You're over-reacting. This is going to stir up a lot of interest in you, just wait and see. By the way, I think I'll stick around for a few days."

"Here? In Turners Bend? I thought you despised this 'vile' place," said Chip, indicating quotation marks with his fingers.

"Well, Lance has this wonderful little idea of having an old-fashioned barn dance at his place for Halloween, and I offered to help with the decorations. He's such a darling, how could I refuse?"

"Lucinda, the guy's a womanizer. You, of all people, should be able to smell a skunk when he lifts his tail."

"I think you're just jealous of him. He's going to grow organic vegetables. He's truly concerned about the environment and eating healthy food and being an authentic person, instead of a corporate drone."

"Since when do you care about any of that rot?"

"I'm sure I'll love eating his organic vegetables," she said, lifting her nose and sniffing.

Her haughtiness irritated Chip to no end. "Right, along with your Skinny Vanilla Lattes," he snapped.

CHAPTER FOURTEEN

Mind Games
St. Paul, Minnesota
Late July

Jo SCHWANN HAD TO PULL OUT her credentials to secure a spot in the parking lot of the *Pioneer Press* headquarters. Every news team in the Twin Cities was already represented by a van full of equipment and impatient reporters, clamoring to get the story about the death of one of their own. The eight-story limestone building, located in downtown St. Paul just a few blocks from the Mississippi riverfront, still looked more like the former insurance company headquarters that it was, rather than a newspaper office.

As Jo moved toward the set of steps leading into the building, she felt her shoulder muscles tightening. Throngs of reporters closed in on her like a swarm of bees, and everywhere she turned a microphone was shoved in her face. Their voices all blended together in their rush to beat their competitors to the story. Jo heard variations of, "Agent Schwann, is it true Annie McDonald and State Representative Freemont were murdered by the same person?" repeated as she moved up the staircase. Jo's head began to throb as she answered, "No comment" over and over again.

Muscling her way through, she looked up to see Marjorie Payne at the top of the steps near the building entrance. Jo sighed. Solving a major murder case was difficult in the best of circumstances, but reporters like Ms. Payne made her job twice as complicated.

Marjorie Payne wore her trademark red suit and high heels. "Ms. Schwann. Is it true that ultra-conservatives all over the Twin Cities are being targeted by a madman?"

Jo was shocked at the audacity of the question. Careless news reporting such as this could lead to panic and, quite possibly, create a copycat murderer. Her eyes narrowed as she focused on the red slash of lipstick across the reporter's mouth. Through gritted teeth, Jo said, "Ms. Payne, I will not comment on such wild speculation."

Jo turned away from the woman and had just reached for the brass door handle when she heard Marjorie speak again. "Any plans to bring Dr. John Goodman in as a consultant?"

Jo twisted around and struggled to keep her voice level as she replied, "I wasn't aware there was a need for a neurosurgeon's expertise. Maybe you've already solved the case for me. If so, I congratulate you."

"But you two are dating, isn't that true?" The reporter's eyes had become cat-like and her smile was all-knowing. Jo wondered what else she knew.

"Where did you hear that?" Jo hated hearing the high pitch of her own voice. She took a deep breath and managed to speak in a lower tone. "I have a case to attend to, Ms. Payne, if you'll excuse me." Jo grabbed the handle of the door once again, desperate to get away from the reporter.

She heard Marjorie say, "Or maybe there's trouble in paradise. Must be hard to carry on a relationship, long distance, two high-powered careers and all that."

Jo whirled around and stared at the reporter. It took every bit of her self-control not to hit the woman. "Good day, Ms. Payne." She pulled open the door with more force than was necessary and it slammed into the side of the building as she strode inside.

A policeman in the lobby directed her to the third floor, where the body of Annie McDonald had been discovered. She skipped the elevator and took the steps instead, giving her a moment to calm down. She mumbled to herself, "Damn that woman." Jo was shaken by the fact the reporter had guessed their relationship was in trouble. The thought depressed her. *Maybe everyone can see we aren't meant to be together.*

* * *

JO CAUGHT FRISCO'S EYE, just as he was talking to a pale, skinny young man of about twenty-five with thinning hair. The detective wrote down a few notes, and then let the man go.

Frisco waved Jo over and she met him by a window. "Hey, Frisco. This is getting to be a habit with us."

"You got that right. Jeez. Haven't been this busy with dead bodies since the NeuroDynamics case."

Jo pointed at the young man standing in the corner, who couldn't seem to stop jiggling his leg. "What's his story?"

"Him? He's the poor bastard who found the body. Says they've never worked together. I gather Annie McDonald works from home, but he knew her by reputation around the office. He came in early to write up his story on the death of State Representative Freemont. Ironic, huh? He comes in here to write one story and finds another."

"The guy looks pretty messed up. Get any details from him?"

Frisco shook his head. "Not much. He went to start up the coffee machine and tripped over the body before he got a chance to flip the light switch. Unfortunately, he managed to mangle the crime scene when he was struggling to get away from the body. Guy was so shook up I had a hard time getting much of a statement, but my gut says he's told me all he knows."

Jo gave the guy one last look. The young reporter had stopped shaking his leg and now repeatedly scuffed the top of one shoe with the sole of the other, as if he was trying to rub off a stubborn spot. He would probably spend some time on a therapist's couch in the near future. She looked around the room. "Anyone else know anything?"

Frisco ran his hand through his hair. "Gotta tell you, I've never read the woman's articles, but the scuttlebutt around here says there are an awful lot of people who hated McDonald. Might be easier to figure out who wouldn't want to shut her up permanently."

"I've read her op-ed pieces. She never pulled her punches, that's for damned sure. Extreme right-wing, with a dollop of religious overtones." Jo looked around to where the ME was crouched down over the body. She snapped on a pair of gloves and followed Frisco to the sprawled-out body of the journalist.

ME Carole Miller looked up from the latest victim. The dark circles under her eyes looked like she hadn't slept much more than Jo the previous night. "Twice in twenty-four hours is too often to see you, Agent Schwann, at least under these circumstances."

"You'll get no argument from me. What have you discovered so far?"

"This is not the original crime scene, I can tell you that. There was some blood, but not like you would expect from this kind of gunshot wound."

Frisco paused from his note-taking and asked another question. "Any idea on time of death?"

"I'd say at least thirty-six to forty-eight hours ago. Rigor mortis has come and gone."

Frisco flipped through his notes, a frown on his face. "Another indicator the body must've been moved. When I talked to the witness and the editor of the paper, they said there've been people in and out of this room every day since the weekend. That means the body was obviously dumped here in the last twenty-four hours."

Jo spoke up, "So, where has the body been stored up to now?"

"That's the sixty-four thousand dollar question now, isn't it? Maybe trace will turn up something."

Jo turned to the ME again. "Lividity give us anything?"

Carole gently turned the body to its side. She lifted the woman's shirt to show them the dark purple splotches covering the back of the neck. "The vic bled out lying on her back. Given it was a shotgun blast to the face, I would guess she was lying prone when she was killed."

Jo studied the dead journalist's face. She noticed some discoloration on the side of the neck, away from the shotgun blast. "What's that?"

The ME gently turned the head toward them and studied the marks on the side of the neck. "Haven't figured that out yet. Could be strangulation marks."

Frisco said, "Why choke the victim if you are just going to shoot her?"

Jo looked closer. "Could it be that the killer was trying to force the victim to open her mouth? See, there are some bruises on the upper lip and jaw line, too."

The ME carefully pried open what was left of the mouth. She flashed a narrow beam of light from her flashlight down into the mouth. "Looks like a piece of paper was shoved down her throat. Hand me those tweezers, will you?"

Frisco handed her the instrument from the medical kit. Carefully feeding the tweezers into the mouth, she pulled out a long, narrow piece of paper. There were smeared letters on the surface.

Frisco leaned closer, "What's it say? Something like, 'marriage bed' and 'God will judge' something, something. Can you guys make out anything else?"

Jo squinted, "It says, 'Let marriage be held in honor among all, and let the marriage bed be undefiled, for God will judge the sexually immoral and adulterous.' It's from Hebrews. McDonald frequently quoted it in her column."

Frisco scratched his chin, "So the killer made McDonald literally eat her words. But what the hell has that got to do with our other case? Any idea?"

Jo said, "I'm not sure. But the killer seems to be focusing on adultery. Wonder what the relationship was between our two vics?"

Frisco raised an eyebrow and said, "You think they were having an affair?"

"Worth checking into. He certainly wouldn't be the first politician to come across as the perfect family man while having a little something on the side. If that's the case, we need to circle back to Freemont's widow. An affair would give her motive."

Jo pointed at the body of Annie McDonald. "What about her? Was she married? If so, we need to check out the alibi of her husband, too."

The detective consulted his notes. "Nope. Her co-workers say she never married."

Jo turned toward the ME. "Find a note like this in the mouth of State Rep. Freemont?"

Carole shook her head. "No, at least not so far. But I haven't started the autopsy yet. Maybe something will turn up there."

CHAPTER FIFTEEN

Turners Bend
Late October

C HIP SAT IN HIS CAR OUTSIDE Jane's veterinary clinic with Callie zipped inside of his down parka. She was warming his heart in more ways than one. On an intellectual level he knew spaying her was the responsible thing for a pet owner to do. But, on an emotional level, he could not bear the image of her going under the knife. Yes, she was a just a stray cat, but she was his stray cat, his baby.

"Sorry, puss," he said as he entered the reception area and deposited the kitten into Mabel's hands. "Please don't hold this against me, Callie.

"Mabel, I'll be working over at the Bijou, if I'm needed. I'll come by later to make sure she's okay. Is Jane here yet?"

At the mention of her name, Jane came through the front door. She was dressed in knee-high Wellies and a long rubber coat. "Just delivered a calf out at the Jensen place," she explained. "She was breach, so I'm kind of a mess. Oh for Pete's sake, what's wrong with you, Chip? You look like you've brought your precious child to be sacrificed. Millions of cats are spayed every day in this country. Relax, she'll be just fine."

"I know . . . it's just that I hate to see her in any pain."

Jane removed her coat and boots and took Callie from Mabel. "I'll call you with a report later today. Oh, by the way, are you going to Lance's barn dance on Saturday? He's decided to make it a fundraiser for the Bijou, so you really should be there."

"I'll think about it," answered Chip.

"I just can't believe your floozy agent is staying in town to help Lance. She obviously has her sights on him, and there's no way he could honestly be interested in her."

"Yes, well, I'll probably show up for part of the party," he said, skirting her remark. He abruptly turned and left the clinic with Jane's words spinning in his head. *Jane usually is not one to speak disparagingly of others. Is she jealous of Lucinda? Are both women lusting after this guy?*

He got in his car and started the engine and let it idle while he tried to process the situation. *Is Lance leading both of them on? What does Sir Lancelot have that I don't?*

He pulled out onto Main Street and headed for home, so distracted that he almost failed to stop at Turners Bend's only stop light. He wondered if he would he end up like King Arthur and lose his ladylove to this knight in shining armor.

Halfway home he remembered he had planned to go to the Bijou. He made a U-turn and headed back to town.

This love life stuff is killing me.

* * *

THE BIJOU PROJECT had resumed and a few volunteers showed up every day to work. The goal was to finish by spring and to have a grand reopening with *The Cranium Killer* movie. The president of the Historical Society, Sylvia Johnson, had already donated a red carpet runner for the gala event. The broken glass in the ticket booth and poster cases had been replaced and new upholstery had been ordered for the seats. Several retired farmers had started to replace the stage floorboards under the guidance of the high school shop teacher. A magical pied piper had lured the mice away, as well as exterminated a few other unwelcome squatters.

Lance had taken on the repair and restoration of the marquee as his personal project. He had studied old photos, drawn up sketches and blueprints and started replacing all the sockets for the lights. He was a man of many mechanical talents.

As Chip walked into the lobby, there he was . . . his nemesis . . . working away. "I didn't expect you today, Lance. I thought you would be getting ready for the barn dance."

"Well, Lucinda has taken charge. I thought I might just finish the marquee today since I had to come into town anyway to order the booze over at the Bend. What would we do without these women? I have to tell you, I never thought I would come to Turners Bend and find the woman of my dreams."

Chip had no idea if Lance was talking about Jane or Lucinda. He had a hard time believing it was Lucinda, but he prayed it was her and not Jane. Just as he was trying to figure out how to tactfully get at the dream woman's true identity, Chief Fredrickson walked into the Bijou with a grim look on his face.

"I hoped I might find you here. I wonder if you could come over to the station and have a look at something, Chip."

"Sure, what is it? Is it something to do with the murder?"

"Don't know. Thought you might have a clue about something I got in the mail."

Chip and the chief silently walked over to the police station, each deep in thought.

As they entered the station, Sharon barked. "Don't even ask me about my day, 'cuz it's horse shit. Oh sorry, Chief, my day got off to a bad start."

The chief motioned Chip into his office and closed the door. "What's with Sharon?"

"Robert's mother moved in with them. I take it there is no love lost between the two women."

The chief sorted through papers on his desk and held up an envelope. "I got this in the mail yesterday. No explanation and no return address. Postmark says it was mailed from Ames. My gut tells me it has something to do with the body we found. What do you make of it?"

Chip unfolded the piece of paper. On one side there was a printed form and on the other side was a strange drawing done in black grease pencil. It was a crudely drawn rectangle marked with five X's inside.

Chip looked at the diagram and then turned it over. "What's this form?"

"From what I can tell, it's some kind of order or delivery form for raw milk. The company name has been torn off. As far as the diagram on the back, I haven't the vaguest idea. It was addressed to me personally. I've sent Jim to get copies of forms from all the milk processors, but each of them probably services hundreds of dairy farmers."

"I'm as clueless as you, Chief. May I have a copy to take home?"

"Sure, I'll have Sharon make one for you."

* * *

CHIP TOOK A COPY OF THE DIAGRAM home and posted it on his refrigerator. His mind wandered to clues . . . clues to crimes. The killer in *Mind Games* was leaving clues, clues on paper stuffed into victims. Writing a trail of clues would be his next task.

CHAPTER SIXTEEN

Mind Games
St. Paul & Minneapolis, Minnesota
Late July

T HIS TIME, WHEN JO AND FRISCO stopped in to see Freemont's widow, they were immediately admitted to a spacious family room. A large plasma TV was mounted above the ornate fireplace and the volume was muted.

Tanya rose to greet them and said, "I've just seen the news report about Annie's death. How horrible! They're saying her murder is tied to my husband's? What's going on?"

Jo glanced at Frisco, who looked surprised. "So, you know Ms. McDonald personally?" he said.

"Why, yes. She went to college with Lee and I. She is . . . was a dear friend." The woman's voice broke on the last word.

"I'm sorry for your loss. I apologize for my bluntness, but is there any chance your husband and Ms. McDonald were having an affair?" Jo asked.

There was a sharp intake of breath from Tanya Freemont. Her words were clipped when she replied, "No. Absolutely not. Annie was gay. She and Lee were very close, like best friends. It was Annie who convinced Lee to go into politics in the first place."

Frisco spoke up. "Mrs. Freemont, could your husband have had a recent affair?"

She furrowed her brow. "I am not a fool, detective. I know affairs happen on campaign trails all the time. Just look at John Edwards, when he ran for president a few years back. However, to the best of my knowledge, my husband was faithful to me." She paused, and then said, "Why do you keep asking me about affairs? Has there been a break in the case?"

Jo shook her head and said, "We have found a puzzling clue, which refers to adultery. I'm not at liberty to say anything more at the moment."

"What *can* you tell me?"

Jo frowned. "At the moment, nothing much. Except to say we feel there may be a connection between the cases. We will be in touch."

Frisco and Jo had turned to leave, when Jo heard Tanya Freemont mutter, "First, Lee. Now, Annie. How much can I bear?"

* * *

AFTER THEY LEFT THE REYNOLD'S MANSION, Frisco said, "It's been a long day already and I'm starving. Let's grab a bite. Know of a good burger joint?" Jo had smiled and driven them to the 5-8 Club.

The waitress set down a pair of Juicy Lucy burgers and French fries in front of them. As she left the bill, she warned, "Be careful. The cheese in these is crazy hot. Anything else I can get you folks?"

Frisco looked up at Jo with a raised eyebrow and she said, "No, thanks. These look great."

Across the booth, Frisco carefully bit into his blue-cheese burger. He closed his eyes, and groaned, savoring the double burger patty with melted cheese inside. Wiping a bit of juice from his chin, he said, "These are fantastic. How'd you find this place?"

"It's a Twin Cities institution. It used to be a speak-easy during Prohibition, can you believe it? Both Matt's up the street and this place claim to have been the first to come up with the idea of Juicy Lucys, but I prefer the history of the 5-8 Club. Besides, it's not far from the Minnehaha trail and Lake Nokomis, so sometimes I treat myself to a burger after a long bike ride."

Her first bite was tasteless. She knew it had nothing to do with the quality of her burger. Jo set the sandwich back on the plate and checked her phone again under the table.

Frisco took another, bigger bite of his sandwich and said, "He call back yet?"

Jo was surprised the detective knew what was on her mind, but didn't bother to pretend she didn't know what he was talking about. *So much for being subtle.*

She fidgeted with the napkin in her lap and after a moment, she quietly replied, "No. He hasn't."

Frisco nodded at her across the table. "He will. He's crazy about you and the Doc's no fool. He just needs time to process. Like you, I expect."

The bright sunshine outside made her squint as Jo looked out the restaurant window. "I know. But I also know this long-distance thing doesn't work." She felt the tears building behind her eye-lids and blinked.

"You know, when Katie got the job offer here, we fought like crazy. I didn't want to give up my seniority at the Duluth cop shop. She said it was her turn for moving up. Said she was taking this job, no matter what. Scared the shit out of me, if you want to know the truth."

Frisco reached across the table for the salt shaker, and gave his order of fries a coating of salt. "When I came to my senses, which took all of twenty seconds, by the way, I realized nothing meant more to me than my family." He pulled his jacket aside with a salt-encrusted finger, revealing his detective's badge. "I love this badge, don't get me wrong."

Frisco reached for a fry and waved it like a musical conductor's baton to make his point. "But my job exists to support what I love the most in this world, not the other way 'round." He shoved the fry into his mouth.

After he swallowed, he pointed to Jo and said, "So, you gotta decide what you love just a little less. The doc or your job. It doesn't get any simpler than that."

"So, you think I should move to Baltimore?" Jo asked. The thought made her stomach flip, but at least it replaced the queasiness that had resided there since she and John decided to call things off.

"I didn't say that." His gray eyes bored into hers. "Only you can decide that. But, if this relationship with him is as big a deal as I think it is, you owe it another look. Is he worth the fight?"

The detective reached for the ketchup and squirted it on his entire remaining order of fries. He dug in with his fingers and clearly relished the results. Once he polished off the order, he pointed to her burger and said, "Aren't you gonna eat that?"

Jo looked at the plate in front of her. She lifted the burger to her mouth and took a bite that would make Frisco proud. Warm Swiss cheese oozed in her mouth, and this time, it tasted every bit as good as the first time she'd tried a Juicy Lucy.

"That's more like it," Frisco said. He finished up the rest of his sandwich and asked, "So, what do you make of these cases?"

Jo's head whirled at the abrupt change of subject. She guessed he'd given out all the advice he was going to. She was startled to realize she felt better. Jo may not have made any decisions about her relationship with John, but at least her perspective, put in Frisco's simple terms, gave her hope.

* * *

AS FRISCO PUT BACK HIS WALLET after paying his share of the tab, Jo's cell phone buzzed on the tabletop.

It was Dr. Miller, the ME. "I've finished the autopsy of State Rep. Freemont. I was wondering if you and Frisco would like to swing by in about thirty minutes and go through my findings. That work for you?"

"Sure, see you then," Jo replied.

Clicking off the phone call, Jo glanced at her watch and said to Frisco, "That was the ME. We're scheduled to review the results on Freemont in half an hour. Ready to go?"

Frisco swallowed the last of his Coke. "Yup. She give you any hints about finding anything unusual?"

"I think she wants to surprise us."

* * *

THEY DROVE TO THE Ramsey County Medical Examiner's office on University Avenue in St. Paul. Jo thought it was fitting that the ME's office was located just a few blocks east of the Minnesota Capitol building. *At least Representative Freemont isn't far from his beloved workplace.* Jo and Frisco walked into the low, red brick building that looked more like a doctor's clinic than a place where the dead received their final examinations.

It was cool inside the building and Jo shivered. After checking in at the information desk, Frisco led the way to the large autopsy suite at the end of the hallway. Carole Miller greeted them at the entrance, a frown evident on her faintly-lined face.

The autopsy suite was large, with white walls changing to turquoise-colored tiles about three-quarters of the way up toward the ceiling. A stainless steel cabinet and sink dominated one end of the room with hoses and equipment neatly in place. Carole led them to the figure draped in sheeting on top of the wheeled autopsy table in the center of the room.

Dr. Miller lifted the sheet and began her assessment. "Cause of death was a perforating gunshot wound to the mouth."

Frisco raised one eyebrow and interrupted, "Perforating. So, meaning there is an exit wound. Is that normal for a shotgun blast? I thought all the buckshot tended to scatter inside the body."

Carole replied, "In this case, the gun was in such close proximity to the jaw that the buckshot blasted all the way through the back of the skull."

"How come we didn't catch that at the crime scene?" Frisco questioned.

"The buckshot that exited the wounds in the back of the head would have been left at the original crime scene."

She carefully lifted the victim's head and turned it so they could see the back of the skull and continued. "Additionally, the victim's hair covered the exit wounds and there was very little dried blood around the area. I found several fibers in and around the injuries that may indicate the head was wrapped in absorbent fabric in order to transport the body to the Capitol with minimal blood trace. Therefore, the wounds were more difficult to observe. I've passed the fibers onto the BCA for further review."

Dr. Miller ran through the specifics of her findings and then said, "The autopsy supports your conclusion that this was a hard-contact wound, since I discovered particles of soot and unburnt powder in the wound track."

She concluded by saying, "I found no other evidence of trauma on the body. Other than minor signs of osteoarthritis around the cartilage surrounding his knees, he was in excellent health for a sixty-two-year-old man."

This time Jo interrupted, "We didn't see any evidence of defensive wounds at the scene. Did you find anything at all to indicate he put up a fight?"

Dr. Miller frowned, "No, none at all."

Jo thought for a moment, trying to sort out why the state representative had not struggled as someone placed the muzzle of a shotgun directly on his jaw. "Even if it was someone he knew, wouldn't he have fought to save his life?"

The question hung in the air, as no one seemed to have an answer.

Frisco spoke up, "So, my big question is, did you find a note in the throat of State Rep. Freemont?"

MARILYN RAUSCH AND MARY DONLON

The ME gave a small, mysterious smile. "Not in the throat, no. But, when I examined the contents of the stomach, I found this." She held up a plastic evidence bag.

The ME handed it to Jo. She studied the contents of the bag for a moment, feeling a combination of excitement and dread at the same time. Jo said, "Another slip of paper with typing on it, like the one we found in the journalist's mouth. I can't make out all the words. Looks like the stomach acids did a number on it."

Jo took the note over to a magnifying glass on the ME's countertop. "Looks like 'folly of his heart.' Wasn't that part of Freemont's speech when he recently condemned a senator caught cheating on his wife?"

Carole Miller chimed in, "It's from Proverbs. It says, 'But he that is an adulterer, for the folly of his heart shall destroy his own soul.'"

"The ME knows her bible," Frisco said with a smile.

"If Freemont was an adulterer, then who wanted revenge bad enough to kill him?"Jo said.

CHAPTER SEVENTEEN

Turners Bend
Halloween

Writing about burgers and fries had at first made Chip hungry for Five Guys—his favorite hamburger joint in his old neighborhood in Baltimore. He could almost taste the bacon cheeseburger loaded with grilled onions and the spicy Cajun fries. When he switched his attention to a web search for photos of bullet wounds, he lost his appetite. He had learned with his first book, however, his readers love gory details, so he did not hold back on the details, like the plastic bag of stomach contents or the description of the bullet's path through the victim's head.

He turned his attention away from his writing and sought out his pets. Honey and Runt were keeping vigil over Callie. They occasionally sniffed her as she curled up on Chip's ratty old terrycloth robe. He had put the robe in a shallow box and placed the box in the kitchen near the radiator to keep her warm. He hand fed her and carried her to her litter box. Her surgery had been tough on all of them. Jane labeled him a "mother hen," but he didn't care. Callie obviously needed his post-op TLC.

Chip was continually astounded at the intellect and range of emotions displayed by his pets. He was sorry that it took him forty-seven years to realize he should have had more pets and fewer wives. Mary, his first wife, had refused any alimony, but Erica and Bambi were sucking him drier than Death Valley. He just received another letter from Bambi's lawyer making more claims on his earnings.

That woman was a piece of work. How stupid could he have been to fall for a pair of super-sized boob implants? It was a Catch 22, the more money he made or she thought he was making, the more her lawyer demanded.

He sat in a kitchen chair staring at the copy of the mysterious diagram on his refrigerator door. He concluded that each "X" must mark the spot, but the spot for what? And what did the shape represent? Did it have to do with the murdered girl or was it some other kind of message? Nothing was clicking for him. He had positioned the form vertically. He re-taped it horizontally and stared at it some more. Still nothing.

He looked at the clock. It was time for him to get ready for Lance's barn dance. He didn't want to go but couldn't think of a good excuse for not attending. He had tried to weasel out of it, claiming a sick cat. Even he knew that was pretty lame, and it only resulted in lots of teasing down at the Bun. The problem wasn't that he had never square danced in his life, which he hadn't . . . the problem was the Lance-Lucinda-Jane dilemma.

He called Jane's cell phone. "Hi Jane, just checking to see if you need a lift out to Lance's place."

When she answered there was lots of noise in the background, and she had to shout to be heard. "I'm already here. I came early to help with the food. Get your rear out here and man the theater donation table. Stop dawdling. This is going to be a fabulous fundraiser. Lance has done a bang-up job. Wait till you see it."

"Okay, okay. I'll be there soon." He was getting sick of hearing Lance this and Lance that. Next thing he knew, Lance would be walking on water.

* * *

LANCE OWNED THE OLD NELSON PLACE, a 360-acre dairy farm twenty miles west of town. Oscar Nelson had died in the tornado that hit Turners Bend the previous spring. The farm was auctioned off and no one came close to Lance's bid. The locals called him a city slicker and speculated the only thing he knew about organic farming was what he read on the Internet. There was a betting pool at the Bend guessing how long he would last. Nevertheless, it hadn't stopped all the naysayers from showing up for the barn dance.

When Chip approached the farm, the pasture was full of pickups and the barn was ablaze with lights. There were strings of lights hanging from all the trees surrounding the farmhouse. The yard was scattered with grinning Jack O' Lanterns with candles glowing through their grotesque features. Ghosts and bats swung from tree branches. He could hear fiddle music and laughter from inside the barn.

Lucinda came out to greet him. She was wearing a short swing skirt and a western-style shirt. The shirt, with its top three buttons undone, looked two sizes too small, and Lucinda's ample bosoms were bursting forth like a pair of ripe melons. *Real deal, not fake*, he thought. To complete the outfit she was wearing tooled, red leather cowboy boots and a white cowboy hat.

"It's about time you got here. Lance has been looking for you. This is just so exciting. I've never had so much fun. Lance contacted the Central Iowa Square Dance Association and managed to get the Barn Owl Band and Hoot Jamison, the best caller in the area. Lance is going to teach me how to do-si-do and allemande right. Isn't he adorable?"

"Who are you kidding, Lucinda? What's with all this gushing sweetness? Where is the broad who can peel paper off the walls with her caustic remarks? I miss her."

"Lance has changed all that. I'm a new woman. I'm in love."

Chip groaned and mocked Lucinda's voice. "Lance, Lance, Lance."

She ignored him, took his arm and hauled him into the barn. "Come on, don't be such a jerk."

Chip had to admit to himself that the barn was pretty amazing. It had been transformed into the set of an old Broadway musical, maybe *Oklahoma* or *State Fair*. It definitely had a 1950s feel. Bales of hay were arranged for sitting. A long table brimming with food ran along one side. Jane was behind the table serving slabs of ribs dripping with barbecue sauce and crispy fried chicken.

"What's that wonderful smell?"

"Oh, it's the mulling spices from the hot cider. Or you could have cold beer, the kegs are over there in the tubs of ice," Lucinda said.

"What are all those kids doing over there?" Chip pointed to a group of children kneeling around a huge sawed-off barrel in one of the empty cattle stalls.

"They're bobbing for apples. Each child who gets an apple can bring it to the prize booth for a Halloween treat bag."

"I remember doing that once as a kid. It freaked out my mother, who was always cautious about communal germs." He watched the children dressed in home-made costumes reminiscent of the era . . .

hobos, gypsies, cowboys and clowns. He recognized a Lone Ranger and a Little Orphan Annie. The Andrews twins were Raggedy Ann and Andy. Jessica Andrews seemed pleased with her appearance, but her brother, Justin, less so. Probably a little too cutesy for his taste.

The Barn Owl Band fiddlers were warming up, and Hoot Jamison was testing the microphone. "One, two, three, testing. Folks, we'll be ready for the first dance in about five minutes, so find your partners."

"I better find Lance. He promised the first dance to me," said Lucinda.

"Guess, I'll just mosey over to the food table and grab me some grub."

Lucinda laughed and punched him in the arm. "Now you're getting into the spirit of the party." Chip watched her as she wiggled her hips seductively through the crowd.

Jane smiled at him from behind the buffet table. Her face was glowing and her blue eyes sparkled. He hadn't seen her look so happy in months. If Lance Williams was the source of that happiness, he feared he would just have to saddle up and ride out of town into the sunset and die in the desert.

"The plates are at that end, down by the salads," Jane said.

Chip followed Jane's directions. He helped himself to cole slaw and potato salad and chose strawberry jello from the gem-colored array of jello salads. He took a foil-wrapped baked potato, a scoop of green bean casserole and sweet potatoes with marshmallows on top. He chose a corn muffin from the basket of breads and moved down to where Jane was serving the meat.

"Ribs or chicken or both?" she asked.

"What the heck, both."

"I'm glad you're here, Chip. After such a difficult year here in Turners Bend, this is just what the town needed. Lance has really knocked himself out with this affair. He'll be the new town hero."

"Do you mean replacing me?"

"Oh, you're still our only celebrity . . . well, our only author. I hope you'll dance with me later." She smiled coyly.

Is she flirting with me? Could this be another "Chip gets lucky" night? Her manner cheered Chip considerably. Maybe he was still number one with Jane. He found a vacant hay bale where he sat and ate his dinner. The dancing had begun and Lucinda and Lance were just finishing dancing to a rousing "Turkey in the Straw." Lucinda threw her arms around him, and Lance lifted her feet off the ground in a big bear hug.

Chief Fredrickson sat down next to him and sipped from a big plastic cup of beer. He licked the suds from around his lips and gazed out at the dancers. "Got another mystery in the mail today. You might want to come by the station and have a look tomorrow."

"Did Jim come up with anything on that form?"

"Turned out to be a generic form used by most of the milk processing companies. Guess the best we can say is that the sender is either a dairy farmer or works for one of the companies. Not much help, is it?"

"What arrived today?"

"Don't think this is the time or place to talk about it. I'll show you tomorrow. I better join Flora and push her around the dance floor or I'll never hear the end of it. Look at her, isn't she a sight?"

Flora was indeed a vision . . . dressed in a traditional square dance dress, complete with puffed sleeves and a full skirt over layers of crinoline. Chip was surprised to see she was a graceful dancer, despite her considerable girth. He was reminded of the dancing hippos in Disney's *Fantasia*.

Chip first danced with Jane, then Lucinda and later with Flora and Bernice. He and Sharon promenaded to "Buffalo Girl." He was always going right when everyone else was going left and up when everyone else was going down.

Despite his initial reluctance and clumsiness, he was enjoying himself. The gaiety in the room was contagious, and his spirit was buoyed by the music and movement.

"How are things with the mother-in-law situation, Sharon?"

"Lordy, if you hear she's been bumped off, you'll know I was the perp. This morning she fixed Robert's eggs 'the way Sonny likes them,' like I can't scramble a damn egg right. Don't get me started on her, Chip."

After a few more dances Chip counted the donations and was very pleased at the amount of money donated for the Bijou renovation.

Fifteen thousand dollars was beyond his expectations. A generous contribution by one anonymous donor added significantly to the total. He strongly suspected that donor was Iver, who in the past had given surprising amounts to the town.

Chip purposely avoided Lance until about midnight, when Lance sought him out. "Are you having a good time, Chip?"

Chip decided to suck it up and be cordial. "Great event, Lance. Everyone seems to be having a wonderful time, and we took in a bundle for the theater."

"How much?"

"Just over fifteen thousand."

Lance whistled. "Not bad, huh? But I can't take all the credit. Lucinda and Jane helped a lot. They're bringing out the desserts and coffee now, so I better get over there and help my fair ladies."

Chip took a breath, got up his nerve and asked the question that had been plaguing him for days. "Is one of them the ladylove you told me about?"

"Sure is," Lance said over his shoulder as he smiled and strolled toward the buffet table. Chip watched as he put one arm around Lucinda and the other around Jane.

Just when Chip was pretty sure Lucinda was Lance's target, doubt raised its ugly head again. Could it be Jane instead?

He consoled himself with a piece of carrot cake, a slice of cherry pie and a cup of hot coffee, then went back for a handful of chocolate chip cookies. He was stuffing his face and stuffing his feelings. He had fun, but still felt like such a loser, especially in contrast to the suave Lance. He wanted to escape unnoticed, go home, and stew in his own self-doubt.

He slipped out the door and returned home to his household of faithful pets. He stayed up until 2:00 a.m. writing another chapter of *Mind Games*.

CHAPTER EIGHTEEN

Mind Games
Minneapolis, Minnesota
Early August

T HE HUNTER CLOSED HIS LAPTOP. The Ghost Rider tracking device he installed on Jo's car showed she was still away from home, but he felt a need to be in her world again.

He quickly crept along the hedges in the alleyway until he reached her home, thankful that Jo kept late hours while the rest of her neighborhood slept. The street was quiet, with only a television screen glowing a bright blue through the curtains of an insomniac's house. The Hunter sank into the shadows until they swallowed him whole.

His ears strained for sounds of late-night dog walkers or other nocturnal activity. He heard the distant thrum of the traffic on Interstate 35W running parallel to the neighborhood and the deep-throated bark of the St. Bernard that lived four houses down. He waited until the dog had settled back down for the night. Finally satisfied that he had not raised any suspicions from the neighbors, he crouched down by the fence surrounding Agent Schwann's house and quickly pushed aside the boards he had loosened earlier in the week.

The Hunter climbed into her yard, feeling a slight tug on his shirt sleeve where it caught on a nail. He reached up to loosen the fabric and once he had climbed through, he pulled the boards back into place.

The night air was sticky and he felt a trickle of sweat down his back. The fluttering grew in his belly. Normally, he was content to watch her on his computer screen. The video cameras he had installed around her house were top-notch.

But it wasn't enough now. Tonight he decided he needed to see her, in the flesh.

He stood on the edge of the yard, where he had an unobstructed view outside her bedroom window. Jo's house was a 1920s, two-story white stucco, with the corners edged in stone. From this side of the house, he had a clear view into the den and the first floor master bedroom.

The agent had security lights, of course, which flicked on with any movement in the yard. However, earlier in the week, the Hunter had lured a wandering dog onto the property with the toss of a hamburger into the yard, and he was able to identify what areas stayed in the shadows.

The Hunter settled in, waiting for her to come home. He pulled the bottle of ibuprofen out of his pocket and shook three pills into his palm. Wincing, he swallowed them dry. He hated to admit it, but the headaches were starting up again. Not as bad as before, but getting there. *They're just stress-related. Nothing more. They will disappear when Jo is mine.*

When he saw the headlights of a car, his heart sped up as he thought about Jo. But when he peeked around the corner toward the front of the house, he saw a green and white taxi idled at the curb. A tall, well-dressed man stepped out with a suitcase. He reached into the open front window of the car and talked to the driver, reaching in his pocket for his wallet.

As the taxi pulled away, the man turned toward Jo's house. In the light of the street lamp, the Hunter had his first good look at the passenger. His breath caught in his throat. The man was Dr. John Goodman.

* * *

JOHN DIRECTED THE CAB DRIVER to the last turn toward Jo's house. He loved this old neighborhood. It felt like coming home, in more ways than one.

Still, he had to stop his leg from jangling every time he thought about what being here again meant. He hadn't called because he knew she would only try to talk him out of coming. *I'm still not quite sure what this is.* Did he want to uproot and live a life here, with her? All he knew for sure was the last few weeks without her had been miserable.

He looked down and was surprised to see he still clutched his boarding pass. John smiled when he thought of Sally, his office manager, since she was the one who was responsible for him being here. She had stormed into his office that morning and announced, "John, you look terrible. You've bitten my head off twice this morning and it's not even nine. If you don't get your head out of your ass and tell that special agent of yours you've screwed up royally and beg her forgiveness, I'm going to quit. So take this ticket and get your butt to the airport. Your flight leaves at five." She slapped the boarding pass on his desk and left abruptly.

Leave it to Sally to cut through all the bullshit. Of course, he knew Sally would never quit. She had been with him from the beginning and was the only one besides Jo who ever called him out on his behavior. At sixty-five years old, she was well past the age when she felt the need to coddle anyone. And besides, Sally was right. He was being an idiot as far as Jo was concerned.

So here he was, in Minneapolis, worried that Jo might just slam the door in his face.

Finally, the cab pulled up in front of Jo's house. His hand shook just a bit as he handed the cab fare to the driver and grabbed his overnight bag off the seat. Rolling his eyes at his clumsy behavior, he thought of the hundreds of brain surgeries he had performed without a tremor, and here he was trembling because he was about to see Jo again. His heart pounded when he looked up at the door to her house. Grabbing the door handle, he took a deep breath and stepped out on to the curb. *Here we go.*

It was a dark, cloudy evening and the vee of yellow light from the light fixture above Jo's front door guided him like a beacon. Climbing the steps, he fought to slow down his galloping heartbeat. He closed his eyes, counted to ten, and then pushed the doorbell, anticipating the look on Jo's face when she opened the door.

When he had waited for what seemed an eternity, he pushed the bell once more, this time peeking into the sidelight beside the door. He was startled to see a small shadow at his shin level just on the other side of the glass. Crouching down, he could hear the plaintive mewling of a kitten, and he saw its eyes glowing. "Well, well, well. Looks like Jo picked up a boarder since I was here last."

His fingers closed around the key in his front jeans pocket. Jo had given it to him the last time he'd been here, because she had to go to work before his flight back to Baltimore. At least that's what she had told him, but he felt it meant so much more, that she would trust him with a key to her world.

The key slipped from his sweaty hand, and he cursed to himself as he bent over to retrieve it. He unlocked the front door and flicked on the light switch. Immediately, the cat wound its way in and out of his legs. He set his suitcase down and scooped up the kitten. It purred contentedly as he stroked its soft fur. John chuckled and said, "Well, at least one family member thinks I belong here. Let's hope your roommate agrees."

He put the cat on the floor and looked around. Everything in the room reminded him of Jo and he felt happy he'd come. In spite of the nervousness he felt about whether or not he'd be welcome after their last conversation, being here, in Jo's house, felt absolutely right.

John turned around at a noise and saw the kitten gnawing on the white and black luggage claim ticket on the handle of his suitcase. Crouching down, he gently pulled the tag away from her and removed it from the bag. "That can't be good for you to chew on. Let's go find you some food, instead."

He tossed the luggage tag into the wastepaper basket next to Jo's desk in the den and then strode into the kitchen, the kitten on his heels. After locating the cans of cat food in her pantry, he filled the kitten's food dish.

John leaned against the counter, watching the little creature lap up her food. He looked at his watch, tempted to call Jo. *She's probably still on duty, but surely she'll be home soon.* He was exhausted from a full day at work, the race to the airport and the long flight here.

He moved back into the den. Stretching out on the couch, his six-foot-four frame spilling over the edges, he thought about what he'd say to Jo when she got home. Would she be glad to see him? Shocked? Or just flat out pissed?

An unsettling thought hit him. *What if Jo isn't simply working late but out on a date?* They had said their goodbyes, after all. And it had been two weeks. Maybe Jo was ready to move on. Suddenly, John felt foolish for charging in here.

Deep in thought, he almost missed the light rap on the front door. He was startled out of his musings and jumped up to answer the door. Jo wouldn't knock at her own house, unless she was startled to see lights on in her house. *Who else would be here at this time of the night?* He called out, "Who is it?"

* * *

WHEN JO ARRIVED HOME, she kicked off her shoes at the door. Cleo came running and greeted her with a happy meow. Jo reached down and stroked her ears, "Good evening, sweet girl. I'll bet you're hungry. Sorry I'm so late."

She walked into the kitchen and grabbed a can of cat food from the pantry. She flipped open the top and spooned the contents into the cat's dish. Cleo neatly sniffed at the bowl and then turned her back on it. Jo shook her head, "Well, aren't we getting finicky? I thought you'd scarf it down, after all this time." She shrugged her shoulders, "It's there if you change your mind. I'm taking a long bath and then you are on your own."

Jo had drawn her bath when Cleo nudged up against her, demanding that she be cuddled. "Oh, now you want my company? You're going to have to wait. This tub and a glass of chardonnay have my full attention at the moment."

As she reached for a towel, she saw the kitten chewing on a piece of paper. She bent over and tugged it out of Cleo's teeth. "Here now, that's not yours."

Straightening up, Jo looked at the paper in her hand. It was a long, skinny tag. "What the hell?" A baggage claim tag . . . where did it come from?

She brought it over to the vanity light for a closer look, and her heart stopped when she read, "J. Goodman."

Jo's hand flew to her mouth. "My God. John! And it's dated today." She ran out into the den, looking for more signs of him. *John was here!* She spun around the room, trying to make sense of things. There was no other sign that he had been here.

She called out his name as she ran from room to room. No sounds greeted her, except the quiet ticking of the clock on the mantle. After searching the entire house, she stood still, just listening. Jo looked down at Cleo, who had followed her in her hunt for John. "Where is he, sweetie? He was here, right?" Elation turned to confusion when she couldn't find him. *Maybe he went back out, running some errand when he didn't find me at home?*

As she stood in the upstairs bedroom, she checked her cell phone for messages once again. Nothing. A seed of panic was growing inside her. Maybe he changed his mind and went back home. *But would he have just left without saying a word?*

She dialed his cell number. After a few rings, it went to voice mail. Jo left a message, "John, it's me. I know about your surprise visit. Please, just come back to the house. I'm . . ." Jo swallowed the lump that had formed in her throat and tried again. "I'm so glad you came. We've got a lot of things to talk about. And, John? I love you."

In a fog, Jo almost slipped on the last step as she walked back down the stairs. "Where is he?"

CHAPTER NINETEEN

Turners Bend
November

W HEN CHIP RETURNED HOME after the barn dance, Callie was sitting by her empty food dish complaining, howling as if she hadn't been fed in days. After eating, she fastidiously licked her paws and used them to wash her face. He was relieved to see she had turned the corner. Again his pets proved to be a calming diversion from his troubles, and after completing his chapter, he went to bed and was able to sleep until dawn.

As he was eating his cold cereal the next morning, however, his mind began to roil and fester like maggots in road kill. His first thoughts were about Lance Williams. He was beginning to really get sick of the guy. If Lance's paramour was Lucinda, it was good news-bad news. Good thing it wasn't Jane, and bad that Lucinda might move to Turners Bend and be on his case 24/7. If it was Jane, he was doubly screwed. He would lose Jane, and Lucinda would return to her she-devil persona and take her rejection out on him. *How did I get to be the loser in this situation?*

Putting the jug of milk away, he again studied the diagram he had posted on the refrigerator door. Last evening's conversation with Chief Fredrickson had definitely piqued his curiosity. He was eager to get dressed and head down to the police station.

The sound of a car pulling up to his house startled him. Out the pet-nose- smeared window he saw Lucinda emerge from her rental car, a white BMW. She looked different somehow, glowing, natural looking, still attractive, but with a softer edge than he had ever seen before. He invited her into the house and poured her a cup of coffee.

"Sorry, I can't make you a fancy coffee. I've got milk if you want it and some sugar somewhere."

"This is fine, Chip. Thanks. I wanted to talk with you before I head to the airport. I've got to get back to the office to finish the publicity for the launch of *Brain Freeze* next month. I know you won't believe this, but I hate like hell to leave here, to leave Lance. I've really fallen for the guy, head over heels, ton of bricks, cloud nine and every other cliché you've ever heard about being in love."

She sighed wistfully. "At times, I think he feels the same about me, but at other times, I have my doubts. I just don't know. He said he would think about coming to New York for Christmas. I told him I would convince Howard Glasser to come to the Midwest premiere of *The Cranium Killer* at the Bijou. I definitely plan to be back in March for the event. In the meantime, could you keep tabs on him? Would you let me know if he says anything about me? God, I sound like a junior high school girl, don't I?"

Chip sipped his cold coffee and gave himself a moment to think how he could approach this question and at the same time solve his own dilemma. "You love New York, the excitement, the clubs, the shopping, the publishing business. You'd never survive out here in the cornfield raising organic vegetables. I just don't see it happening. Your best bet is to lure Lance to New York and convince him to stay."

"You're one to talk, Chip. You ended up here, and I don't see you running back to Baltimore and your playboy life. Something is keeping you here, and I know who she is. You're not giving up on Jane, are you?"

"The question is . . . is Jane giving up on me?"

Lucinda checked her watch, a wide gold bangle with a face the size of a silver dollar. "I've got to make tracks to the airport. Oh, just because I'm in love, it doesn't mean you're off the hook. Keep writing; I need another book from you."

* * *

ON THE DRIVE TO TOWN Chip prided himself on his brilliant idea—Lance in New York and Jane in Turners Bend would be the best of all possible worlds for him, positively Machiavellian. He'd have to continue to promote Lance's move to the Big Apple.

At the police station he found Sharon in the outer office at her desk. She had been in good spirits last evening at the barn dance, but her mood had obviously swung in the opposite direction by this morning. She grumped, "In there," and motioned her head to the chief's office.

The chief and Jim were leaning over a table. They both wore purple evidence gloves. "Take a look at this, Chip, but don't touch. This is what I got in the mail yesterday. Came in a plain manila envelope mailed from Sioux City this time. I wanted you to see them before we send them to the Iowa Bureau of Investigation. What do you see?"

"Looks like pieces of fabric to me."

"What else?"

"Well, they are all the same shade of blue, some kind of shiny silky material."

"Sharon, would you please come in here." Sharon appeared at the door and slouched against the doorframe.

"Do you have any idea what kind of fabric these are?"

She walked to the desk, put on a pair of gloves and picked up each piece, rubbing them between her thumb and fingers. "I'm no Martha Stewart, but I'd say it's nylon with a mesh weave."

"Five X's on the diagram and five pieces of blue cloth. My gut tells me they're connected," said the chief. "But I just don't know how. Jim here has some hair-brained idea about a serial killer."

Jim, at age twenty-four, was a fresh-faced deputy just three years out of the Police Academy. He immersed himself in TV cop shows, much to the chief's vexation. "On that TV show *Criminal Minds* a serial killer always sends clues to the FBI, and they profile him," said Jim.

"We only have one body. According to the coroner, the murder wasn't recent, so we don't have anything that says serial killer to me," said the chief. "What's your opinion, Chip?"

"I don't know. I think Jim might have something there, and if he's right, this won't be the last message you get. I remember reading about how the Son of Sam and the Zodiac Killer sent clues to the police and media. Let me know if anything else shows up."

* * *

ON HIS WAY HOME, Chip spotted two pheasants alongside the harvested corn field on Hjalmer Gustafson's farm. They were a pair; the cock a thing of beauty with his white-ringed neck, vibrant blue-green head and red face wattles, and the hen a plain buff brown. He heard a shotgun blast, followed by two more. Pheasant hunting season had started the last week in October, and Chip feared the two birds would soon be served on a platter in one of Turners Bend's households. Never having been a hunter, Chip had a hard time understanding why shooting these marvelous creatures qualified as sport.

Thinking about hunters reminded him he had the Hunter on the loose in Minneapolis with the lovely Jo Schwann as his target. Lucinda's parting salvo about working on his book entered his head, and on the remainder of the trip home his mind was occupied with the developing plot of *Mind Games*.

CHAPTER TWENTY

Mind Games
Minneapolis, Minnesota
Early August

Jo SANK INTO THE COUCH in the den, her mind whirling with possibilities. Maybe there was some kind of mistake. Maybe John hadn't been here at all, and she just wanted to believe he had come back for her. She thought she'd go crazy with all the "maybes" in her head. She sorted through the scenarios out loud, "How do I explain the baggage claim tag?" She pinched her lower lip between her teeth. "Maybe I read the date wrong and it was from a previous trip."

Feeling foolish about how she had allowed her hopes to conjure up a visit from John, she looked down at Cleo, who had curled up on the sofa next to her, "Did you pull it out from under a bed or something?" The kitten had no answers, except a sympathetic meow.

Jo stood up and walked back to the kitchen table where she had left the tag in her search for John. She hesitated a minute to pick up the tag, half dreading the moment when she would realize she had made a huge error and that John really had not been here today. Jo shook her head at her foolishness, and then raised the ticket up to the light to read it more carefully. No, she hadn't been mistaken; the claim ticket was dated for a flight today.

Pulling her cell out of her pocket, she called John once more. As she waited for his deep voice on the other end, she heard a strange humming sound emitting from the den. Stepping back into the room, she realized the hum was in sync with the ringing on her phone. She dropped to her knees on the thick Oriental rug and reached under the sofa trying to locate the source of the vibrations. Her heart beat faster as her fingers located an object. She pulled it out and gasped as she recognized John's cell phone in her hand. "Oh my God, John was here!"

Jo's chest felt tight. Something was definitely wrong. Where was he and why was his phone under her couch?

Panic was setting in. Her watch showed it was late, almost midnight. Where would he have gone on his own at this hour AND without his phone?

Jo dashed out the front door, desperate to find any additional signs of John. Her eyes adjusted to the dark and they darted around the yard. The wind picked up her red curls and blew them around her face. Clouds scudded across the night sky. As she was about to go back into the house, she heard someone call out, "Jo!"

Jo spun around, praying it was John. Her heart dropped in her chest when she saw it was her new neighbor, Stephen, out for a walk with a tan and white Jack Russell terrier. "Evening, Jo. I thought that was you."

Jo was eager to go back inside and figure out what she was going to do next. "Hi, Stephen. I'm sorry I can't talk right now. I'm kind of in the middle of something. See you soon."

He reached out to grasp her arm when she turned to leave and said, "I've left a few messages for you, to see if we could get together for that coffee I owe you. Why haven't your returned my calls?"

Jo looked down at his hand lightly gripping her arm and then up at his face. His touch irritated her, and she pulled away. "I've been working a case that's been eating up all of my time."

The corners of Stephen's mouth turned down, and she could see the hurt in his eyes. For a moment, she felt a sliver of guilt. *He's just trying to be nice, after all.*

"Look, I'm sorry I haven't called you back. I'll touch base as soon as my schedule eases up a bit. Now just isn't a good time."

Jo turned back toward her front door when Stephen said, "Must have been quite a party at your house tonight."

She faced him once again. He had moved to the base of her steps and looked up at her, the frown now replaced by a sly smile. He ignored the terrier tugging at the leash in his hands. She raced back down the steps and said, "What do you mean, party?"

Stephen said, "I saw two guys stumbling down your front steps and into a cab."

Jo felt her heart thudding in her chest. She forced her voice to be calm, "Are you sure it was my house? I didn't have a party. I just got home from work."

Stephen's smile widened, "Oh, they were definitely coming from your house. I know, because I was admiring the shutters on your house and was thinking I should ask you where you got them." He cocked his head to one side, "So, maybe you weren't quite honest with me about how busy you've been . . . or maybe you've just been too busy partying without me."

Jo bristled at his tone, and any regret she had about hurting his feelings evaporated. She could hear the sharpness in her voice when she replied, "As I've said, I just got home from work. Tell me what you saw."

Stephen's smile faded and his eyes narrowed. "Oh, I don't know. It was pretty dark . . ."

Jo grabbed Stephen by his upper arm, frustrated that he was playing games when John was missing. She forced herself to be more civil, "A close friend of mine was here and now he's not. This is important. Please tell me everything you remember."

Stephen watched Jo for a moment, until she dropped her hand from his arm. His voice was tight when he replied, "A close friend, you say? Well, let me think."

The dog uttered a sharp bark. Stephen yanked on the leash and said, "Hush now, Max." He looked back at Jo, as he said, "Ms. Schwann needs our help."

There was no mistaking the mocking, bitter tone in his voice, and Jo wondered if he was lying to her about what he saw earlier. *But how could he have known I was looking for someone when he told me about the two men?*

Jo recognized it was time for a different tack. She needed to pacify her neighbor, even when all she wanted to do was shake him. John could be anywhere by now. *He could be in trouble and this guy is acting like a jilted lover.*

She took a deep breath and forced her voice to be soothing, "I know I hurt your feelings by not returning your calls and I regret that. You are a nice man and you deserve better.

"But please, don't let my rude behavior stop you from helping my friend. I would appreciate anything you can tell me about the two men you saw, any detail at all. My friend could be in serious trouble and I know you would like to help."

Jo reached out to touch his shoulder. "Please."

Stephen looked down into her eyes. He took a minute to speak and Jo wondered if she had overplayed her hand. A clock ticked furiously in her head; time for John could be running out.

Jo was startled when Stephen finally replied, "One guy was definitely tall, taller than me. I'd say about six-foot-three, six-four. White, kinda good-looking, if you go for that type. He seemed to be the drunker of the two and was leaning heavily on the shorter guy."

Stephen looked skyward, as if concentrating on what he had seen. "I would say the other guy was maybe five-ten, give or take. Hispanic or something; dark-skinned. He had on a Twin's baseball cap." He wrapped Max's leash around his hand a few times to reel him in as the terrier tried to wander to a nearby fire hydrant.

Jo's heart raced. The taller guy Stephen described could certainly be John. "If you saw a picture of the tall man, do you think you'd recognize him?"

"Maybe. I don't know."

"Would you mind coming inside with me? I have a picture."

Stephen looked eager and uncomfortable at the same time. "You know, it's late and Max here is getting antsy. Can we do this in the morning?"

Jo was at the end of her rope. She briefly thought about arresting him for failure to assist in a case, but she knew that was desperation whispering in her ear.

Jo took a deep breath and let it out slowly. "I really need to make sure my friend is all right. It'll only take a moment. It could make a huge difference."

Stephen blew out a heavy sigh. He said, "Oh, okay. But just for a sec." He bent over to pick up Max and followed Jo into the house.

Jo grabbed the picture of John and herself which had been taken in front of the Captain James Landing restaurant in Baltimore's Inner Harbor the previous spring. They were sitting on the deck, with a huge plate of steamed crabs piled in front of them. John's nose was peeling from a day out on the boat, and both of them grinned from ear to ear as they sat close together.

She walked back to where Stephen stood in the doorway with his dog. "This is my friend, John. Could this be the man you saw stumbling as the other guy helped him into the cab?"

Stephen took the photo out of Jo's hands, studying it carefully. A double frown line formed above the bridge of his nose, and Jo saw a muscle bunch along his jaw line.

When he didn't say anything, Jo prompted him, "Stephen, do you recognize him?"

"Yeah, yeah. I guess it could be him. I didn't get a really good look." He tried to return the photo back to Jo, but she ignored his gesture and he held the photo awkwardly in his hands.

"Did it look as if the other man was forcing him in any way?"

He cocked his head to one side. "What do you mean?"

"Did you have reason to believe he was being dragged to the cab against his will? Did you see any evidence of a weapon of any kind?"

"No, nothing like that. They looked pretty chummy, as far as I could tell."

"Do you remember anything specific about the cab? The name of the taxi company, the color of the vehicle . . . anything at all would be helpful."

"No, I didn't give it much thought. I guess it might not have even been a cab at all, now that I think about it. I had the impression since it was idling by the curb, so I assumed it was a taxi."

Stephen looked down again at the photo. Jo saw he gripped the frame tightly in his hands, until his knuckles showed white. His voice was cold as he held up the photo. "You're pretty happy with him in that picture. Looks like more than just a friend to me."

He shoved the photo back to her and said, "Your friend really should be more careful. Never know what sort of person you are going to run into in the dark."

Jo sucked in a breath and she felt a chill run its finger down her spine. "What do you mean by that? Did you see something else I should know about?" She grabbed his shirt as he turned to go.

Stephen pulled from her grasp and bent down to pick up Max, who had been yanking on his leash and was barking madly. Jo realized the dog probably had picked up Cleo's scent. The terrier wriggled in Stephen's arms, ready to hunt down his prey. Stephen ignored the dog and said, "I think maybe I was mistaken about seeing your friend. It was dark and it could have been anybody out there. Look, it's late. I need to be getting home."

He turned around and let himself out the front door, not bothering to close it behind him. Jo fought the urge to run after him; she knew he wouldn't tell her anything more tonight. But she was just as certain he saw more than he was telling her.

Jo walked over and closed the door. She wasn't sure what to think of Stephen's behavior. Would he lie about what he saw?

When she came back into the den, she heard the plaintive meows of her cat coming from upstairs. She ran up the stairs and found Cleo huddled beneath her bed. She cautiously reached under the bedskirt and scooped the kitten out, pulling her into her chest.

Jo could feel the small body shaking against her. She rubbed the cat's ears and murmured, "Did Max's barking scare you? It's okay now."

But as Jo thought about John, she wondered if she was saying that for Cleo's benefit or for her own.

CHAPTER TWENTY-ONE

Turners Bend
Thankgsgiving

CHIP SPENT HIS SECOND Thanksgiving at Iver and Mabel's house. This year the guest list was expanded to include Jane's children, who had spent the holiday last year with their father, and Lance.

Chip gazed out Mabel's kitchen window and watched Lance getting Iver's full litany, verse and chorus, praising deep-fried turkey. Last year that guy had been him. A lot had changed since then. He was feeling like leftover turkey or worse, Tofurkey . . . soybean curd pressed into a mold . . . doesn't look like turkey, doesn't taste like turkey.

As Mabel and Jane busied themselves in the kitchen with all the side dishes and pies, and Sven and Ingrid sat in the living room watching football, Chip reminisced to the women.

"Gosh, it was just about this time last year that Honey had eight puppies right here in this kitchen, and the last one was Runt. Hard to believe that eighty-five-pound boy once weighed just a few ounces. They grow up too fast."

Jane took a taste of the gravy she was stirring and added some black pepper. "That's the same thing I say about Ingrid and Sven. Just yesterday they were babies and now they're almost adults." She sighed wistfully.

Chip thought about Honey, Runt's mother, the stray who had arrived at his door one stormy night and never left. "How old do you think Honey is, Jane?"

"Hard to tell exactly, Chip, but I'd guess she is seven or eight. Why do you ask?"

"She just hasn't been herself lately. Doesn't want to play. Kind of off her feed."

Jane moved on to the potatoes. She started mashing them by hand, using Mabel's old-fashioned masher with a wooden handle. She stopped to add a dollop of sour cream. "I better have a look at her. I can come by on my way home tonight and check her over. Sven and

Ingrid are going to a youth event at First Lutheran this evening, so I'll have to drop them off first," she said, as she added a chunk of butter to the potatoes.

The idea of having Jane to himself elated Chip. His thoughts went right to their previous sexual romps, the first being the time she had come to the house to de-worm Runt and ended up in his bed. He felt better with each sip of the Pinot Grigio he was nursing, even though it was far too sweet for his liking. He knew full-well Jane's visit may not be a repeat of previous magical evenings, but just to have Jane alone, no kids, no Lance, would be a step in the right direction.

Watching Lance charm all three ladies during dinner punched a hole in his happiness balloon. Lance was funny and sweet and flirtatious in turn. Mabel was calling him "my dear boy" and Jane was forever touching him. When Lance complimented Ingrid on her hair, she blushed and demurely thanked him. It was obvious to Chip that she was thunder-struck by his attention. Chip tried to derail his nemesis.

"What do you hear from Lucinda, Lance? She said you might be spending Christmas in New York with her. Sounds pretty serious to me."

"Yes, Lucinda is a lovely woman, but Turners Bend has no lack of lovely females, as I'm sure you have found," said Lance, gesturing to the three women around the table and winking at Jane in particular.

Chip had to admit to himself that Lance was as smooth as honey on a hot biscuit. The guy was acting way too much like Dr. John Goodman, his dashing hero. *I could learn to hate both of them . . . Lance and Goodman.*

* * *

CHIP ARRIVED HOME AND QUICKLY picked up dirty laundry, made the bed and cleaned out the litter box before Jane was due to arrive after dropping off her kids at church. He surveyed the living room, shooed the animals off the furniture, dimmed the lights and put Ella Fitzgerald in his i-Pod dock. Hearing Ella's lilting intro to "Dedicated to You" quelled his nerves. He looked around, it wasn't perfect, but it would have to do.

Jane arrived carrying her medical bag. She called Honey to the kitchen and looked in the golden retriever's eyes and ears. She ran her hands along the dog's back and underside, all the while asking questions about the dog's energy, food, elimination, and sleep. Honey was compliant and wagged her tail in response to Jane's gentle touch and soothing words, as she repeatedly palpated her abdomen.

"Good girl, Honey. You can go lie down now," Jane said, as she finished her exam. "Let's sit in the living room a minute, Chip."

They settled themselves on the couch. It had been a halfway decent piece of furniture before the dogs appropriated it for their daytime naps. Now it was snagged and dirty and covered with animal hair.

"I'm sorry about all the pet hair. I just can't seem to keep up on it. It's everywhere. I guess I could get one of those special pet hair attachments for the vacuum cleaner. That is, if I had a vacuum cleaner."

Jane did not laugh. Instead she had a grave look on her face, as she reached out and took Chip's hand. She looked directly in his eyes and did not sugar-coat her findings. "I felt a mass in Honey's belly, a rather large one. I'm sorry, Chip, I think it's on her liver. I can't be sure without further tests, but I can tell you it may not be good, but then again it could be benign."

Chip felt like the air was being sucked out of his lungs, he couldn't speak or swallow, and there was an odd ringing in his head. Jane put her arm around his shoulders and gave him time to absorb the news.

"I deal with this all the time, but it never gets easier. Pets become like family members. I even see it with farm animals. People love their animals and seeing them sick or losing them is sometimes harder than losing a human friend. I promise I'll do all that I can for her. Bring her into the clinic tomorrow."

"Jane, I . . ." He couldn't go on, tears started to blur his vision and a lump gathered at the back of his throat. Jane held him, gently rocking until he quieted. Then she kissed him lightly on the cheek, slowly rose, gathered her supplies and prepared to leave.

"I'll see you tomorrow, Chip. In the meantime, try to get some sleep."

* * *

SLEEP ELUDED HIM. He lifted Honey onto his bed, whereupon both Runt and Callie joined them. The three animals slept soundly. Runt nipped in his sleep, Chip assumed he was dreaming about chasing rabbits. Callie curled up near the top of his head, her usual spot. Finally about 3:00 a.m. he maneuvered himself out of bed without unduly disturbing the animals and went into the kitchen. He poured himself a glass of orange juice and stared at the diagram on his refrigerator without really seeing it. His mind was on Honey, when another thought jumped to the forefront of his consciousness.

"Iowa," he whispered. "It's a map of Iowa."

He wondered how many times he had looked at the diagram and not seen the obvious. It was roughly the shape of the state of Iowa with five locations; each marked with an X. He had never been so sure of anything in his life. It was exciting and scary at the same time . . . five locations around the state. *Does this mean five bodies?*

He called Fredrickson's number, got his voice mail and left a message about his theory. Then his mind wandered to the body count in *Mind Games. How many bodies should I pile up in my story? One never seems enough in a good crime story.*

CHAPTER TWENTY-TWO

Mind Games
Minneapolis & Brooklyn Center, Minnesota
Early August

Jo WOKE WITH A START when Cleo walked across her legs, sharp claws demanding attention. Her head pounded in the rhythm of her heartbeat. She was sprawled across the couch in her den, the notes and plans she had made throughout the night scattered across the coffee table. The temporary relief she felt at the realization she had been dreaming evaporated when she remembered John was still missing.

She swiped a hand across gritty eyes, and blinked a few times. To locate anyone who might have a record of picking up John at her house, Jo had spent the better part of the night calling all of the major cab companies in the Twin Cities and the surrounding suburbs, beginning with AA Airport Taxi. Around 3:00 a.m. she found the cab company who brought John from the airport to her door, but no indication anyone else had driven him after that. After finishing up with Zipp Taxi, she started in on the list of hospitals. Absolutely no sign of John, as if he had ceased to exist.

She looked at her notes, trying to clear the cobwebs from her sleep-deprived brain. Her analytical mind kicked in and she began plotting her strategy. An hour later, she leaned back against the sofa, her neck stiff. *Why does it feel like Stephen sent me on a wild goose chase?* Jo intended to have another little chat with him later this morning, but first she had other business to attend to.

Jo glanced down at her watch. 6:00 a.m. She dug under the pile of papers in front of her and located her cell phone. She stared at it for a moment, trying to decide whether or not to call John's office. Jo had met Sally, John's office manager, at a hospital function and felt an immediate connection to the older woman. Sally loved John like a son, and Jo sensed there were few things that escaped Sally's notice when it came to her boss. Jo finally dialed the phone number for his office.

As she waited for a response, she padded into the kitchen when Cleo meowed impatiently. Jo wedged the phone between her ear and shoulder, reaching up into a cabinet to grab a can of cat food. A voice across the miles answered, "Neurosurgeon Specialists. How may I direct your call?"

"Good morning. This is Jo Schwann. I'd like to speak to Sally Townsend, please."

"One moment." Jo thought about what she would say to Sally. She needed to find out about John's plans, but she wanted to avoid alarming his office manager until she knew more.

Just as she flipped back the top on the cat food can, Sally's voice resonated in her ear. John's office manager sounded a bit confused when she spoke, "Hi, Jo. This is a pleasant surprise. What can I do for you?"

She cleared her throat and said, "Well . . . I feel awkward asking this, but do you know if John flew to Minneapolis yesterday?" Jo already knew the answer, but she needed to hear Sally say the words.

Jo gripped the phone tighter, waiting for Sally's response. An irrational voice in her head said, *Please say no. Tell me he's just down the hall, safe in his office. This was all just a screwy mix-up.*

There was a moment of silence on the other end of the phone and then Sally answered, "Yes, I booked the flight and then drove him to the airport myself. Was there a problem?" Jo's stomach churned. *So he had come, then.*

Jo closed her eyes and said, "It appears he made it as far as my house, but I haven't heard from him. Did you happen to book a hotel room for him?"

Sally sounded bewildered when she replied, "No, he said he would book a room himself, if, um, things didn't go as well as he hoped when he saw you again." Sally hesitated, and then said, "What do you mean, you think he made it as far as your house?"

The throbbing in Jo's head increased, and she rubbed her temple. "I worked on a case last night and didn't get home until late. I had no idea John was even coming. By pure luck, I found his luggage tag and his cell phone, but there was no other sign that he was here."

Sally's voice raised a few notes. "He left behind his cell phone? That makes no sense at all. I always give him a hard time about that phone. It's an extension of his hand, for heaven's sake. Jo, what are you not telling me?"

Jo was beginning to regret her call to John's office manager. Sally obviously didn't know anything and Jo had only succeeded in scaring the poor woman. She knew, however, any attempt to brush off Sally's questions would lead to panic. Jo took a breath and said, "I ran into one of my neighbors who may have seen John leaving in a cab with another person. Does John know anyone else in the area that he might have gone to visit?"

"He's had some business colleagues in the Cities over the years, but I can't imagine he would run out to meet one of them when he was hell-bent on setting things right with you."

Jo felt a stirring in her heart. "Really? Hell-bent?"

Sally's voice was soft when she said, "Honey, that man has been a bear since you both decided to call things off." Sally's voice took on a stern tone, "What the hell were you two thinking, anyway? You think love like that happens to everyone? Anyone with half a brain can see you two are meant to be. The rest is just nonsense."

In spite of her fears about John's whereabouts, Jo found herself smiling at Sally's words. "John always said the smartest thing he ever did was to hire you. I have to say, I couldn't agree more." Jo looked down at Cleo who wound around her legs, having finished her breakfast.

"Look, Sally, I've gotta go. I'll let you know if I hear from John. Will you do the same?"

"Sure will. And, Jo?"

"Yes?"

"Don't let that man slip through your fingers again. Do you hear me?"

Jo's smile widened. "Yes, ma'am. And Sally, thanks for everything." She clicked off the phone, feeling a little more hopeful. She wasn't quite sure why. Sally certainly didn't know anything more about John's whereabouts. But she had shed some light on John's feelings about their relationship.

Jo stood up and headed into the shower. Quickly, but carefully, she got ready for the day. It was important she look professional when she met with her boss this morning, because she had a feeling he would think her plan was most decidedly unprofessional.

* * *

JO TAPPED ON HER BOSS'S DOORFRAME and poked her head into his open office. "Tom, gotta minute?"

Tom Gunderson looked up from the papers scattered across his desk. There were dark circles under his eyes and a hank of his thick black hair hung down on his forehead. She couldn't remember seeing her boss looking so harried before. "Schwann? Tell me you've gotten a break in the Freemont/McDonald cases. The governor just called and reamed me out. God, that man is obnoxious. You would think he was my boss."

"Not just yet, but we're making progress. Since both victims were moved from the original crime scenes, Frisco cross-checked the cleaning crew staff for the Capitol with that of the newspaper headquarters. So far, there doesn't seem to be any commonalities."

"Did the alibis for all the construction workers and the cleaning staff at the Capitol check out?"

Jo frowned. "Yes. Unfortunately."

"And what about Freemont's wife?"

"We've checked out the widow's alibi and it's airtight."

Tom was thoughtful for a moment. "I presume you've checked into threats made against either one of them."

Jo nodded. "We've been digging through the reams of hate mail both of our victims accumulated over the last six months." Jo shook her head, still amazed at the vitriol the state representative and the op-ed columnist received on an almost weekly basis. "We've come across several letters that appear to have been sent by the same person to both of them. Of course, there was no return address and no fingerprints. And the postmarks are never the same, although they all originate in the metro area."

"Any trace of DNA on the envelopes when they were sealed?"

Jo shook her head. "No, but we sent them on to the BCA lab. Maybe we'll get lucky and they'll find some epithelial tissues from a paper cut or something. In the meantime, we're still processing trace evidence found at the scenes and on the bodies. Not much to work with, but we're due for a break."

"Seems we're dealing with one smart son-of-a-bitch. Thank God we haven't had any more victims, though I don't expect this nut-job is quite finished yet."

"Yes, sir." Jo shifted on her feet, unsure of how to broach her real reason for being in her boss's office. "Um, Tom. There is something else I want to discuss with you."

Jo took a deep breath and spoke quickly before she lost her nerve. "Look, something has come up and I would like to be reassigned to another case."

Tom furrowed his brow. "Are you joking? The Freemont/McDonald cases are the most important thing this office has seen in years and you're talking to me about changing mid-stream . . . what's going on, Schwann?"

"Something's happened to John."

"What do you mean, something's happened to him? If this is about your personal life, I . . ."

Jo interrupted, "Tom. Listen to me. John has disappeared. I have proof he came to visit me, but he's disappeared into thin air. I have reason to believe he's been kidnapped…"

"Maybe you should start from the beginning."

Jo ran through everything she had discovered so far and Tom listened carefully, occasionally asking questions and jotting down notes.

When she had concluded her report, he said, "So, you want me to assign you to his case? Has it occurred to you that you are the *last* person who should handle this? You know that's against regulations. You cannot be on a case when you are personally involved with the victim."

Tom ran his hands through his hair. "Look, Jo, I'm sorry to hear about John. He's a great guy and I know how much he means to you. And he's done a hell of a lot of favors for the FBI. But I can't put you in charge of the investigation of his disappearance."

Even though Tom reacted the way she had expected, it still rankled that he wasn't putting her on the case. Hot tears of frustration welled up in her eyes and she dug her fingernails into the palm of her hand to halt their progress. Between clenched teeth she said, "Tom, I chose this badge over John once before and I'll be damned if I'll make that same mistake twice. I'll quit if I have to. But I will find him, with or without your support."

Tom stood up from his desk and stared at her for a moment. Jo wondered what he would do, and part of her was worried he would accept her resignation.

Finally, he heaved a heavy sigh. "Schwann, you're killing me. You know I'm not going to let you quit. Tell you what. We're going to classify the investigation as a disappearance until we receive a ransom note or some other solid proof this is a kidnapping. That works out better for us. If it were a kidnapping, we'd have to let the state take the lead for twenty-four hours, until the Lindbergh Law kicks in. I don't want to wait until we have to assume John was transported across state lines before we can take over."

He held up a hand when Jo started to interrupt. "I'll assign John's case to Agent Daniels. You've worked with Daniels before and you know he's the best we've got at working missing person cases. Would that satisfy you?"

Jo put her hands on her hips, not backing down from his stare. "Daniels is an arrogant jackass. *I* have to do this."

Tom poked a finger in her direction. "And I'm telling you that even if I could assign this case to you, you would screw it up. You can't expect to be objective, and you could jeopardize John's life, you know."

His words stopped Jo cold. Tom's last words reminded her when they worked the NeuroDynamics case, she and John had both almost lost their lives because she was too personally worried about John's welfare. Deep down inside a nagging voice said Tom was right.

Jo's voice was weary when she mumbled, "Damn it."

Tom pounced on the waver in her resolve. "You will be kept in the loop, of course. I'll have Daniels update you every step of the way." He grimaced and said, "He won't thank me for it, mind you. Just promise me you'll keep plugging away at the Freemont/McDonald cases and leave the rest up to Agent Daniels."

Jo heaved a heavy sigh. The analytical part of Jo's brain knew Tom's plan had the best chance at finding John alive. *Doesn't mean I like it.* "Not giving me much of a choice, are you?"

Tom smirked. "Nope. I'll give Daniels the heads up, and then I want you to brief him and turn over all your notes as soon as humanly possible. We'll find him, Jo. I promise you that."

CHAPTER TWENTY-THREE

Turners Bend
December

CHIP REALIZED HE HAD TWO CRIMES running parallel in *Mind Games.* It was getting complicated, so he was working on a diagram in an attempt to keep them both on track. The phone startled him. He grabbed it and recognized Sharon's voice on the other end. "Hi, Sharon, what's up?"

"Your favorite FBI agent is here and requesting your presence. Actually it was more a command than a request; better get your keister down here pronto."

* * *

I CAN'T BELIEVE I'M SAYING THIS CHIEF, but it looks like you and your ace crime writer are on to something here," said FBI Agent Masterson.

Chip observed Masterson carefully as she spoke. He guessed she was ex-military. She was all spit and polish with nary a wrinkle, rarely a smile. No make-up on her face, no jewelry, and short cropped hair. She was small and wiry and gave the impression of being able to handle herself in hand-to-hand combat. At first he thought she was totally humorless, but occasionally he witnessed her razor-sharp wit. She said "ace crime writer" with just the right intonation to turn a compliment into sarcasm.

"Our lab has done an overlay of the diagram onto several types of maps of Iowa. One of the X's is located in or near Turners Bend. Locations of the other four X's have been determined and 'Bingo,' one of them is the Iowa City area where Tracy Trent was abducted. We now have local authorities checking all the abandoned buildings within a ten-mile radius of those locations. It's going to take some time, but I think we're on to something here, and it may lead us to a serial killer."

She consulted her iPad, scrolling through screens until she found what she was looking for. "Your fabric swatches are surely related to this case. Our forensic people are analyzing them now, trying to trace them back to a manufacturer. So far nothing in their preliminary report. We are also following up on the milk delivery form. Apparently there are many drivers in the state who deliver to the areas we are searching. None of them have a criminal record, but we'll investigate and interview all of them." She turned to the chief. "No more mysterious mailings, I presume."

"Not as of today's mail, but we'll keep a close look out," he said. "Anything else we can do for you, Agent Masterson?"

"That's it for now." She turned toward Chip. "I'm warning you, Mr. Collingsworth, no meddling, no amateur sleuthing like you have been known to do." She stood, preparing to leave. "By the way, I picked up *Brain Freeze* at the airport. Just published and flying off the shelf, I understand. The jacket blurb says it's about a female FBI agent. Should be good for a laugh. Good day, gentlemen, I'll be in touch." She shook hands with both of the men, donned her mirrored sun glasses and departed without a smile.

The chief blew out a puff of air. "That woman intimidates the hell out of me, Chip. I need a decent cup of coffee. The stuff here tastes like mud from the bottom of Beaver Creek. Let's head over to the Bun."

* * *

BERNICE WAS BUSY DECORATING the Bun for Christmas. The running lights around the front window looked like mice chasing each other. On every table she placed a snowman surrounded by fluffy fake snow. The radio was tuned to an all-holiday-music station and she sang along with "I Want a Hippopotamus for Christmas."

"We can serve ourselves, Bernice," said Chip, as he went behind the counter, grabbed two mugs and filled them from the chrome coffee pot. He spied a copy of his new book, which had just been released on December 1st. "So what do you think of *Brain Freeze*, Bernice?"

"Well, I think you're improving. It was a little on the gory side for me, but I do love the spunky FBI agent. Sort of part Jane and part Agent Masterson. And I'll take the dashing Dr. Goodman, if it doesn't work out with Jo. You know, he reminds me a lot of Lance. Don't you think?"

Chip choked on a sip of coffee. He had almost forgotten everyone in Turners Bend was a literary critic. He got no end of advice when the town folks read *The Cranium Killer*, his first book, and he could expect no less with *Brain Freeze*. But the comparison between Lance and Dr. Goodman was more than he could take. "Lance, really?"

"Yeah, tall, handsome, charming, a real lady's man. If I wasn't married to Chester, I'd be chasing after him. I've noticed more than a few eligible gals in this town fawning over him." She glanced out the café window. "Speaking of Prince Charming, I see him crossing the street, right now." Bernice fluffed her hair, straightened her apron and batted her eyelashes.

Lance entered the Bun and gave Bernice his Crest Whitening smile. He praised her decorating style, and she melted like a cheap candle. Then he approached the counter. "Just the guys I wanted to see. Mind if I join you?" Lance took the stool beside Chip. Bernice poured his coffee and offered him a slice of pecan pie, which he accepted.

"I'm going to be gone over the holidays. I've drawn up a work plan for the Bijou so you can keep on schedule while I'm out of town. I have the marquee just about done—weather permitting it can be installed out front. That's going to take a forklift and quite a crew. Sven will be home for break, so he's offered to get a crew together." He forked a big piece of pie. "Uhm, Bernice, this is heavenly." He gave her a wink, and she blushed.

"You wouldn't be going to New York to visit a certain literary agent, would you?" asked Chip.

"Yes, she made me an offer I couldn't refuse. Got tickets for the *Radio City Rockettes Christmas Show* and a free room at the Plaza, compliments of a client, promised me an unforgettable New Year's Eve in Times Square. I've never seen the ball drop in person, so it should be fun." He lifted his coffee mug, and Bernice obliged with a refill.

"Go, have a good time. The chief and I can handle things at the Bijou while you're away. Who knows, you might never return after you've seen the lights on Broadway."

* * *

CHIP WENT HOME WHISTLING "Give My Regards to Broadway." He was a happy man with a plan brewing. Step one was an email to Lucinda.

December 15, 3:30 p.m.
Lucinda,
Congratulations, I hear you have convinced Lance to join you in NYC. After you wine and dine him and show him the glories of the Big Apple, maybe he will give up his quest to be a vegetable farmer and make NYC his permanent residence. Good Luck!
Chip

She responded immediately.

December 15, 3:35 p.m.
Chip,
Yes, isn't it marvelous? I plan to pull out all the stops for my Lancelot. In the meantime, did you see this week's New York Times book section? You got a rave review and my phone has been ringing off the hook with requests for interviews and talk show appearances. I've already ordered a second printing. You must blog, blog, blog every day for a couple of hours at least. Your fan base is very important. Plus, no holiday from writing for you. Get humping, country boy.
Lucinda

Oh, crap, Chip hated blogging. It was so tedious. He needed time for step two, which was to win back Jane. This step would take some planning and finesse.

In addition, something was nagging him. Despite what Agent Masterson had said about interfering, he was pretty proud of his part in the Iowa map solution, and he was sure he could be of further help with the fabric swatches. *Blue nylon, blue nylon, what is made of blue nylon and how can it be connected to the possible abduction and murder of women?*

His mind was reeling with crimes, both on the home front and in *Mind Games*. Write or blog . . . writing was the lesser of two evils, he decided. He had murders to solve and John was still missing. A phone interview with the Bureau of Criminal Apprehension's communication manager had given him lots of details about the BCA in St. Paul and led to a second interview with one of its forensic scientists. He was eager to write his next chapter.

His concentration was broken momentarily by Honey. She was whining to be let out. First he gave her the Tramadol Jane had said would give her some temporary comfort. She did not seem to be getting worse, so he continued to be in denial about Jane's recent diagnosis of liver cancer and the inevitable. He was not ready to lose her.

CHAPTER TWENTY-FOUR

Mind Games
Brooklyn Center & St. Paul, Minnesota
Early August

AFTER FILLING AGENT DANIELS IN on everything she knew about John's disappearance and after providing him the information about her neighbor, Jo gave Daniels the key to her house. She knew the crime scene techs would go through her house with a fine-toothed comb, looking for fingerprints or any sign of struggle. She had told Daniels nothing seemed out of place, but then again, she might have missed something. She was not at her most observant after such little sleep. And so much stress.

Jo spent the next four hours sitting at her desk at FBI headquarters, trying to stay focused on the cases in front of her. She had to force herself to stay in her seat; another part of her brain kept urging her to get up and run out to look for John.

Work only occupied half of her brain as her mind wandered again and again to what Stephen had said. She found herself checking her cell phone every fifteen minutes or so, hoping to get an update from Daniels. At one point, she had even dialed the agent's number, then quickly disconnected. *I've got to trust him to do his job. He may be a pompous jerk, but he's a good agent.*

Her phone rang around 1:15 p.m. and she almost dropped it in her scramble to answer it. She was disappointed to see the caller was Frisco, not Agent Daniels. "Hey, Frisco. Tell me you've figured out this whole mess."

Jo heard Frisco's raspy laugh on the other end. "No such luck. However, the BCA boys and girls may have found another big piece of the puzzle. Seems they found some DNA in one of those envelopes after all."

"I thought they said the sender was smart enough not to lick the envelope."

"True, but he or she left behind a strand of blond hair, which we didn't see 'cause it was so light colored. No hair root for standard DNA testing, but they've got some information for us. Feel like a field trip to the BCA?"

Jo felt an adrenalin rush. At least progress was being made, even if it wasn't the news she was waiting for. "Oh, yeah. Anything to get away from this desk. Meet you there in twenty."

* * *

SUNLIGHT POURED THROUGH THE SKYLIGHTS as Jo and Frisco waited in the lobby of the BCA for one of the technicians to escort them to the labs. Jo shoved her phone into her purse, frustrated since she still hadn't heard from Agent Daniels. It felt like all she was doing today was sitting around and waiting. She wasn't very good at waiting, but she was especially bad at not having something to do to find John.

She watched Frisco look around the building and saw him peer up at the soaring ceilings. "What a place. It's like a mini-college campus, or something," he said.

Jo appreciated the distraction of Frisco's fascination with the BCA. She hadn't yet told him about John's disappearance because it was easier to work the routine of the Freemont/McDonald cases and shove her fears in the back of her mind. Knowing the detective as well as she did, he would want to be out there looking for John, too. Regardless of his jurisdiction.

She agreed, "It is pretty impressive. For instance, did you know they have a library here with over fifty-five hundred different weapons and every ammunition you can imagine?"

"Amazing. We always worked directly with the BCA's regional office in Duluth, so I never had a chance to visit the main building." His head swiveled around and he said, "Hey, what's that thing over there?"

Jo turned to see where Frisco was pointing above her shoulder. On the second level balcony above them, a row of metal rings ran along the railing. "Oh, that's called the 'Exquisite Corpse'. Come on. Let's take a closer look. It's my favorite artwork here. Always reminds me of why I do this job."

They climbed the steps to the second floor and stopped at one end of the artwork. "These rings represent giant magnifying glasses, all lined up. And do you see the stained glass at the center of each ring?" Jo asked.

Frisco leaned closer and squinted. "Yeah. What is that? Kinda looks like the cross section of a brain."

"That's exactly what it's supposed to look like. If you look at each one of the magnifying glasses, you will see pieces of stained glass that look like horizontal slices of an entire human body, from head to toe."

"Very cool. In a clinical, sort of creepy, way."

While Frisco spent some time quietly studying each ring, Jo thought about John again. Her mind wandered to the horrible possibility if he were killed, details from his case might be examined under a BCA magnifying glass. She swallowed a few times, trying to regain her composure before the detective noticed.

"Sounds like you've spent a lot of time here," Frisco finally said.

"Since the FBI doesn't have a lab in the state, we rely on the BCA to process quite a bit of our evidence."

Just as Jo finished her comment, she looked up to see one of the technicians she had worked with in the past coming toward them. She smiled and said, "Clara. So good to see you. I hear you have some results for us."

"Special Agent Schwann, always a pleasure. Sorry to keep you waiting." The sunlight filtering in through the skylights lit up Clara's blonde ponytail and her blue eyes were inquisitive as she turned to Frisco. "And you must be Detective Frisco. Pleased to meet you." Frisco shook her hand and they followed in Clara's wake to the lab area labeled W335 MITOCHONDRIAL DNA LABORATORY. In the window of the lab, someone had pasted up a sign that read THE MIGHTY MITES. Following the directions on the door, they donned blue face masks before entering the lab.

DNA processing equipment sat on neatly organized white countertops. Several technicians looked up from their work as Jo and Frisco entered and a few nodded their greetings before focusing on their work once more.

Clara walked over to a desk and handed a file to Jo. "Here are the results of the DNA testing. As you know, we were only able to run the mitochondrial DNA on this hair sample, since no root tag was present for nuclear DNA testing."

Frisco pinched the bridge of his nose and muttered, "I never can keep this DNA mumbo-jumbo straight. Remind me again of the difference in the nuclear and mito . . . mito . . . whasits DNA testing?"

Clara chuckled. "Mitochodrial DNA. Nuclear DNA analysis is what you hear about most in law enforcement. We used to only be able to determine a DNA match when we had trace such as blood, semen, or hair follicles, etc. Basically any cells containing a nucleus. The problem was that if we had evidence like hair without a root tag, teeth or a bone, we were out of luck.

"With mitochondrial DNA testing, we can narrow down to a finite list of suspects. For some types of evidence like teeth and bone specimens, there are no cells that contain a nucleus. In these cases, mitochondrial DNA can be used to identify the sample."

Frisco rubbed his chin. "You said narrow the list of suspects. Why not the exact suspect?"

"You see, mitochondria are the DNA inherited from the mother only. So, it is not unique to one specific individual, like nuclear DNA, but it at least gets us in the right family."

Clara pointed to the report in Jo's hand. There was a ghost of a smile on her face as she said, "The trace you brought in has given us a maternal match."

Jo could feel her heart pounding. She had a feeling Clara was about to hand them a very important piece of the puzzle. "So, who was the match?"

"Robert Clarence Bishop. He was involved in two aggravated assaults here and one drug bust."

Frisco's excitement was obvious in his rapid-fire questions, "Aggravated? So the guy had a weapon. What kind?"

"A Remington 12 gauge, pump-action shotgun."

Jo groaned. "The most commonly purchased shotgun out there. Could be the same type used on our victims, but who knows? Can't run a ballistics test on buckshot." She caught her lower lip between her teeth, thinking. "And where does Mr. Bishop currently reside?"

Clara's smile disappeared. "Underground, I'm afraid. He died in a shoot-out with police officers at the scene of the drug bust."

Frisco's face fell. "And I suppose this death-by-cop took place before State Rep. Freemont was murdered?"

When Clara nodded, Frisco said, "Well, damn. I guess we couldn't have gotten that lucky."

Jo said, "But don't forget, we now have a family connection to work with. Remember, mitochondrial DNA is about matching trace with family members, all having the same mother. We just have to track down Mr. Bishop's siblings."

Frisco grunted. "I guess I can live with that. Let's hit the birth records and see what pops up."

CHAPTER TWENTY-FIVE

Turners Bend
Mid-December

IT WAS A WEEK BEFORE CHRISTMAS, and Chip had put off calling his mother about the holidays, but he couldn't stall any longer. He took a deep breath and dialed his parent's home number. "Hi, Mother."

"Hello, Charles. Are y'all coming to Baltimore for Christmas?" Maribelle Collingsworth, who was born in South Carolina, had never lost her southern accent. As a kid Chip found it embarrassing, but now as an adult he thought it was ridiculous. He was sure she was faking it for affect. Once a Southern Belle, always a Southern Belle, he guessed.

"No, that's what I'm calling about. Honey is sick, and I have lots of work connected with my books. I'm staying in Iowa."

"Oh dear, my little Colette will be so distressed to hear her mama is ill. Your father has agreed to be on call for your brother so Parker and Francesca can take Lucia and Roberto to Tuscany for the holidays. I was hoping you would come and keep me company." She heaved a guilt-producing sigh. "Well, I guess that's what I get for marrying a prominent doctor and producing two successful sons. I'll just have to celebrate by myself. Give my love to all our friends in Turners Bend and give Honey a get-well kiss from me."

"Bye, Mother. I'll call again on Christmas." Chip heard her kiss-kiss sounds as she hung up.

He was glum. Jane was taking her mother and kids to San Diego to visit her brother Larry, a small animal vet, for Christmas. It was snowing every other day, and Iver was working day and night plowing roads. His own days were filled with blogging and keeping up with his Facebook fan page and his website updates. He was finding it hard to concentrate on *Mind Games* and was spending way too much time thinking about the possible real life serial killer in Iowa. Working on the Bijou was the only way he could escape his troubles and worries.

He got into his car, and gunning the engine to get through the drifts in the driveway, he drove slowly into town. The bleakness of the snow-covered fields added to his melancholy.

All the regular volunteers were busy with holiday preparations; he had the theater to himself. The restoration cheered him a bit. A mechanic from the farm equipment store had fixed the popcorn machine. It was ready to pop Iowa's best corn and top it with real butter, none of that fake stuff for the Bijou. The marquee had been returned to its former state, and Sven had a crew lined up for the installation. The glass poster cases had been repaired and were already mounted out front. Best of all was the discovery of beautiful mahogany wooden chairs with flip-up seats under the old, deteriorated cushions. The committee decided to cancel the order for upholstery fabric and refinish the wood, a project which required the sanding, staining and varnishing of 125 chairs.

Chip got out a can of stain and began on the chairs that had already been sanded. It gave him pleasure to see the stain bring out the dark grain of the wood. He was sitting back admiring his work when Chief Fredrickson appeared.

"You alone today, Chip?"

"Yes, I guess everyone has more important things to do this week."

The chief flipped down one of the unfinished seats and sat down. "Got a call from Masterson today and they found something. There were some fibers in all the evidence Jim bagged in the prop room. They match one of the five fabric samples. She's proceeding under the assumption each piece of fabric belongs to a victim. She is trying to match one of the pieces of blue cloth to Tracy Trent. Pretty tough after five years to find out if Tracy owned any clothing to match. They do think she might have been on her way to Iowa City Fitness the morning she went missing, and the swatch could be some kind of jersey or gym shorts or maybe a warm-up jacket. If so, we could identify one of the victims."

Chip wiped his hands on a rag. "I hate to say this, but I almost wish you would get another communication from the killer. I wonder why they are coming to you, instead of the FBI."

"My guess is that we were the ones to find the first body. Or, maybe our killer knows me or lives around here." The chief rose, picked up a hand sander and plugged it into a wall socket.

"That thought's enough to make a guy plenty nervous," said Chip.

"Damn right." The chief switched on the sander and the two worked side-by-side, each lulled by the grinding buzz of the sander.

* * *

DURING THE NIGHT OF DECEMBER 23rd it snowed again. It did not just snow; it was a full-out blizzard with wicked winds and below zero temperatures. Chip tried to clear a small patch in the yard for the dogs to do their business, but it kept filling up with snow. He heard the rumble of a snow plow. It was Iver.

He went to the window and began to scrape away the frost so he could peer outside. Sure enough it was Iver. His passenger, who resembled a grizzly bear, was dressed in a huge fur coat and matching hat. Iver followed the bear-like figure, carrying two Saks Fifth Avenue shopping bags, as they exited the plow and began trudging toward the house. Chip thought it could only be one person . . . his mother.

As they entered, the wind caught the back door and slammed it against the house. Snow blew into the kitchen, delighting Runt and causing Callie to run for cover.

"Well, I must say, that was an adventure," said Maribelle Collingsworth. "Frightened me more than our cruise down the Amazon in '82. Now let's get this food in the refrigerator, and Iver, dear, those presents can go under the tree. Do you have wine glasses? I certainly could do with a drink." Maribelle pulled a shivering puppy out of her large tote bag. "It's okay, Sugar, you're safe now."

"Mother, how did you and Colette get here? With the storm and . . ."

"Charles, you know when I decide to do something, I can make it happen. Iver, of course, was instrumental in the last leg. I just couldn't let you be alone with a sick dog over the holidays. Now, you get some coffee going for Iver, while I heat him the oyster stew I brought."

Iver hadn't attempted an explanation. He sat in a kitchen chair with a fur-lined hat on his head, the flaps still down over his ears. He smiled at Chip and shook his head from side to side.

Maribelle was in her full take-charge mode. In the past her behavior, as well as her fake southern accent, had alternatively embarrassed and irritated Chip, but he was surprisingly glad to see her and to let her order him around. *I may be forty-seven years old, but I'm not too old to let my mother take care of me once in a while.*

Honey rose from her bed by the radiator, walked over to sniff Collette and began to wag her tail, welcoming her daughter. Collette wagged in return. The three adults said "aah" in unison. Collette, like her sisters and brothers, was part golden retriever and part who-knows-what, but the dogs were cute as heck.

"How are you doing with your next book, Charles?" asked Maribelle, as she rummaged through the cupboards. "Heavens, what do you eat? Don't you have any decent crackers for my stew?"

"I've got a few saltines, that's all. And to your question about my book, my FBI agent has her hands full of crimes and her romantic life is in turmoil."

"Speaking of romance, how is Jane? Not that I'm the kind of mother to meddle, but . . ."

Chip thought about all of the meddling women in his life: Lucinda, Flora and now his mother. At this moment, the only person he wanted to talk to was Jane.

CHAPTER TWENTY-SIX

Mind Games
St. Paul & Brooklyn Center, Minnesota
Early August

FRISCO AND JO WALKED OUT into the parking lot of the BCA together. White, cottony clouds dotted the cornflower blue sky. When they reached her car, Jo brushed the curls away from her face as she dug in her purse for the keys.

Frisco said, "So, what's going on with you today? I can tell something's rattling around in that brilliant brain of yours, and I get the feeling it has nothing to do with our case."

Jo looked into Frisco's eyes and saw the concern. She wanted to brush him off, to tell him he was imagining things, but he hadn't become a detective without having a keen sense of observation. She took a deep breath and said, "It's John . . ." She stopped, not sure where to begin her explanation.

"Still haven't heard from him, huh?" Frisco said with a frown.

Jo blinked, at first assuming he had somehow found out John was missing. However, the lack of panic on Frisco's face made her realize he was still referring to her relationship with John being rocky. She relaxed a fraction. Jo hated not being entirely truthful with Frisco, but one person had to have their focus entirely on the Freemont/McDonald cases, and it certainly wasn't going to be her.

Jo shook her head. Her voice cracked when she said, "I'm pretty worried." *At least that part isn't a lie.* Even though she didn't want to distract Frisco with John's disappearance, talking to him relieved some of the tightness in her chest.

Frisco reached out and awkwardly patted her shoulder. "He'll show up. I have faith in him."

Jo bit her lower lip until she had her emotions under control again. Finally she nodded. "Me, too. Thanks, Frisco. You are definitely one of the good guys." She unlocked her SUV and said, "Now, let's figure out who's related to our mitochondrial DNA match Robert Clarence Bishop and see if we can't solve this case."

"Sounds like a plan to me. Meet you at your office."

* * *

FRISCO AND JO SAT SHOULDER to shoulder in Jo's cubicle, sifting through various databases, including birth and death certificates, and criminal records on her laptop. Three hours later, they discovered Bishop had an older brother and two younger sisters. They were all born in the Baltimore area, but their father was listed as unknown. Their mother, Karen, had committed suicide a couple of decades ago, after a long battle with alcoholism. Robert had been shuffled from one relative to the other, until he finally did his first stint in prison at the age of nineteen. It had been all downhill from there.

Thomas, the older brother, evidently had risen above his rough beginnings and was a successful stockbroker on Wall Street. According to property tax records, he lived in a mega-mansion in Connecticut with his wife.

Of Bishop's sisters, Sarah had a brief career as a prostitute until she cleaned up her act and started a shelter for runaways. The youngest sister, Michelle, had led a surprisingly normal life with a Washington, D.C. couple who adopted her when she was four. However, in the middle of her junior year at the University of Maryland, all records of her existence completely disappeared.

Jo did a quick search on the Internet for Michelle, but nothing popped up. "Very strange. She makes the Dean's list every semester and then, out of the blue, she drops out of college. From there, she goes completely off the grid."

Frisco rubbed his chin and Jo could hear the rasp of his whiskers. Jo glanced at the clock in the corner of her computer screen. She hadn't realized it had gotten so late in the afternoon. "And no missing person reports were filed?" Frisco said.

Jo clicked away at the keyboard. Finally, she said, "Nope. Nothing at all. You would think the school or her parents would have been looking for her. I'm going to call our Baltimore office and see if they can drop in on her adoptive parents."

Frisco nodded and said, "In the meantime, I'll take a closer look at the family's history, along with old Robert's criminal records, both here and in Maryland. Maybe Michelle's big, bad brother had something to do with her disappearance."

Jo thought for a moment. "Good idea. And I'll dig around in the other siblings' lives a little bit, too. Just because they aren't in the system, doesn't mean they haven't been up to something they shouldn't be."

Frisco grinned. "Feels good to have some leads to follow for a change, doesn't it?"

Jo felt her lips curve upward. "Oh, yeah."

* * *

JO WAS PICKING OUT HER DINNER from the vending machines down the hall from her office when the call came. Her heart began a rapid staccato when she saw the caller was Agent Mark Daniels. "Tell me you found him."

Mark sounded exhausted when he replied, "No, not yet. We've had no luck reaching your neighbor. We stopped by his house, banged on the doors, but the guy hasn't been home all day. We'll keep trying."

Jo couldn't keep the disappointment out of her voice. "Did you try reaching him at work?"

"Well, we ran into another snag there. There are no Minnesota tax records for Stephen Paulson, so we're checking the IRS and Social Security data bases."

Jo's stomach fell. "So, our only witness has disappeared into the wind."

"For now, Jo. I'm not giving up on finding him. Guy's probably going to show up, sooner or later." Daniels paused, and then he said, "We found something at your house, though."

Jo was intrigued. The agent sounded mysterious, and he was much more civil than the last time they spoke. "Fingerprints?"

"Yes, but all of them belong to either you or John. Not surprising, since you two have been seeing each other. But, no others. The odd thing about it is that it appears your front door knob and several other surfaces in your home have been wiped completely clean of prints."

The tightness in Jo's chest was back. "Only people with something to hide wipe away their prints."

Daniels response was quiet. "Yup. However, that's not what I meant when I said we found something at your house. Or, rather, *somethings*. Did you know that your house was wired?"

Jo's eyes widened. "Wired? As in, bugged?"

"Wired, as in set up for sound and video. We suspect it's throughout the entire house."

Jo couldn't take a deep breath for a moment. When she found her voice, she said, "Wha . . . what are you telling me?" She couldn't quite get her head around this new piece of information. "Who would do such a thing?"

"Good question. What I need to know is, do you want us to shut it all down, or . . ."

Jo interrupted, and she could hear the anger in her voice, "Of course, I want it shut down! What kind of perverted question . . ."

In a patient, deliberate tone, Daniels said, "What I was going to say is, maybe we should leave it up and running. At least for the short-term. We could play him for awhile. He might reveal himself."

The thought of living in her house, full of recording devices, made her skin crawl. However, she saw that Daniels had a point. "You mean, put on an act to draw him out."

"Something along those lines."

Jo's mind buzzed with what he was asking of her. She put off answering his question and asked one of her own. "You said you suspect the entire house is wired. Does that mean you don't know for sure?"

"No. When we found the first device, we immediately stopped looking for more. If the guy who set up all this equipment was watching, then he would know we were on to him. We found the first gadget by mistake, and the tech was low-key about it, so I think we're good." He hesitated, and then restated his earlier question. "So, Jo. Are you game?"

She knew immediately she would do anything, put up with anything if it meant finding John.

And then, before she answered him, it hit her. *John's disappearance is tied to someone who was spying on ME!* She felt her knees go weak and she sat on the floor to steady herself.

Why would anyone spy on me?

And, how could I not have known?

Through the phone line, she heard Daniels's voice. It sounded tinny and far away. She realized he was shouting at her, "Jo! Can you hear me?"

She forced the sound out of her mouth, "Yes, I'm here."

"Jesus, are you all right? I just asked again if you want us to remove the surveillance equipment."

"No, no. You're right. Everything should stay where you found it. We don't want this prick figuring out we are on to him."

"In that case, I'm going to put a couple of agents outside your house."

Jo shook her head. "Absolutely not. I already feel like my every move is being watched and you're just going to scare the guy off."

Agent Daniels heaved a heavy sigh, but didn't argue with her.

Jo felt like she was returning to herself. "And have the technicians check my car for tracking devices, while you're at it."

Through clenched teeth, she said, "This bastard is going to be sorry he ever thought about messing with us."

CHAPTER TWENTY-SEVEN

Turners Bend
January

CHIP CONCLUDED WHEN T.S. Eliot wrote "April was the cruelest month of all," he had never been to Iowa in January. He was waiting for the "January Thaw" the natives told him was coming soon. Winter's trick of making you think spring was on the way, only to turn around and slam you with three more months of wretched weather.

It was a period of extreme grief for him. His precious Honey had passed. Watching her painfully waste away had ripped his heart to shreds. Her eyes had glazed over and she no longer seemed of this world. Eventually she couldn't eat and became incontinent. Jane humanely put her down, and her ashes were in a box next to his computer. Jane reminded him Honey's six daughters and eight sons, one of whom was Runt, were living proof of her greatness.

Runt, too, was grieving. It was breaking Chip's heart to see him searching bewilderingly for Honey. Although Runt had grown to over eighty pounds, he wanted to be held on Chip's lap and did so with his head resting on his shoulder. Callie, being an independent feline, was the only household member to continue as if nothing had happened to disturb her realm, although she too was seeking extra lap time with Chip, especially when he was working at his computer. She seemed to sense he needed comforting.

The holidays were over. His mother had returned to Baltimore and Jane and Lance were home. All had resumed their normal routines, including their visits to the Bun and the Bend. As Chip walked into the Bun one frigid morning, he saw Lance at the counter appearing to have Bernice rapt in his spell.

"Bernice, I swear if it weren't for Chester, I'd be on your doorstep with flowers in my hand. You are one fine-looking woman," Lance said, as Bernice laughed a girlish twitter and batted her eyelashes.

Much to Chip's surprise, Jane was sitting at "their table," the table for two they used to share on a daily basis. He approached her with some weariness. "May I join you?"

"Of course, I've been waiting for you. Sit, and tell me how you and Runt are coping."

Chip sat across from her, took a deep breath and let it out slowly. "It's hell, Jane. Never having had a pet before, I had no idea it would be this hard, and poor Runt . . ." He signaled Bernice for a cup of coffee.

"Animals grieve just like humans do. Ever read James Herriot? He's a wonderful veterinarian author from Yorkshire Dales in England. He says when you lose a dog you should go right out and get another one, preferably a mixed-breed rescue animal."

"I can't think about that now, Jane. Let's talk about something else."

Bernice arrived with his coffee and a warm caramel roll encrusted with pecans and topped with a scoop of whipped butter.

"Sorry to hear about Honey, Chip, damn shame." She started to tear up, sniffed and said, "Rolls are on the house."

Jane and Chip sat in silence each picking nuts off the sweet roll and licking caramel off their fingers. Jane finally broke their reverie. "I want to thank you for letting Sven supervise the installation of the marquee. When he comes back in March for the premiere, he's bringing his whole Film Making 101 class. I have to find lodging for twenty students."

"Maybe you could house them at First Lutheran. They could camp out in the Fellowship Hall."

"Good idea, I'll give Pastor Henderson a call."

More silence followed until Chip changed the subject again. "Have you seen the theater recently? It's almost done. We just have to hang the new curtain when it comes and then do some clean-up. We got the projector and sound system working."

"Mabel has decided we should all wear ball gowns and tuxes to the premiere. She's sewing dresses like crazy, and Sylvia has ordered tiaras for all the women."

Bernice returned to refill their coffee cups.

"Hey Bernice, is Lance regaling you with stories of his Christmas visit to New York City? He told me all about it yesterday when we had lunch," said Jane.

"Yes, did he tell you about shopping with Lucinda? He bought her a Versace knock-off to wear for the premiere. Damn lucky woman, if you ask me."

Chip was in no mood to talk about Lance or formal wear. He was relieved to see Chief Fredrickson open the door and motion for him to leave the café.

"Sorry to depart. This conversation about dresses and tiaras is too much for me," said Chip, rolling his eyes. He followed the chief out of the café.

As they walked to the police station, the chief said, "Your Christmas wish has come true. I got another message from our killer. This one's from Waterloo."

In the inner office, the chief took out another delivery form, identical to the first one. On the back was a message composed of letters cut from a newspaper. It read:

SτaRτ/NG 5 DϵaD. T/$\mathbb{M}$E TO GϵT NEW RϵcRU/Ts.

Chip stared at the message, and he felt snakes slithering up and down his spine. "Have you notified the FBI yet?"

"Masterson is on her way as we speak"

The chief leaned back in his chair. "Here's what I think. This has something to do with basketball. The starting five could be five dead girls from a basketball team. So, maybe now this monster is moving on to other girls, girls who play basketball, looking for recruits. Those pieces of fabric could be from basketball jerseys. It's all coming together. I think we're looking for a coach or an ex-coach or maybe a disgruntled player or fan. Basketball is the key. I feel it in my gut."

"Interesting theory, Chief; you may have something there. If Tracy Trent was on a basketball team at some time, the FBI can track down her teammates. Let's hope they are alive and well. I have a feeling we're closing in on this guy."

* * *

WITHIN HOURS ANGELA MASTERSON, two male agents and a van loaded with equipment had arrived in Turners Bend. They took over a vacant space above Harriet's House of Hair and set up a temporary field operations office. Chip and the chief were summoned to her office.

"When I heard the message and your thoughts about what it might mean, I tracked down Trent's high school yearbook. She did play basketball, but the uniforms were red and black not light blue, and the coach has been dead for years. She didn't play on the University of Minnesota's team, but we're looking into other teams she may have played on. We're also checking to see if there are any milk delivery guys who are or have been basketball coaches. Right now we're only working on hunches, so no leaks to the press. We don't want every girl's basketball team in Iowa in a frenzy."

"Oh, my God." Chief Fredrickson had turned ashen and beads of sweat appeared on his forehead.

"What is it, Chief?" asked Masterson.

"Our high school . . . the Prairie Dogs wear blue and white uniforms."

CHAPTER TWENTY-EIGHT

Mind Games
Minneapolis, Minnesota
Early August

Jo Schwann sat in her SUV inside the detached garage of her house, long after she had turned off the engine. The thought of going inside made the bile rise in the back of her throat. Some stranger had been in and out of her home, probably on more than one occasion. He had watched and listened. For God knows how long. It felt like a heavy hand was pushing down on her shoulders, holding her in her seat.

She felt depressed and angry, all at the same time. Her privacy had been invaded. Worst of all, the man she loved was missing. Just because he had been in her home at the wrong time. Jo didn't believe in coincidences. John's disappearance and her house being bugged had to be related. She slammed her bunched up fist against the steering wheel, impotent rage coursing through her.

After a while, she rubbed at the ache in her hand and gathered her belongings. Out loud, she muttered, "Showtime." Before she stepped out of the vehicle, she double-checked that she had easy access to the side pocket of her purse, where she had slipped her loaded Glock before leaving the office. Part of her longed for an excuse to use it on whoever was responsible for this.

Jo unlocked the side door by the kitchen and let herself in, flipping the light switch with her elbow. Cleo immediately rubbed against her, meowing for dinner and companionship. Jo bent down to rub her behind the ears and said, "Hi, Sweetie. You are getting tired of these late nights, aren't you? Me too."

She kicked off her shoes and did a quick, surreptitious peek around the room. Jo didn't think the creep would be in her house, but she couldn't take any chances. Nevertheless, she had to be careful not to let whoever was watching know she was on to him. It was a fine, delicate dance between caution and nonchalance.

The opening act of the play had begun.

Jo fed Cleo and then opened a bottle of cabernet. She poured herself a full glass, and padded into the den. Settling into her chair, she trailed her finger through the dusting of silvery-gray fingerprint powder on the table next to her. The techs had conducted the search for evidence and had done their best to clean up, she knew, but the residue settled in after they left, like a fine mist. Her stomach clenched as she pictured her house being examined by the crime lab people just hours before. It was another sort of invasion of her private space, even though she was the one who had set it in motion.

Jo put her feet up on the ottoman. *I need to relax. I have to look like I'm just coming home from a regular day at the office.* She wondered what the bastard was thinking as he watched her. Jo was convinced he was looking at her right now and the hairs on the back of her neck rose.

Which pissed her off.

How dare this asshole invade my life. How dare he take John. She could feel an ache in her jaw where she had clenched her teeth.

Enough! Abruptly, she stood up and strode into the kitchen. She pulled out her work files and set up her laptop on the pine table. In her haste, she knocked over her glass and the blood-red wine spilled over her papers.

"Shit." She jumped up to grab a towel and sopped up the mess, the papers stained purple. She poured another glass and then sat down in front of her laptop. Working the Freemont/McDonald cases were the closest thing she had to having something to control. Because everything else definitely felt out of control.

She spent the next couple of hours reviewing every data base at her fingertips, trying to locate any information on Bishop's siblings. Thomas, the stockbroker and Sarah, the director of a runaway shelter, had spotless records. The big unknown was still the missing youngest sister, Michelle. The only thing she discovered was an old DMV photo, issued when she was still in her teens.

Jo printed out the photo for her files and then studied the girl's picture. Michelle had a small, shy smile, her eyes bright. According to the record, Michelle was five-foot-three, had brown hair, hazel eyes and weighed 110 pounds. She looked vaguely familiar, but Jo realized that it must be the resemblance to the girl's older brother.

Jo thought the girl looked happy, hopeful. *What happened to you, Michelle?*

Which only brought up the question Jo had been carefully avoiding all night. *What's happened to you, John?*

Jo stood up, restless once more. She poured herself another glass of wine, noting the bottle she had just opened was nearly empty. Still, the wine had no relaxing effect on her. If possible, she was even more wired than before.

She walked through the den and over to the sidelight next to her front door and stared out into the road lit by the streetlights. John had been missing for twenty-four hours now, the point when the FBI assumes that kidnapping victims had been taken across state lines.

The rational part of her brain said it was likely he was still somewhere in the Twin Cities. If her stalker spent so much time shadowing her every move, then he probably wouldn't go far.

Jo couldn't get it out of her head that John was out there, somewhere. Likely hurt; quite possibly dead. It was the first time she had consciously allowed the last thought to fill her head and it felt as if someone had reached inside to squeeze her heart. She rubbed the spot on her chest and huffed out a puff of air. *Damn it! I'm sick of not doing anything to find him.*

She felt like she wouldn't be able to draw another breath if she stayed in her house a minute longer. Somewhere, eyes were watching her every move and she needed to get out. Jo snatched the black hoodie she kept on the coat rack and opened the front door. The cooler night air rushed in. Hearing the throaty croaks of frogs coming from the direction of Minnehaha Creek a couple of blocks away, she slipped on the sweatshirt and wrapped her arms tightly around herself.

She looked toward Stephen's house. The windows were dark and there was no sign of him. Agent Daniels had mentioned they were still looking for her neighbor, but since he was only a witness, not a suspect, Jo knew there would be no one watching Stephen's house.

As she stood on her front stoop, she mentally argued with herself, trying to decide if she should take her gun with her. Releasing a grunt, she muttered, "So, now I am so friggin' paranoid that I need my friggin' gun in my own friggin' neighborhood." She dashed back inside to grab it.

She closed the front door behind her to keep Cleo from escaping. Heading in the direction of Stephen's house, she told herself, "I'm not interfering in Daniels' case. I'm just checking on a neighbor."

Or at least, that's what she would tell the agent if he caught her peeking in her neighbor's windows.

She walked up the driveway, eyes and ears alert for any movement. Climbing the stairs to his front door, she rang the doorbell. She muttered to herself, "Please be home. Please tell me something more that will lead us to John."

The house remained dark and quiet, so she pounded on the door. Still no sign of life. She went back down the front stoop and walked to the side of the house. Jo pulled the hood of the sweatshirt up over her head to cover the bright copper of her hair and looked up and down the street. Seeing no one about, she shoved aside the tall rhododendron bushes which crowded the den windows, and climbed behind them. The branches tugged at her clothes and she felt a scrap against her cheek. Jo stood on tiptoes, trying to get a glimpse inside.

The room was dark, except for a small night light which illuminated the far corner. A dog bed and chew toy sat next to a recliner, but she didn't see the dog. *Must've taken Max somewhere with him.*

She crept along the house until she came to a six-foot fence that lined the perimeter of the backyard. The gate was closed. She noticed the wood of the fence was raw, not yet painted. She realized it had been recently installed and was certain the elderly widow who lived here before did not have a fence. Jo whispered to herself. "Awfully tall fence, just to keep in a little dog. Wonder why Stephen needs so much privacy."

As she pulled on the latch of the gate, she knew she was definitely crossing the line. She would have a hard time convincing Agent Daniels and Tom that she was merely checking on an absent neighbor's well being by entering his private back yard. And she knew she was about to trespass. If an ordinary citizen were to do this, they could claim they were just worried about a neighbor, making sure they were okay. But an FBI agent? It was clearly an unlawful search. Between the wine she had consumed and her concern about John, she had moved way past caring what would happen to her career if she were caught.

The new gate opened with a squeak, making Jo's heart pound. The evening air carried sounds far and the last thing she needed now was to alert anyone to her presence. As if collectively listening for an intruder, every other night sound halted. Jo held her breath, waiting for a house light to turn on or a face to peek out of a window. Even friendly neighbors would ask a lot of questions about her snooping this late into the evening. They would remember she had been here, if Agent Daniels or Stephen asked later.

When the evening hum resumed, Jo stepped through the opening in the fence. The clouds hiding the moon parted and Jo caught a glimpse of the back yard. Over to the right, she saw a newly planted garden, along the fence line. The patch was large, running most of the length of the yard. The ground had been carefully tilled, but the plants had withered and weeds had crept in.

She walked along the back of the house, and leaned against the window, cupping her hands around her eyes to gaze into the kitchen. There was a light above the sink that revealed a tidy room, with lacy curtains. Jo had been inside the house a few years ago when the elderly Mrs. Matthew still lived there. Strangely, the kitchen looked pretty much the way she remembered it from before. Jo shrugged, maybe Stephen hadn't had the time to make changes yet.

Frustrated that she hadn't found any signs of Stephen at home, she was about to walk back through the gate when she noticed a dusty window at the ground level of the house. Jo bent over and tried to see inside, but there was no light and the room was pitch black. She straightened and walked through the gate, closing it quietly behind her.

Walking back toward her house, she felt a bit ridiculous for snooping. She had accomplished nothing and was no closer to finding John than when she got out of bed this morning.

Jo felt bone weary. The stress of John's disappearance and her caseload was a weight slowly crushing her. She couldn't remember the last time she had slept for more than an hour or two at a time. Jo longed to sink into oblivion. Anything to stop the grief that was settling around her heart the longer John remained missing. *Why hasn't the kidnapper reached out to me, to any of us?* She was afraid the answer was one she never would be able to face.

She let herself back into her house and went from room to room, snapping off the light switches as she went. Never forgetting someone somewhere was watching her every move, she quickly washed the day's grime from her face, brushed her teeth and then slipped into her darkened, walk-in closet to change out of her work clothes. Jo climbed into bed. The last thing she remembered as her head hit the pillow was the weight of Cleo curling up next to her on the comforter.

CHAPTER TWENTY-NINE

Turners Bend
February

No respectable groundhog would poke its head out in Iowa in February. The "cruel" month of January had morphed into another equally bitter month weather-wise. Chip's old farmhouse was under-insulated and drafts rattled the windows. He covered them with plastic, using a hair dryer to shrink the film, making it taut. He stuffed bath towels along the bottom of the doors. He wore socks and gloves to bed. Cabin fever had set in, and he began to envy the locals who had headed south right after Christmas—the snow birds who had flown the coop.

The murder investigation seemed to have intensified, and Agent Masterson had suddenly shut Chip out. She was keeping the developments hush-hush. His only news came via Chief Fredrickson, who had discretely been keeping him abreast of the progress. The chief was not a stickler for protocol and relished sharing details to get Chip's insights.

Chip headed to town, his Volvo's engine complaining, the icy leather seat crackling the whole way. He made a mental note to order seat warmers on his next vehicle. He was eager for an update from the chief. Being involved in this real-life crime was providing good material for *Mind Games*.

The road ahead looked clear, but all of a sudden, he lost control of his car. It careened across the road into the oncoming lane and then into the ditch. He gripped the steering wheel and over-corrected right into a utility pole. Steam began to rise from under the hood of the car. He pushed open the driver's side door, plowing it into a snow bank. Wading hip deep in snow he made his way to the road and retrieved his cell phone from his jacket pocket. "Bars . . . thank God!" Chip said out loud.

"Iver, remember when you warned me about black ice? Well, I've just experienced it firsthand. I'm in a ditch about three miles from town out on 25." He paused. "Yes, I'm fine but freezing cold. My car is pretty banged up."

* * *

WITHIN FIFTEEN MINUTES CHIP'S Volvo was being towed by Iver's snowplow truck, and he and Iver were on their way to Willis Volvo in Ames.

"The first time I rode in this truck was the night I met you and Honey," said Chip.

"Yup, that was quite a snowstorm. And Honey was one damn good dog."

The two rode in silence for several miles, Iver with his eyes watching ahead for patches of potential black ice, and Chip staring out at the empty farm yards and desolate fields of corn stubble. Iver finally broke the silence. "Hard to remember the sweet smell of grass and the chirping of song birds, isn't it? Spring will come, Chip, and life will emerge out of this bleakness."

"You're quite the philosopher, and a damn fine friend, Iver."

"You too, buddy."

The rumble of the truck tires lulled the two for several more miles, until Iver again spoke, trying to lighten the mood. "Your mother . . . she's a pip. Don't think I've ever met anyone quite like her. That ride to your house at Christmas was non-stop yakking."

"Yes, she's a piece of work, all right, but I can always count on her in a pinch. She has a way of showing up right when I need her."

"What about your dad? You don't talk much about him."

"We aren't on the best of terms, haven't been since the day I dropped out of med school and became the black sheep of our family. He and my brother, Parker, are both brilliant neurosurgeons and ass-holes. The two often go hand-in-hand. I don't think he'll ever accept who I am; I'll never be good enough to be a Collingsworth in his eyes."

"He'll come around, Chip, but you have to meet him halfway. It's never too late to mend fences . . . trust me, I know."

Chip sensed there was a story there, something Iver might be willing to share with him, but they had arrived at Willis Volvo's auto body shop.

* * *

CHIP GOT A LOANER CAR from the dealer in Ames and headed for the police station back in Turners Bend. He found Fredrickson in his office, clipping his fingernails. Sharon and Deputy Anderson were nowhere in sight. "Slow day in the world of police work?" Chip asked, as he took a seat, shedding his gloves, ski hat and muffler.

"Jim's off looking for outdated license tabs and Sharon is taking her mother-in-law to the clinic in Ames. As a matter of fact, there's been a huge break in the murder case. Seems Tracy Trent played on an intramural basketball team when she was at the University of Minnesota. The coach was asked to resign after a number of complaints from the players. There's nothing in the official records, but a dean who was interviewed recalls it had to do with her anger control problems on the court and in the locker room. Back then it was pretty common to shove that kind of stuff under the rug. It didn't get the media attention it would today."

"Bingo, there's the basketball connection. Agent Masterson must be pretty eager to track down a coach with a hot temper and an axe to grind."

"The kicker is the coach wasn't a guy, it was a woman. They're looking for her, but she seems to have dropped off the face of the earth. Her name is Elizabeth Brown, but the FBI likes to use code names. They're calling her Knight Rider. Don't know why, but maybe it has something to do with the hot-tempered Indiana basketball coach." The chief scooped his nail clippings into his hand and tossed them into the wastepaper basket beside his desk.

"I would never have guessed the killer was a woman. Doesn't fit the usual serial killer profile," said Chip. "Only female serial killer I can think of is Bonnie . . . you know, Bonnie and Clyde. I'm having trouble visualizing this . . . a woman, huh?"

"The Minnesota job wasn't the first one she lost because of her temper and coaching style. She's got a rap sheet with three assault charges, even did some time in the Shakopee Women's Correctional Facility up in Minnesota."

"What about the other women on the team?" asked Chip.

The chief leaned forward and began to talk in a hushed tone. "Here's where it gets real interesting. Tracy and the other four starters of the team are all missing."

"Holy crap! And they didn't put this together when it happened?"

"Two of the gals were assumed to have run away on their own accord, and the other two were thought to be abducted, one in Michigan and one in Wisconsin. They think our body is the girl from Wisconsin, but forensics hasn't confirmed it as of yet. She's been missing for three years. The searches in the other four locales on the map have intensified. FBI agents are now aiding the local guys. I suspect they'll find the other bodies here in Iowa soon, and one of them will be Tracy Trent. Just think, she has been missing for five years and all the time her body was hidden somewhere around here."

Chip's mind began to race as he tried to put everything together. "Are there any women who drive milk delivery trucks in this area?"

"Not one. The milk delivery forms I received are probably a false lead, just some paper the killer had handy. Masterson isn't totally dismissing it, but it's not likely to lead us to the killer."

"What about the blue swatches?"

The chief laughed. "You're a regular Sherlock Holmes, aren't you? This is where the plot really thickens, but I don't know if I should be sharing this with you. Masterson would have my hide if she knew."

"Masterson doesn't need to know. Come on, Chief, don't mess with me."

The chief pulled a copy of a photograph from a file on his desk and passed it to Chip. "Tracy's mother found this snapshot of the team wearing blue jerseys. The girls might have hung on to them after college, maybe wore them to work out in or something. Or, maybe Elizabeth Brown kept a jersey and cut it into five pieces."

The chief slid the photo back into the file. "Only the Michigan abduction is recent, just two months before we found the first body, all the others go back a few years. Our killer finally located the last of the starting five, it seems. Guess the authorities never linked them together because of the time and geography spans or maybe it was just plain shoddy investigative work. To be safe, they're contacting all the other team members to tell them they could be in danger. Masterson is also trying to locate others who were in the athletic department about that time, coaches and administrators."

"From the message you got it doesn't look like the killer is going to stop with the five. What kind of psycho is she?"

* * *

CHIP LEFT THE POLICE STATION deep in thought about the mental state of the killer and headed back to his loaner car outside of the Bun. He couldn't imagine such extreme revenge and such persistence over the years to find and kill her accusers. As he walked back to the Bun, he saw Ingrid enter her mother's veterinary clinic. She was wearing a Prairie Dogs warm-up jacket. The blue color of the jacket, coupled with the news he had just heard, gave him a foreboding feeling. He changed his destination and entered the animal clinic.

Mabel was at her front desk, stitching sequins on a piece of emerald green satin. "Hi Chip, I know this doesn't look very professional, but I've got to finish this dress for Flora. The premiere is less than a month away. Jane and Ingrid are in the treatment room. You can go in. We don't have any patients right now."

When he entered the treatment room and saw Ingrid, still in the warm-up jacket, his first impulse was to grab the jacket and tell her to never wear it again. He frantically tried to think of a way to warn them without revealing information he was privy to and without arousing unnecessary fear.

"Hi, how are the Swanson women today?"

Ingrid tucked her long, red hair behind her ears and gave Chip a big smile, revealing braces. They were multi-colored; it looked like she had two bracelets running across her teeth.

"We're so excited about the premiere," said Ingrid. "I get to wear my first formal and tiara and see *The Cranium Killer* movie at the Bijou. Good thing it's rated PG13 and not R." She stopped gushing and turned abruptly to her mother. "Mom, can I go to the Bun before practice? I'm starving. Can I have a couple of dollars?"

"Sure, honey, ask Mabel to give you some money from the front desk drawer."

Chip plunged in. "Ingrid, I know you feel safe walking around by yourself in Turners Bend, but until the murder is solved, it would be best to always walk with a friend. You can never to too careful," said Chip. "I'll walk you to school."

Ingrid rolled her eyes. "Oh, Chip, you sound like my mother. I know there are some people who are freaked out by the body you found in the theater, but they're all just being paranoid. Jeez, this isn't Minneapolis. I'd be scared stiff walking around by myself up there like Sven does, but get real, this is Turners Bend. Anyway, I can take care of myself. Nothing is going to happen to me."

Ingrid grabbed her duffle bag and kissed her mother on the cheek. "I've got to run. Coach Whittler goes postal if we're not there on time. Bye."

"Call me when you get to practice, okay?" said Jane. "And don't roll your eyes at me, young lady. Remember it's better to be safe than sorry."

After Ingrid left, Jane bit her lower lip and gave Chip a quizzical look. "What was that all about? You don't really believe all the fear mongers in town who think we have a murderer in our midst, do you?"

"I don't know, but what I do know is that there's no harm in being cautious. Humor me and keep a close watch on Ingrid and pass the word around among the other parents, okay?"

"Until now I haven't taken too much stock in the local talk about the 'skeleton in the closet.' According to the autopsy, it was a crime from years ago, and what's to say it happened here in Turners Bend? The worst of the talk is speculation about farmers who keep to themselves, guys who don't frequent the Bun or the Bend. I know most of these men, they're my clients. A couple of them are a little strange, but I trust them. I'm worried this situation could turn into a witch hunt, Salem-style, with innocent men being accused of unspeakable crimes."

Jane squinted and gave him a penetrating look. "I sense you know something you're not telling me."

"Let's put it this way, Jane. I'm not telling you something I know and can't tell you." He looked at her gravely, trying to convey more than he could say in words.

"Fair enough, thanks for the warning. This whole thing is kind of creepy, isn't it?" Jane shivered as if to shake off an unpleasant feeling. "I've always felt so sorry for Tracy Trent's parents. Imagine going five years not knowing what happened to your child. I know losing Ingrid like that would be more than I could bear."

"I'm not a parent, Jane, but it doesn't take much to imagine that kind of heartache." Chip checked his watch. "Crap, I'm sorry, Jane, I've got to run. Got a podcast interview in half an hour. How about breakfast tomorrow morning?"

"I'm having breakfast with Lance. I promised to help with the party planning for the premiere celebration. He's quite the event planner. You're welcome to join us."

"I wouldn't want to butt in on you and Lance."

"Don't be silly. Come."

Hell, lunch yesterday and breakfast tomorrow . . . she's spending a lot of time with that guy. What's he up to?

* * *

CHIP THOUGHT ABOUT LANCE as he sped home for his interview. One minute the guy was buying a fancy dress for Lucinda and the next he was logging time with Jane. He had to admit he was jealous to the point of wanting to confront him, slap Lance's face with a glove and challenge him to a duel. *With my luck, the dude is probably an ace shot. Man up, Chipster, enough of your petty jealousy of a relatively decent guy.*

The FBI investigation was equally disturbing to him. The closer they got to the killer, the scarier it got. Waiting for the killer to strike again was like watching a horror movie unfold. What would her next move be?

He rushed into his house and got ready for the NPR podcast interview. It was the fourth interview he had done in the past three weeks. Every radio announcer or newspaper editor had asked the same inane questions. He was in a foul mood, so he decided to make up a bunch of phony answers for this one.

He logged in and waited for the interviewer to begin. He recalled his uncomfortable interview with Amy Chang and steeled himself for possible trick or leading questions. A female voice broke into his thoughts.

"Today's guest is crime writer Charles Collingsworth."

"Please call me Chip, only my mother calls me Charles."

"Certainly. Tell us about where you do your writing."

"I have a lovely log cabin by a lake. I sit by the fire and write long hand on a yellow legal pad." He looked out at his deserted farm yard piled high with dingy snow, dotted with dog turds.

"Sounds idyllic. Describe what you see out your window."

"Cardinals are gathering around my bird feeder and a lone ice fisherman and his dog are on the lake."

"What authors have influenced you?"

"I'd have to say Proust and Tolstoy. Oh, and Zane Grey."

"Odd choices for a crime writer. What are you reading right now?"

"The Decline and Fall of the Roman Empire, the third volume."

"And are you enjoying it?"

"Well, after the previous two volumes, it's getting a little stale."

"What do you do when you have writer's block?"

"I'm training for the Boston Marathon, so I go out for a seven or eight mile run, or I bake a cherry pie and take it to my elderly neighbor."

"What are you writing now?"

Chip began to sense doubt in the interviewer's voice. He thought she was probably on to him, but he persisted with his charade. "I'm working on a biography of Dr. Kevorkian."

"Dr. Death? I'm sure that will surprise your publisher."

"Yes, I suppose it will."

"I see our time is up. Thank you, this has been an enlightening interview."

He expected Lucinda to call any second. There would be hell to pay. He was feeling a little foolish, but why not; he was a fool and had just reinforced his self-image, hadn't he?

Fortified with a mug of burnt-tasting coffee that he had reheated and a package of somewhat stale Double-Stuffed Oreo cookies, Chip turned the switch in his head to *Mind Games*.

CHAPTER THIRTY

Mind Games
Minneapolis, Minnesota
Early August

WHEN THE ALARM WENT OFF the next morning, Agent Jo Schwann was groggy and for a brief moment, she couldn't remember what day it was or where she was. She had been in the middle of a lovely dream, in which she and John were out on a sailboat on the Chesapeake, the sun warm on their backs. Her hair had been blowing around her face and John had just reached out to tuck a strand behind her ear when the bleat of the clock radio woke her with a gasp.

And then, reality slammed into her.

She curled up in a ball on her bed, pulling Cleo close to her chest. The kitten purred and tucked her head under Jo's chin. Jo's tears fell on the fur of the little creature. *What am I going to do if I never see John again? I have so much to say to him. We have so much to say to each other.*

Cleo squirmed out of her arms, bounding to the floor in a silent leap. Jo sat up and rubbed the sleep out of her eyes. She snatched the cell phone off the nightstand, checking for any missed calls. She swore under her breath when she saw there were none.

She decided it was time to give Agent Daniels a call. She couldn't risk the kidnapper overhearing her conversation, so she got out of bed and grabbed the robe that lay in a crumpled pile at the end of her bed. Throwing it across her shoulders, she surreptitiously slipped the cell phone in her pocket and walked out to her garage. *Hopefully, the asshole will just think I went out to get the newspaper from my driveway.* She got into her car and flicked through her contacts until she found the number for Agent Daniels.

He answered on the third ring and said, "Schwann, you know I said I'd call you if there were any new developments. Stop trying to micro-manage this case. We still haven't been able to reach your neighbor and there's been no word from the kidnapper."

She leaned back into the leather seat of her Highlander. She swallowed and said, "Still think this is a kidnapping? Seems like . . ." Jo shook her head in frustration when she heard the crack in her voice. She cleared her throat and began again, "Seems like we should have heard from the guy by now."

Daniels' voice was less gruff when he spoke again. "Jo, it's only been a little over twenty-four hours—"

"We always tell people that the first twenty-four hours are key in cases like this. So far, there is no news. At all," Jo interrupted.

"I know. We're not giving up." He hesitated, and said, "Have you given any thought to why someone would want to wire your house? Any threats or ties to a recent case?"

Jo rubbed her forehead, trying to wipe out the throbbing that had taken up residence there. "I've been wracking my brain. My most recent case was the NeuroDynamics investigation up in Two Harbors. Even though the Bureau is still fighting the widow over Candleworth's death, I can't see her being the type to put cameras in my house and kidnap my boyfriend. All the suspects involved in the case are dead."

Jo could hear Daniels shuffling papers. "Anything else? No cases involving sex crimes or anything like that?"

Feeling a need to do something with her hands, she fiddled with the rear view mirror and said, "You think it's related to a sex crime?"

"Jo, someone wants to watch the intimate details of your life. Maybe gets off on seeing you." He cleared his throat and continued, "Seems like the work of a stalker, to me."

Of course, Jo had considered it, but hearing Daniels express it out loud turned her stomach. Her mind flipped through the cases she had worked over her career. After a minute, she said, "A few years ago, I put away a guy for harassing a woman he had met on a dating site on the Internet. We caught him entering her house when she was sleeping. Turns out he installed home security systems for a living."

"Now, that sounds like a possibility. What's his name? I'll follow up and see if he's still in prison."

She gave him the information and then said, "You mentioned we should leave the cameras in place, so we can draw the kidnapper out. What did you have in mind?"

Jo heard Daniels swallow at the other end of the line, like he was drinking his morning coffee. "We need to prompt the guy a little, get him to contact you. Maybe if you acted more upset by John's disappearance for the cameras. You know, perform a little."

She huffed out a laugh. *As if I haven't already been showing the creep how upset I am.* "It wouldn't be much of a stretch."

Daniels' voice was firm when he said, "One thing. Don't forget for one second that this guy is unpredictable, so don't do anything stupid. We want him to reach out to us, but it's a fine balance. The last thing we need to do is provoke him into attacking John."

Jo swallowed and said, "Thanks, Daniels. I'll keep that in mind."

* * *

JO GRABBED HER NEWSPAPER and walked back into the house. She went into the bedroom and shrugged out of her bathrobe. She lay back on the bed, thinking about all the cameras that might be scattered around the house. Jo briefly considered climbing back under the covers and shutting out the world.

But then HE wins. I can't let that happen.

Daniels' parting words kept replaying in her head. She had to do something to get the kidnapper to contact them, but she had to be careful. She stood up and began making the bed, trying to look as normal as possible, the whole time thinking. *If I were to hide a camera in this room, where would I put it?*

She quickly surveyed her bedroom. Her lamp on the nightstand was a likely target. It had been her mother's and it was heavy with ornate scroll-work in the base. As she reached across the bed to pull the comforter in place, she looked to the opposite side of the room, toward her dresser. Nothing on the surface was wired and therefore, unlikely to contain a camera.

Tossing the throw pillows into place, she looked up. As she dragged her eyes away, she realized that she had discovered where she would put a surveillance camera. In the ceiling fan.

She sat down on the bed she had just made up. Still thinking of Daniels' comments, she knew she had to do something. Take some action. It was time she figured out just what made this guy tick.

Mindful of the camera watching her, she stood up and grabbed the work files she had placed on her nightstand the previous evening. They provided a prop to appear as if she were thinking about her caseload, not plotting what she would do to provoke the kidnapper.

As she absently flipped through the files, she considered doing what Daniels had suggested, showing how distraught she was. *But I've been doing that and it hasn't gotten us anywhere.*

Jo pulled out another file and turned to the first page. Without seeing the words in front of her, she thought about Daniels' observation that it could be related to a sex crimes case. *Sex crimes are all about control of the victim.*

It made her skin crawl thinking about letting the perp control her. *Isn't that exactly what he's been doing since he put these cameras in here? From the moment he took John he's been in control.*

She set the files aside. As she thought through her options, one plan kept springing up in her mind. It might backfire. He could get very angry. However, she was determined to find out what had happened. Determined to face the truth. *Can I go through with it?*

Jo took a deep breath and stood up. For a moment, her hands hovered near her waist. Finally, she let out a puff of air, grabbed her shirt and yanked it over her head, tossing it on the bed. Carefully, she shed the rest of her clothes. Once she was completely nude, she spread her arms wide and turned in slow circles next to her bed. *Take a good look, you bastard. Come and get me. I dare you!*

Her face burned with shame, but she forced herself to keep from covering her nakedness. She needed to egg him on, force him to show his hand. She tilted her head toward the ceiling and sent a defiant look toward the ceiling fan where she assumed he had hidden the camera. Her hair tumbled down her back and she could feel the curls glide across her shoulders as she made one more turn.

Finally, she walked into the master bathroom and turned on the shower as hot as she could stand. After steam filled the room, she climbed in and stood in the scalding spray, trying to wash away her humiliation.

* * *

CRACK! Somewhere in Dr. John Goodman's subconscious he felt the slap to his cheek, but he slept on, because the dream was more seductive. In it, Jo's arms wrapped around him, and he felt her warm, moist breath in his ear when she told him they would be together always.

Another hit. This time, John felt his head snap back at the vicious backhanded blow and it thumped against the surface behind him. Jo vanished like a vapor and his cheek burned where he had been struck. Bright points of light flashed behind his eyelids. He blinked a few times, trying to make sense of what was happening to him.

A gruff voice next to his ear growled, "Wake up, Goodman. I've got something to show you."

He forced his bleary eyes open and he turned his head to see who was speaking. The man standing next to him wavered in and out of his vision, but John saw he had pale gray eyes and black hair. He wore a green plaid shirt. A part of John's brain registered the man was about his own age, maybe a few years younger.

John tried to speak, but his mouth was dry. Swallowing, he felt saliva loosen his tongue. He managed to croak out, "Who . . you?" He tried to pull his thoughts together, but they were fuzzy and he couldn't seem to form his words properly. *Have I been drugged?* "Where . . . where am I?"

A sly smile crossed the man's features. "That's not really important for your purposes. What you should be asking me is, why are you here?"

His mind wandered away from the man and the aches in his body began to register. His neck was sore, probably from being at an uncomfortable angle when he was unconscious. He felt a dull pain throbbing throughout his body. He looked down and saw he was sitting upright in a solid, old-fashioned office chair, with casters on the bottom of the legs. His wrists and ankles were strapped down with zip ties. Experimenting, John tugged at his restraints and realized he was only making them tighter, so he stopped struggling.

The man clapped his hands in front of John's face and the sharp sound set off the over-worked nerves in his head. "Pay attention. The drugs should be wearing off by now, so listen up."

The man grabbed John's chair from behind and pushed it along the floor. John realized the man was right, he was starting to feel a little less woozy. He took the opportunity to look around and saw he was in the middle of a cavernous room, with exposed brick walls. The cement floor beneath his feet had rust spots and holes, where it appeared manufacturing equipment had once been mounted. The windows high above were dingy, letting in sickly daylight. The last thing he remembered was sitting on Jo's couch in her den, waiting for her to come home. *How did I get here?*

The man pushed him in the chair until he was seated in front of a laptop on a scarred oak desk. "Here's what I want you to see." He clicked the mouse and the screen lit up. A grainy image appeared and John leaned forward slightly to get a better glimpse.

On the screen, he saw a nude woman, standing next to a bed. She spun in slow, lazy circles and John wondered why the man was showing him this video.

And then it hit him like another physical blow. *Jo!*

His befuddled mind cleared with the shock. John recognized Jo's bedroom. The red curls he loved to wrap around his hands cascaded down her strong back.

Seeing her in this vulnerable state made him realize she would go to just about any length to save him. Jo kept her eyes averted from the camera until the very end, when she looked directly at the lens. John knew her well enough to see the humiliation in her eyes, but he also saw defiance. She had purposely provoked the kidnapper. Not in a sexual way, but in a "C'mon and get me" sort of way. Jo was poking the man with a very sharp stick and the acid in John's stomach churned.

He tugged at the restraints, until he felt a trickle of warm blood at his wrist where the tough plastic of the zip ties cut into his flesh. John's head flew up, searching for the man who made him watch Jo on the screen. "Who are you? Why are you doing this?"

The man's sly grin was back, wider than before. He froze the screen with Jo's face staring upward at them both. "Special Agent Schwann has become very important to me. Let's just say I have a vested interest in keeping an eye on her."

"You sick bastard! You put cameras in her house."

"I've been watching for several weeks now. Until Agent Schwann looked up at the camera, I was convinced they had remained hidden. The FBI was snooping around, looking for signs of you, by the way. When they didn't find my surveillance cameras in the search, I thought my secret was safe." He pointed to the frozen image of Jo. "However, now there can be no doubt that she knows I am watching."

He tilted his head to one side and added, "I think she looks pleased by my attention, don't you? Enraptured, even."

John shivered. This man was clearly out of his mind. And Jo was in terrible danger. As he watched Jo he knew she had performed for the camera, knowing that it would taunt the bastard into revealing himself.

* * *

JO STAYED IN HER SHOWER until the water turned cool. When she stepped out onto the tile floor of the bathroom, she heard her cell ringing in the bedroom. She wrapped a towel around her wet body and dashed for the phone. She saw it was Frisco and she asked, "Find any more background on our DNA match?"

He spoke in a rush, "Just for kicks and grins, I called the Baltimore PD about the death of Bishop's mother, Karen. She died in 1987, of a self-inflicted gunshot wound. You're not going to believe this . . . it was another shotgun blast to the mouth."

Jo sat down on the edge of the bed and tucked the towel tighter around her body. "Really? That can't be a coincidence. Is the BPD certain it was a suicide?" Jo questioned.

"Well, that's where things get even more interesting. The detective who pulled the file said there was an interview with one of the children, who was present at the time of the shooting. And guess which kid that was?"

Jo could feel Frisco's excitement. "Robert."

"Uh-huh. Seven year-old Bobby swore his father was responsible. He was hysterical and couldn't give them any specifics, so the cops assumed he meant Karen was so depressed over a bad breakup that she took her own life. In light of our recent shootings with the same gunshot to the mouth, I wonder if there is some other explanation for Karen's quote-unquote suicide."

Jo's heart pounded and she stood up, remembering to grab her towel just before it fell away from her body. "Are you thinking maybe Freemont was the father?"

"The thought crossed my mind. His wife did say he wasn't the best husband in the early stages of their marriage."

"So maybe someone is going after Freemont for revenge. But why now? And who? We know it couldn't have been Robert Bishop, because he was already deceased at the time of Freemont's murder."

"I would say we're back to looking at Bishop's siblings."

Jo sighed. "I already researched Thomas and Sarah. They were clean as a whistle. The only loose end is Michelle, the sister who disappeared in college."

"So, it would appear we need to solve an old missing-persons case to solve our current cases. I wouldn't mind taking a peek at the visitor logs while Robert Bishop was incarcerated in Baltimore. Never know who might pop up on his visitors list," Frisco said.

"You mean, like a missing sister."

"Exactly."

Jo sat up and said, "You know, something else just occurred to me. I think it's about time I look into Robert Bishop's death. Everything about this family is screwed-up. Maybe his mother's death wasn't the only one made to look like something else."

Frisco whistled. "You think Robert may have been killed on purpose, to cover something up?"

"What if Robert Bishop moved to Minneapolis to finally confront his father about his mother's death? Maybe even blackmailed him. Don't you think it's awfully convenient Robert died in a shoot-out with the cops, not too long after he relocated to the Twin Cities?" Jo said.

"That's a big 'what if.'" Frisco paused and then continued, "But, you know, stranger things have happened. Let me know what you find out and I'll do the same."

CHAPTER THIRTY-ONE

Turners Bend
March

THE COUNTDOWN TO THE PREMIERE of *The Cranium Killer* was on. Chip had assembled all the key players: Myrtle Bauer, who was in charge of ticket sales, Mayor Johnson, Lance, Chief Fredrickson and a few other committee members.

They met in the theater and sat bundled in their outerwear because the heat was being kept low in the building. At 7:00 p.m. the temperature outside had risen to twenty-three degrees with a wind chill of minus two degrees. Chip had thought January and February were brutal, but March was proving to be the icing on this winter's cake.

"Thank you everyone for coming. This is our final volunteer committee meeting. You have put in a lot of hours and have done a great job. The Bijou looks spectacular. Now on to the celebrating," Chip said to the group gathered in the newly finished seats of the theater. "First on our agenda is Myrtle Bauer to outline the timetable of events for next Friday."

There was hardly a person in the assembled group who had not been in Ms. Bauer's History or Government class at Turners Bend High. She was just over five feet tall and almost five feet wide. She waddled to the front of the stage, lifted her glasses from the chain around her neck and gave the group a stern look, as she waited for complete silence.

"The day will start with the ribbon cutting at 9:00 a.m. Mayor Roger Johnson and Mr. Collingsworth will cut the ribbon, and the Mayor will give a brief speech." She scowled at the Mayor. "Keep it short Roger, no droning on as you are prone to do."

She checked her note cards and cleared her throat. "Then the showings will begin and continue all day and into the evening. I am happy to report the pre-sale of tickets will insure a full house for each showing. We have a waiting list for those who still have not learned procrastination leads to poor results. The red carpet will be rolled out for the 6:00 p.m. show. Dignitaries will be interviewed by reporters from Ames and Des Moines TV and radio stations. Once all are seated, Mr. Howard Glasser, the film's producer, will give a short address. The gala will follow the performance. This event is bigger than the day Pope John's motorcade drove through Turners Bend on the way to the basilica in Dyersville. I expect you all to be on your best behavior."

"Can I get a ticket for my cousin from Perry?" asked the man in charge of ushers.

"I cannot grant special favors. Put his name on the waiting list," answered Myrtle.

"Thank you, Myrtle," said Chip. "Next on the agenda is Chief Fredrickson to detail security measures. Chief."

The chief helped Ms. Bauer to her chair and began his briefing. "The State Patrol will be on hand to control traffic. Extra-duty officers from Perry, Grimes and Webster City will be here to monitor the crowds and provide back-up for Deputy Anderson and myself. If our good citizens just obey Ms. Bauer's request for good behavior, we will have a safe and trouble-free event."

"What about the killer that's on the loose, Chief? Will our young women be safe? I think every girl should be escorted by a patrolman."

"Rest assured, Myrtle, the safety of everyone is of utmost importance to us." The chief hopped down from the stage.

"Last on our agenda is Lance Williams with his report on the gala." Chip nodded toward Lance.

Lance, dressed in Ralph Lauren from head to foot, took over. "In keeping with our 'Return to the Glamour of 1930s Hollywood' theme, we will decorate the school gym starting Thursday as soon as classes are dismissed. Our wonderful committee, led by Dr. Jane, has booked a dance band from Chicago. The Starlights will be playing music from that era. The Bun and the Bend will be providing food and libations for the evening. In addition to dancing, we will have a casino set up in the lunchroom and at midnight there will be a drawing for an all-expenses-paid trip for two to Hollywood. Thanks to an anonymous donor, it should be a night to remember."

"Who's the donor, Lance?" asked the mayor.

"Mr. Anonymous, Mayor."

There was laughter and a smattering of applause as Lance returned to his seat. Chip checked his notes. "That's it for this evening.

Thanks again for your work on this project. It's time to polish those dancing shoes and tiaras."

The group exited the theater literally buzzing with excitement. Chief Fredrickson hung back, waiting to lock up. When only Chip remained, he took a seat and sighed deeply.

"We've got a problem. I got a phone call today. The voice sounded mechanical, but the message was clear. Our killer is going to be here next Friday to scout for recruits. Those were the exact words, 'scouting for recruits.' I called Masterson immediately, and the FBI is trying to trace the call. She also informed me another body has been found."

"Where this time?"

"In an abandoned silo in Iowa City. She's 99% sure that it is Tracy Trent. Seems Trent had two pins in her right arm from a break she had as a child, so identification is pretty simple. Masterson warned me, when it's confirmed, there will probably be a public announcement about the serial killer. Because of the phone message she will stall until after the premiere, but then all hell is going to break loose. She's setting up FBI surveillance and calling in a squad of agents. We'll be swarming with dudes in black suits and sunglasses and plugs in their ears."

"You know, Chief, this serial killer thing is straight out of that TV show that Jim likes so much. This is like a friggin' episode of *Criminal Minds*."

* * *

CHIP WAS FINDING IT HARD to concentrate on *Mind Games* with so much happening on the home front. The chief had described the voice on the phone as "mechanical." He wondered how a mechanical voice was produced. He heard it frequently on TV interviews where an identity was being hidden, along with a blurred face. He wondered if a mechanical voice would be just the thing to add to his story. A mechanical voice will keep readers speculating about John's abductor.

CHAPTER THIRTY-TWO

Mind Games
Brooklyn Center, Minnesota
Early August

JUST WHAT THE HELL WERE YOU THINKING?"

Agent Jo Schwann stood in front of her boss's desk, feeling like a school girl called down to be chastised by the principal. Tom's assistant had requested her presence in his office shortly after 10:00 a.m. Jo wasn't sure what exactly he was referring to. Looking back over her actions in the last twenty-four hours, it could have been several things, including trespassing. So, she waited until Tom continued his diatribe.

She didn't have to wait long. Tom's face was red when he said, "Don't you already have enough on your plate? You can't stay out of Agent Daniels' case?"

Well, that narrows things down some. Jo was about to open her mouth to explain exploring her neighbor's back yard without permission, when Agent Daniels walked into the office and said, "Here's the flashdrive we received."

The agent handed over the portable drive and Tom inserted it into his laptop. He walked around to the other side of the desk and turned the computer around so they could all view the screen. Jo was curious about the flashdrive, and wondered if it could have something to do with John.

An image of John appeared on screen and Jo gasped. There were purple smudges under his eyes and his normally ruddy complexion was pale. Silver duct tape covered his mouth and his eyes were dilated. She realized he must have been drugged. Jo was desperate for him to speak, to give her a clue of where to find him.

She scanned the screen, frantic for a date and time stamp. When she saw the video was dated earlier the same morning, her knees almost gave way at the sudden relief. *He's still alive!*

Jo was startled when at last she heard an electronically altered voice in the background, even while the camera remained focused on John. Tom reached over to the volume control and turned up the sound. "Agent Jo Schwann performed an interesting little dance for me this morning. I am rewarding her resourcefulness by showing that Dr. John Goodman is alive and well."

Jo watched John turn his head and look off screen. A pair of gloved hands reached out and twisted his head back toward the camera. Then she heard the disembodied voice again. "Here's my proposition. I would like to meet with Agent Schwann. Alone. I will not tolerate anyone tagging along, thinking they are going to be the hero. My audience will be with Jo. I will be in touch to let you know where and when we will meet."

On screen, John's eyes grew wide. Jo could tell he was upset with the man's terms and was trying to convey she should not come. *I will go, wherever he tells me to go. Because this is our best shot at getting John out alive.*

As if reading her mind, John frantically shook his head back and forth. The distorted voice spoke again. "Doctor, you think you can convince your girlfriend to stay away from me? Of course, she'll come. To save you. But in the end, she'll come to love *me*."

Jo gasped at his final words. For a brief moment, she felt dizzy. *Love? Love is what I feel for John, not the sick obsession this crazy bastard has for me!*

To Jo's horror, the gloved hand raised up, holding a gun. The weapon crashed down on the back of John's head and it lolled forward, his chin hitting his chest.

Jo's heart raced. She heard some scuffling sounds, a yelp and then the screen went blank. Jo stared at the screen. The image of an injured, vulnerable John burned into her retinas.

Tom spoke. "Just what did you do to get him this interested?"

Jo felt herself flush when she looked him in the eye and replied in a hoarse voice, "Like he said. I performed for him. Naked."

Jo watched the jaws of her boss and co-worker drop in unison. Under normal circumstances, she would have found their looks of astonishment comical. As it was, nothing about John's disappearance was remotely amusing to Jo.

Agent Daniels was the first to recover his voice. "Are you fucking kidding me? You really thought that was the best approach? I guess it didn't occur to you to let me in on your little stunt."

Jo whirled around to face him. She snapped, "Well, it worked, didn't it? I got him to contact us and now we know John is alive." Her voice was bitter when she continued, "It's not like you were getting anywhere with this investigation."

Agent Daniels' face turned crimson and he moved to stand right next to her. Jo could smell the stale scent of coffee on his breath. "Damn it. Did anything I said on the phone this morning register with you? I very clearly recall saying that we didn't want to provoke him to the point of violence. And, gee, Jo. Guess what? The guy smacked John with the butt of his gun."

A part of Jo's brain registered that Daniels was right. She had poked a crazy man and he had hurt John. She clenched her jaw and said nothing.

Daniels continued. "This is still my case, Schwann." He pointed to the computer screen. "That may be your boyfriend, but this is exactly why you weren't given this case in the first place. You purposely taunted a guy who is stalking you."

Daniels threw up his hands. "For chrissakes, are you trying to get yourself kidnapped, too? Like I don't already have enough on my hands with trying to save Goodman. You screwed up with that 'girls gone wild' routine."

Jo's fist balled up and before she even realized what she was going to do, she punched Daniels in the jaw. All the stress, anger and helplessness she had stored up ever since John disappeared went into the blow. She felt the force of it all the way to her elbow, and her knuckles crunched on impact.

Agent Daniels had a good foot on her height, but she had caught him unaware. He reeled backwards against the desk and lost his balance.

Tom had watched the argument with a wry smile on his face, but as soon as it became physical, he said, "Jesus, Jo. Have you lost your mind? That's enough." Tom reached for Daniels and helped steady him once more. The agent shrugged off Tom's hand and straightened his suit coat.

Jo's anger disappeared with the hit, and she was horrified at what she had done. *Maybe I'm losing it.* On top of all that, her hand hurt like hell. She was pretty sure she hadn't broken any bones, but it was going to swell if she didn't get ice on it soon.

She knew she had overstepped quite a few boundaries and probably one or two rules, as well. Daniels had been doing his job. John just wasn't safe yet. "Daniels, I'm sorry. I overreacted. You were right; I should have told you what I was going to do. I . . . I guess I just didn't want you to stop me. Look, I'm tired. And scared."

She looked down at her bruised knuckles, and said, "I shouldn't have hit you."

Daniels rubbed his jaw, working it one way, and then the other. "Man, for a little bitty thing, you pack a wallop. I went too far with what I said." He shrugged. "And you did manage to goad him into contacting us, so I guess I should be grateful you jump-started our investigation. Just wish you would've told me about it first."

Jo gave him a small smile. "I'll let you know the next time I'm planning a . . . what did you call it? Oh, yeah. A 'girls gone wild' routine."

The agent colored. "Not my best choice of words. I apologize. I know I've been resentful of your successes, but you've got great instincts."

She reached out to shake his hand. "Thanks. And I accept your apology. You can make it up to me by finding John. ASAP."

Daniels smiled and shook her hand. "You've got a deal."

* * *

THEY SPENT THE NEXT HOUR replaying the video, pausing it here and there to study the background details. From the exposed brick walls, large industrial garage door and wide open expanses, they decided John was most likely being held in an old warehouse or factory of some sort. However, in the large metro area there were many buildings which could fit that description and nothing stood out on the video to identify which one.

They listened again and again to the scuffling noises at the end of the video. Something about the yelping sound tweaked Jo's brain. It wasn't John who made the noise; it was clear that he had lost consciousness before the sound occurred.

Agent Daniels said, "It almost sounds like a dog."

Tom said, "That's what I was thinking. Doesn't help us much, though."

Jo turned to Daniels and said, "I'm assuming you already dusted the flashdrive for prints. How was it delivered?"

"Carol was at the front desk when a teenage boy dropped it off. Kid was pretty pleased with himself. He mentioned some guy paid him fifty bucks to bring it here. It was in a sealed envelope that had 'Investigator for Goodman Disappearance' typed on the front. No prints there or on the drive."

"Can we bring the kid in to talk to our sketch artist?" Tom asked.

"Nah. By the time Carol realized what she had in her hands, the kid had disappeared."

Jo's boss shook his head and said, "What about our security cameras? There must be something on one of the tapes to identify this kid."

Agent Daniels shook his head. "I tried that route. He was wearing a ball cap and we didn't get a good look at his face. We've got Carol's description, but it's pretty basic, 'A kid in a plain black hoodie with a Twins baseball cap.' Could describe half the teen-age boys in the greater Twins Cities area. The only odd thing about him was that he was wearing gloves. I think this kid was coached to keep his head down and stay out of the cameras."

Tom grunted and said, "Damn. I hate when these guys get smart. Sounds like a pro. No fingerprints, no direct trace back to him. Give me a garden-variety dumb crook any day."

They resumed their review of the video, but after another half hour, they gave up and Agent Daniels pulled out the flashdrive. He held it up and said, "I'll take this to the computer gurus and see if they can't isolate some of the sound bites and pictures." As he left Tom's office, he rubbed the spot on his chin where Jo had tagged him.

After the agent had closed the door, Tom frowned and said, "You know, I should suspend you for that stunt. That, and the interference with Daniels' investigation." He shook his head. "Hell, I should fire you."

Jo looked down at the papers scattered on Tom's desk, unable to meet his eyes. "Yeah. You should."

Tom massaged his temples. "What's gotten into you, Schwann? You used to be so level-headed and now you are taking crazy chances and punching fellow agents."

She wasn't sure if he really was looking for answers, or was simply blowing off his frustrations so she remained silent.

Finally, Tom huffed out a loud sigh. "But you know I won't fire you." He shook his finger at her. "Although I might still suspend you after this is all over with. Unfortunately for me, I need you on the Freemont/McDonald cases. Bring me up to speed."

Jo walked him through what she and Frisco had discovered, ending with her plan to talk to the cops involved with the shooting death of Robert Bishop.

"You really think Bishop's death was a set-up?" Tom said.

"That's what I want to find out. Look, I know it's a long shot. But put yourself in Freemont's shoes. You are a powerful man, running for the governor's office. Out of the blue, you are confronted by your long-lost son who can prove that you murdered your mistress to cover-up the existence of another family. What line wouldn't you cross? Freemont would have lost everything. His wife's millions, for starters."

He frowned and said, "Okay, I'm willing to give you some leeway on this, since we haven't had any new leads lately. Make damned sure all the t's are crossed."

Tom was silent for a moment. When he spoke again, Jo was startled by the change in subject. "Wonder when we'll hear from the kidnapper again. You know he's setting a trap for you, right?"

She felt the weight of Tom's words settle on her shoulders. She shrugged and then replied, "No doubt about it. But tell me, Tom. What choice do I have?"

* * *

JO HELD A BAG OF ICE on her throbbing hand as she stood next to her office window, absently staring off toward the distant Minneapolis skyline. Scenes from the video played over and over in her head, always pausing on the final shot of John's bowed head, as he sat unconscious in a warehouse. *But what warehouse, John? Tell me where to find you.*

After a few minutes, Jo shook her head, trying to expel her musings. *I'm not getting anywhere this way.*

She dropped the bag of ice into the trash can next to her desk and sat down in her chair. As she dialed the phone number of her contact at the Minneapolis PD, she knew this was going to be tricky. She would be calling into question any actions they took during a raid of Robert Bishop's home, maybe even accusing them of a cover-up.

When Alex Cohn answered, Jo said, "Hey, Alex. I have a case I need you to research. Last year, there was a drug bust at the home of a Robert Bishop. Ring any bells?"

"Uh, yeah. I remember it. The guy was killed, right?"

"That's the one. Can you put me in touch with the officers involved?"

Alex sounded leery when he said, "Why don't you tell me what this is about, Jo?"

"I'm following up on a trail of clues and it led me to Bishop. Just making sure I have a complete picture of what went down." She hesitated. Something in Alex's voice made her say, "Did I step into something?"

"Yeah, you could say that. The officer in charge of the raid on Bishop's house was just arrested last week on suspicion of taking bribes, among other charges. His name is Ben Johnson."

Jo let out a puff of air and felt the adrenaline flow through her. "Holy crap! I read about Johnson in the paper. Wait, was he the cop that killed Bishop?"

"Yeah, he was. That's why I remembered the case without having to look it up. We're reviewing every damned case Johnson was ever involved in, to make sure there was no improprieties. What a nightmare."

"Sorry to hear it Alex." She paused, and then added, "Well, to be totally honest, I'm not really sorry. I think you just proved a theory of mine. Where can I find Johnson?"

"He's being held at the Hennepin County Jail. Glad I could help."

Jo smiled at Alex's sarcasm. She didn't blame him. The court dockets would be a mess for years to come, once the lawyers started claiming their clients were framed by a crooked cop.

* * *

Jo was in an interrogation room with Ben Johnson. He stared at a spot on the table in front of him and mumbled, "Why would I tell you about the drug raid on Bishop's house? Read the police report. It's all there."

"What if I could get you a lighter sentence in return for your cooperation on my investigation?"

Officer Johnson looked up from the table and his eyes narrowed, "Maybe I should talk to my attorney first."

Jo stood up and made a show of packing up her files. "You know, I don't think I have the time to deal with a dirty cop like you, after all. I've obviously made a mistake."

"Wait. What do you want to know?"

Jo sat back down and took out her notepad. "Let's start with how you knew there were drugs in Bishop's house?"

The cop sat back in his chair, and fidgeted with the zipper on his prison-issued jumpsuit. "They were there because I put them there."

Jo blinked. "The whole thing was a set-up? Who hired you?"

"First, you got to tell me what's in it for me."

Jo sighed. "I will put in a good word with the DA for you. The FBI carries some weight in her office. Now, who paid you to frame and kill Robert Bishop?"

Johnson smirked. "It was that state representative that was found dead in the Capitol a couple of weeks ago. If you ask me, he got what he deserved."

Jo's heart pounded and she leaned forward in her seat. "Did Freemont tell you why he wanted to get rid of Bishop?"

"He said there were some loose ends from his past that he needed to tie up. Said Bishop was blackmailing him. He paid me seventy-five grand to make the problem go away. I knew what he was asking me to do."

CHAPTER THIRTY-THREE

Turners Bend
March

T HE EXCITEMENT OF THE PREVIOUS WEEK had turned into a buzz filled with tension and frenzy the day before the premiere. The two beauticians at Harriet's House of Hair were booked solid with customers wanting upsweeps. In the FBI office above, Agent Masterson was briefing the newly arrived agents. Chief Fredrickson and Chip were invited to relate the details for the next day. When they were finished, Masterson took over with her usual no-funny-business style.

"We now have confirmation that the body in the silo is that of Tracy Trent. Here is a ten-year-old photograph of our suspect, Elizabeth Brown, and here is an age-updated, computer-generated image of what she might look like now. We expect the town to be crowded with movie goers and media people. Every venue needs to be closely watched, every suspicious person detained. State Patrol will check the license plate of every vehicle entering the town. Remember that young women and possibly teen girls are the killer's targets. If this woman is in Turners Bend, I want her found and apprehended before another woman is abducted. She has murdered five times and tomorrow is the day the madness ends."

Chip and Fredrickson passed the photo between them. "Wow, she's not what I expected at all," said Chip, as he gazed at the picture of an attractive, middle-aged woman with shoulder-length, medium brown hair, dark eyes and sweet smile. "Guess I shouldn't stereotype women coaches."

"Sure doesn't look like a woman with a hot temper," said the chief. "Looks more like the woman on a Betty Crocker cake mix box to me."

"Looks can be deceiving, Chief. I've seen plenty of baby-faced killers in my day," said Masterson. "Oh, by the way, we weren't able to trace your phone call with the mechanical voice you received. It was from one of those throw-away cell phones. We do know the phone was purchased in Ames last week. The second it's turned on we should be able to triangulate the location."

She grabbed her vibrating phone for a call. Chip observed a tiny crack in her demeanor as she listened, and muttered "Damn, damn, damn." She asked a series of rapid fire, where, when and who questions, then hung her head after she disconnected to compose herself before continuing.

"I have to leave for Iowa City immediately for damage control. Someone on the police force leaked the Tracy Trent story to the press, including a tie-in to the Turners Bend body. Things are about to blow-up and tomorrow this will be headline news across the country. Chief, prepare for a media flood of national reporters, photographers, gossips, and thrill seekers. This town and Iowa City are going to be swarming like a hornets' nest. Trent was a popular radio announcer and interest in her disappearance has never waned."

Masterson took out a key and opened a desk drawer. She withdrew a shoulder holster and revolver, removed her suit jacket and strapped it to her side. Nodding to one of the agents, she said, "Klein, you're in charge here while I'm gone."

Turning to Fredrickson, she added, "Chief, listen to me very carefully. You are going to tell the press that this is an ongoing investigation, you are cooperating with the FBI, there is no confirmed connection between the two murders and you have no further comments at this time. Do you understand?"

The chief stood and, almost shouting, said, "Yes, Ma'am."

After leaving the meeting, Chip wandered over to the Bun. It was full of unfamiliar faces, except for one. Iver was behind the counter pouring coffee and nuking cinnamon rolls. Chip joined him.

"Jeez, Iver. What are you doing here?"

"My house is like a chicken coop today. Mabel was up all night making alternations and now the place is full of hens having their final fittings. I came here to relieve Bernice, so she could join them. Mabel was 'letting out the bust darts' on Flora's dress. I don't know what in the hell that means, but the image I have is pretty hysterical."

"Who are all these customers?"

"Most of them are with the press crews, I guess. They've blocked off Main Street with all their vans. The chief or Jim should be out there getting the traffic flowing."

Chip began to survey the women scattered throughout the café, searching for the face he had just seen in the photograph. She wasn't there. Most of the women were twenty-something with blonde, asymmetrically cut hairdos, wearing brightly-colored wool blazers. Reporters, he assumed. He was struck by a sick feeling . . . one of them could end up a victim of the serial killer.

"Where's lover-boy Lance and your spitfire agent?" asked Iver, as he started another pot of coffee.

"He called from Des Moines this morning. He went to the airport to pick-up Lucinda and my parents. My parents arrived on time, but Lucinda's plane was delayed out of JFK. I pity the poor airlines that caused Lucinda Patterson to be late, and I pity Lance who has to wait in the airport with my parents . . .my nattering mother and my father, the doctor who waits for no one."

"Remember what I said the day you put your car in the ditch, about your relationship with your father? My pa was sort of like yours, a hard-nosed Norwegian who made a lot of money farming, but not the easiest guy to get along with. As kids my brother, Knute, and I hated him and feared him, but as the old man began to fail, he softened. Or, maybe we softened. Whichever, it doesn't matter. Our last few years with him were good, and I miss the old coot like hell. End of story." Iver blew his nose on a big red bandana and switched topics, leaving Chip to ponder his story.

"Well, I hope Miss Lucinda's bust darts are okay, cause I tell you, Mabel's got no time to fix them," Iver said, chuckling and returning to his jovial self.

Bernice returned. She had been to Harriet's before work and her hair looked like a bakery shop confection. She carried a clear plastic bag, which contained her gown, a gold satin, full-length dress.

"Thanks, boys, I can take over now."

Iver removed his apron and returned it to Bernice. "Where to?" he asked Chip.

"Let's get out of here and check on how things are at the Bijou."

Iver and Chip crossed the street, squeezing between vans and stepping over cables. The door of the Bijou was open, and as they approached the smell of burned popcorn wafted into the street. Inside the theater it looked like a disaster zone.

"What happened?" asked Chip.

"We were popping a test batch, and it didn't turn out too good," offered one of the volunteer concessionaires. "We're going to give it another go."

As they moved through the lobby another odor assaulted their nostrils. "Phew, what's that smell?" Iver asked.

They followed their noses to the men's bathroom, peeked inside the door marked Gents and saw a denim-covered butt sticking out of one of the stalls.

"George, that you?" Iver asked.

A voice echoed out of the stall. "Yup, it's me. Crapper over-flowed this morning. I just about got it fixed. Think we're going to need some air freshener, though."

* * *

Chip's head was pounding as he drove home. He felt like he was on a ship going down in flames. The scenes in the FBI office, the Bun and the Bijou were straight out of B-Grade movies. He took a stiff drink of bourbon and waited for the arrival of his parents. He had gone all day without thinking about Jane. He stretched out on the couch and quelled his thoughts by imagining what she might look like in her ball gown. He grabbed his cell phone to call her, checked for reception and got no bars on his phone, just what he would expect on a day when the Titanic was headed for an iceberg and the passengers were clueless as to the perils ahead.

CHAPTER THIRTY-FOUR

Mind Games
Minneapolis & Shakopee, Minnesota
Early August

Jo Schwann called Frisco as soon as she climbed into her SUV. She turned the AC on high while she waited for the detective to answer.

When she heard Frisco's voice on the line, she immediately said, "Frisco, you're not going to believe this, but Freemont paid to have Bishop killed."

"No friggin' way! How d'ya figure that out?"

Jo quickly ran through her conversation she'd had with the crooked cop.

"Man, when the pieces come together, they really come together," Fisco said.

"What do you mean?"

"I found some interesting details myself. Guess who was a regular visitor of Bishop's when he was an inmate at the Chesapeake Detention Center in Baltimore. Marjorie Payne, ace reporter."

Jo was shocked. "I did not see that coming!"

"Me, either. She was working for WBAL-TV in Baltimore at the time. She supposedly was working on a three-part series on Bishop and his life of crime, but it never showed up on television. So, I did some more digging. Marjorie Payne lived in Baltimore the same time as Bishop. Then, shortly before Bishop moved to Minneapolis, Payne took a job here with KSMN-TV."

Jo leaned back into her seat. "I wonder what she and Bishop talked about." Jo thought for a moment and then continued. "Do you think there was more than a professional connection between Payne and Bishop?"

"I wondered that myself," Frisco said.

Something clicked in Jo's brain. "Frisco, hang on a sec. I have an idea."

Jo dug into her briefcase and pulled out her files on their case. She sorted through the documentation until she came to the DMV photo of the teen-aged Michelle Bishop.

Next, she turned on her tablet and pulled up the website of Payne's TV station. She clicked through the links until she came to the promo shot of

Marjorie Payne. She held up the DMV photo and compared it to the one of Payne on her screen.

Other than the hair color and a few years in age difference, the two women in the photos looked strikingly similar. She could feel her heart pounding. "Frisco, is there any possibility that Marjorie Payne really could be Michelle Bishop?"

"Whoa! But how could she have pulled that off without someone noticing? And why would she?"

"As to why, Michelle had a rough family history. Maybe her big brother Robert filled her in on their mother's murder. Who would want to be a part of that family tree?"

"But why would Marjorie willingly trade identities with her?"

Jo studied the pictures again. "I don't think it was done willingly. Remember the Baltimore cold case we found a few weeks back about the unidentified female who died of a shotgun blast to the face, just like our vics? Wouldn't Marjorie Payne have been about the same age as that victim at the time?"

"Yeah, I guess, but I'm not following the connection."

"What if that victim was the real Marjorie Payne and Michelle Bishop or her brother killed her, so that Michelle could assume her identity?"

Jo could hear Frisco's whistle through the phone. "You think?"

"There is something not right about Bishop's connection with Marjorie Payne. Also, I'm looking at the old DMV photo of Michelle Bishop right now. She sure looks an awful lot like Marjorie Payne. We can have the Baltimore PD run a DNA test to verify."

"A DNA test will take some time, though." Frisco sighed, "This just keeps getting better and better. Man, this is turning into a real shitstorm."

The corners of Jo's mouth turned up into a wry smile. "Funny, my boss used that same expression . . . even before we suspected the Payne link. Now, how are we going to prove it?"

"Beats the hell out of me," Fisco said and paused. "I . . . Hey, Jo, can you hang on a minute? I've got a call on the other line."

The detective was gone so long that Jo wondered if they had lost the cell connection. She was about to hang up and call Frisco again when he came back on the line and said, "Got another one missing."

She raised an eyebrow and said, "Damn. Who is it this time?"

"Sandra Womack."

It took Jo a moment to make the connection, but when she did, she inhaled a sharp breath. "The wife of the ex-Viking football player, 'Mountain Man' Womack? That Sandra Womack?"

"Yup, the same woman who co-founded the mega-church in Shakopee with her husband."

Jo had a sinking feeling in the pit of her stomach. "Another outspoken, ultra-conservative."

"Uh-huh. Not only that, but she and her husband were pretty chummy with Freemont."

"How chummy?"

"They went to college together and the Womacks donated a bunch of money to Freemont's campaign."

"Well, shit."

Frisco's chuckle was gruff. "That sums up my feelings precisely. So, I was thinking, we need to get over to the church and talk to the folks out there. Where are you now?"

"I'm still in the parking lot at the Hennepin County Jail. Why?"

"I'm right near there. How about I swing by and pick you up? We can talk more about the case on the way."

Jo turned off her engine. "Wouldn't it be great if we could actually find Sandra Womack before it's too late?"

"That would be a nice change."

* * *

DETECTIVE FRISCO DROVE WESTWARD along highway 101, which followed the south side of the Minnesota River. Jo tapped away on her iPad, researching the Womacks and their church. As they passed the turnoff for the horse race-track at Canterbury Park, Frisco cleared his throat and looked over at Jo.

"No offense, but you look like hell. Can't just be this case. I know you are having a hard time with John . . ."

Jo stowed away her tablet and quietly said, "John's been abducted."

Frisco swore under his breath and Jo felt the slight sway of the car as he inadvertently jerked the steering wheel in shock. "Abducted? When did that happen?"

"Two days ago," Jo said looking at the floor. She was surprised when she thought about the time frame. It had seemed like weeks ago when she stood in her den and held John's luggage tag in her hands.

"And just when were you planning on telling me?"

She finally looked at Frisco's face and she could see the anger and hurt that crossed his features. Jo felt the heat in her face when she responded, "Look, Frisco. I just couldn't bear to talk about it. It's killing me."

Frisco turned his attention back to the highway and Jo could see a muscle jump in the detective's jaw. He was silent for a moment, and then he said, "Tell me what happened."

Jo began her story, starting with the night of John's disappearance when she discovered he had been in her house and concluding with the video she had watched earlier in the day. She left nothing out, including the swing she took at Agent Daniels in her boss's office.

Frisco didn't say anything at all during her monologue and Jo wondered if he was still angry with her or just processing the information.

He pulled into the parking lot of Heaven's Crossing church and turned off the car. Jo could hear the quiet ticking of the engine as it rested on the pavement of the enormous lot. Frisco stared out the windshield for awhile, making no move to get out.

Jo could take his silence no longer. "Frisco, say something. What do you think?"

The detective turned toward her and his eyes were tired when he finally spoke. "I think Agent Daniels is right. You painted a big-ass target on your back with that dance routine of yours. Not your brightest move."

Then he grinned. "But you don't lack for guts, that's for damn sure."

Jo was shocked. "So, you aren't pissed at me?"

He shrugged his shoulders. "Nah. Well, maybe just a little bit, seeing how you left me out of the loop for so long. But how can I be mad when I probably would have done something just as stupid?"

He stared off toward the mega-church, but didn't seem to be seeing it, as if his mind was a thousand miles away. He finally spoke, "I was also thinking that sometimes life just doesn't make a damn bit of sense. The doc finally comes to Minneapolis to work things out with you and then some psycho-stalker decides to nab him, to use as bait to get to you. Here we are trying to solve a couple high-profile cases and you have to deal with this, too." He paused and then gave her a small, crooked smile. "No wonder you look like hell."

Leave it to Frisco to cut through the bullshit. Jo felt her lips twitch in return, grateful that Frisco had apparently forgiven her. It had relieved some of the tightness in her chest to finally be able to talk to her friend. "Thanks, Frisco."

A frown appeared between his brows. "For what?"

"For being you." She unlatched her seat belt and opened the car door.

As they strode across the huge parking lot, Jo heard Frisco whistle. "Would you take a look at this place? Looks more like a place built to worship money than a place to worship God. Sure don't have places like this up on the North Shore."

Jo looked at the sprawling complex. Frisco was right; it did look more like a corporate headquarters building than a church, with a large center building and several wings spilling to the sides. It was an impressive monument to adoration.

Frisco followed Jo into the building. Here again, everything was done on a massive scale. The large atrium area was filled with light from windows that soared above their heads. Every detail was constructed to draw the eye upward.

Frisco was about to head through an open doorway, when they heard a voice off to their left. "May I help you folks? Worship is not scheduled for another two hours, but you are welcome to go into the private sanctuary just down the hall, if you'd like."

Jo and Frisco turned to see a tall, powerfully built man walking toward them, dressed immaculately in a dark gray custom-tailored suit, a crisp white shirt and an eggplant-colored tie. He was instantly recognizable. Kent Womack was nick-named "Mountain Man" not because he resembled a person that lived in some back hills country, but because he looked like a mountain. And seemed just as immovable.

According to his professional stats that Jo had read on the drive out to the church, Womack stood six-foot-eleven inches. In his days as an offensive tackle for the Minnesota Vikings, he weighed in at 410 pounds, which made him one of the biggest players in the NFL. Even the mega-church's interior could not diminish his size. When Jo stood next to him, she had to tilt her head back to look into his eyes.

What Jo saw there was a combination of fear and bone-deep sadness. She thought the pain in his dark brown eyes mirrored her own.

Jo was the first to speak, "No thank you, Pastor Womack. We're not here to pray. My name is Special Agent Jo Schwann, with the FBI, and this . . ." She waved her hand in Frisco's direction, ". . . is Detective Mike Frisco. We're here to speak with you in regards to the disappearance of your wife."

The big man's eyes filled. "Thank you for coming. Won't you follow me? If you don't mind, I would prefer to talk in my office, where we will have some privacy." The thick carpet muffled their footsteps as he led them down a long corridor.

Womack quietly closed the office door behind them and said, "What can I do to help you find my wife?"

Jo thought the man looked like he was barely hanging on to a thread of control. It made her think about her own worries about John and she found herself empathizing with the giant in front of her. Her voice was gentle when she said, "First of all, Pastor Womack, we want you to know that we will do everything in our power to bring your wife back to you."

Kent Womack's chin quivered a bit as he struggled to hold back the tears that threatened to slip from his eyes. His booming voice was raw when he replied, "Please, call me Kent. Thank you for that. Sandra is everything to me. Did you know we were high school sweethearts?"

Womack's voice cracked on the word "sweethearts" and he reached out for the water glass on his desk, taking a deep swallow.

"No, I hadn't heard that," Frisco said.

Jo hated to be abrupt, but time was of the essence, so she said, "Do you know of anyone who would want to hurt your wife? Or you, through her?"

"Sandra is loved by everyone who has ever met her. I'm sure I've accumulated my fair share of enemies over the years, but I can't think of a single person who would do such a thing."

"So, no hate mail or anything like that? I know that both of you have frequently spoken out against some hot-button topics, such as gay rights and abortion, for instance," Frisco questioned.

"Yes, and we've received some pretty ugly letters and emails. But nothing that we deemed threatening."

Jo looked briefly at Frisco, who raised an eyebrow as if to say, *I wouldn't be too sure of that.* "We'll need to see those notes, just to cover all bases," Frisco said.

"Of course. We didn't save all of them, but I'll give you what we have."

Jo changed the subject. "What can you tell me about your connection to the Freemonts?"

"We've been close friends since college. Tanya and my wife were in a sorority together. We've contributed to Lee's political campaigns over the years . . ." He stopped for a moment, and then his eyes widened. "Wait. You, um, you don't think Lee's murderer took my wife, do you?"

"We're looking into all possibilities. Were you also friends with Annie McDonald?" Frisco said.

"Um, yes, of course. We were all friends. It was Annie that talked Lee into running for office in the first place."

"Did you know that Lee Freemont had another family in Baltimore?" Jo asked. She held her breath, waiting for Kent's response. They still didn't have proof that the state representative had fathered the Bishop children, but she was hoping they would get some answers, here and now.

The big man's face turned white and he sank deeper into his chair. He eventually nodded and said, "Yes. I did. I found out at Lee's first campaign party. He'd been drinking for most of the evening when he pulled Annie and my wife aside and told them. Tanya, his wife, didn't know a thing about it and he was freaking out that she would find out."

When he paused, Jo said, "And what did your wife and Annie do about it?"

"They told me. We confronted Lee the next day, when he sobered up. Annie convinced him to offer a settlement to his mistress, so she and her children would quietly disappear from his life. I gave him the money to do it. We couldn't risk Tanya finding out. She would have divorced him and he would never have been elected. Not with a scandal like that hanging over his head. "

They were all silent for a moment, absorbing the latest information. Jo took no joy in having been proven correct.

Finally, Frisco said, "When was the last time you saw your wife?"

"This morning, around six. We had breakfast together in our home and then she was coming here, to get things rolling for the day."

"I have to ask. Since she's been gone less than a day, what makes you so certain that she's missing and not just out running errands?" Jo said.

Womack looked Jo in the eyes and said, "Sandra never misses the morning service. Never. She would cut a meeting or appointment short, if that's what it took to be here at 10:00 a.m. on the dot. Today we were going to hold a special memorial service for Lee Freemont, and she would never miss that."

Frisco looked up from his notes. "So, she hasn't answered her cell?"

Womack shook his head and looked down at his hands. Jo was relieved to see a bit of color coming back into his cheeks.

Frisco wrote in his notebook and then looked up. "Did anyone see her here this morning?"

"No, but she always arrives before the rest of the staff and she could have gone back out before anyone saw her. When we realized that she was uh, missing . . ." Womack stopped and swallowed, struggling to continue.

"Take your time, Pastor," Jo said.

He nodded and then continued, "Sorry. I . . . well, by the time we realized that she wasn't here, we just started calling everyone we know. No one had seen her. Not since the interview."

Frisco's head shot up from his note taking. "Interview? Who was the interview with?"

"Marjorie Payne, a reporter for the local NBC station. She was doing a special interest piece on our church, how it was founded, and so on."

Jo's heart sped up. *Holy God!* She looked at Frisco, who stood up in his excitement. The detective said, "Pastor, your wife had an interview this morning with Marjorie Payne and you're just now telling us about it?"

A puzzled look crossed Womack's features. "I'm sorry. I thought I mentioned it when I reported her missing to the police. Guess I was so frantic that I forgot." He looked back and forth between Detective Frisco and Jo, the crease between his brows becoming a deep furrow. "Why? Is it important?"

Jo said, "Yeah, it just might be. Do you know where they were meeting?"

"Some coffee shop, over in Minneapolis." He paused, and looked upward, as though the answer could be found on his office ceiling. "She said somewhere along St. Anthony Main, near the Stone Arch bridge."

His eyes brightened. "Wait, it's called The Bean Counter."

"We'll check it out. Maybe someone there will remember seeing them. Do you have a recent photo of Sandra?" Jo asked.

Womack grabbed the picture frame on his desk and extracted the picture of his wife. He handed it to Jo, who tucked it in her suit jacket for safekeeping.

Frisco began packing up his notes and then he reached out to the pastor, who stood up from his chair and enveloped Frisco's hand in his own mammoth paw. "Thank you for your time. We will be back in touch as soon as we know anything."

Jo stood up as well. She didn't bother reaching out for the pastor's hand, because he had crumbled back into his seat. Looking small for the first time since they had arrived, the tears had finally started to flow down his fleshy cheeks. "Please. Do what you can to get her back to me. I'll . . . I'll do anything they ask."

She patted his beefy shoulder before they walked out of his office. Jo felt the panic rolling off the man like fog on a lake. She thought about her own fears about John. *There's a lot of that going around.*

* * *

FRISCO RACED BACK THROUGH the suburbs and headed for downtown Minneapolis. "I wonder if Freemont ended up using the money he received from the Womacks to kill Karen Bishop," Jo said.

"Makes sense. Maybe his initial plan was to buy her off, like Womack said. But if she refused, then he might be desperate enough to have her eliminated."

Jo pulled out her phone. "You know, I could swear Annie McDonald had an appointment in her calendar the day of her disappearance. Remember? We couldn't figure out who it was because all we had were initials."

Frisco nodded and said, "Yeah. That sounds right. What were those damned initials?"

"I'll call my office right now and have them check."

When her co-worker answered, she said, "Shane. Do me a favor. Dig out the evidence files for Annie McDonald, the op-ed columnist. I'm looking for her day planner."

"Sure thing. Hang on."

Jo stopped her leg from jiggling as she waited, listening to the hold music on the FBI's phone system. Shane finally came back on the line a few minutes later. He said, "Okay, what am I looking for?"

"What's the notation on her calendar the day before her murder?"

Jo could hear Shane flipping through pages. "Um, it looks like some initials and then 2:00 p.m."

"Can you make out the initials?"

"N.P. No, wait, I think it might be M.P."

Jo looked at Frisco and nodded. The detective smirked and high-fived Jo. She said into the phone, "Thanks, Shane. I owe you one."

Clicking off the phone, she immediately dialed the phone number for State Representative Freemont's head of staff, Kim Clark.

When she answered, Jo said, "Ms. Clark, this is Special Agent Jo Schwann. Did State Representative Freemont have any appointments the day of his disappearance?"

Jo was surprised when the woman answered without hesitation. "Why yes, he did. He had an appointment with Marjorie Payne."

Jo's heart sped up. "Are you quite sure? Don't you need to check an appointment book to verify?"

"Oh, no. I'm quite certain. Um, and that appointment wouldn't have been in his planner. You see, they had a standing appointment for the last three months. Ms. Payne was covering State Representative Freemont's campaign for governor for her TV station."

If Jo could've reached into the phone line to shake the woman, she would have. "Why didn't you tell us this before? You didn't think this was important in our investigation?"

Kim Clark's voice sounded defensive when she replied, "I didn't think that it mattered. It was most likely a man who killed him. It's not like Marjorie Payne could have been involved, right? She's so smart and attractive."

Jo gritted her teeth. "Ms. Clark, I wish I could press charges against you for utter stupidity."

When Jo clicked off the phone, she rolled her eyes and muttered, "God, help me."

CHAPTER THIRTY-FIVE

Turners Bend
March

IT WAS 5:00 A.M. and Chip gave up trying to sleep. He was on his couch along with Runt and Callie. His mother and father, who had finally arrived after midnight, were asleep in his bed. He turned on CNN and muted the sound on his TV. He didn't need to hear the words to figure out that Masterson's warning had materialized. There were replays of her press conference in Iowa City, and of Chief Fredrickson's in Turners Bend, the chief repeating Masterson's instructions to him almost word for word. There was a recap of the Tracy Trent story, and even clips from his interview with Amy Chang. There was an announcement that the governor of Iowa was sending a National Guard troop to Turners Bend to provide support during the premiere of *The Cranium Killer*, followed by a trailer for the movie.

His mother emerged from his bedroom in a pink fuzzy robe and matching slippers and went to the kitchen. Her hair was in rollers the size of juice cans. Pots and pans began to rattle and dishes clinked. His father in his matching silk pajamas and robe came and sat beside him. Chip turned the sound back on, and the two of them watched without exchanging a word, until his father uttered, "Quite a media circus isn't it? Can't say I'm very happy about the Collingsworth name being associated with all this sensationalism."

Chip ignored the comment. It was so like his father to make everything about himself and their precious family name, yet he had to agree it wasn't the kind of press he liked either.

The unmistakable aroma of frying bacon began to fill the house.

"I say, your mother never fixes me bacon anymore, too much salt, fat and nitrates. But I do love a strip or two of crisp bacon. Turn off that brouhaha. Let's indulge in some breakfast before we get on with this auspicious day."

Maribelle had outdone herself with buttermilk pancakes, scrambled eggs and bacon. "Heaven knows when we will get another decent meal today. You boys eat up. I suppose I should have invited that nice Lance Williams and your agent. She certainly seems to be attracted to him. She was all over him like Saran wrap when she came off the plane from New York. Your father thinks she is quite attractive, don't you, Doc?"

Ignoring his wife's comment, Chip's father reached for a third strip of bacon. Chip followed suit as his mother prattled on and on, as only she could do.

"I brought your tux for tonight, as you requested. I bought a new dress for this occasion, an understated gown, of course. I wouldn't want to look out of place. Now, your father and I will be at the ribbon cutting. Then we'll return here to rest and go back to town for the red carpet events. Imagine us on a red carpet, and with Howard Glasser. I remember when he was that cute little guy on the TV series in the '60s. What was the name of that show? We saw the last movie he produced, didn't we, Doc? What was the name of that movie? Do you think I should prepare something witty to say, if I'm interviewed?"

She never seemed to notice when no one responded to her questions.

* * *

WHEN CHIP AND HIS PARENTS reached town it was so crowded you could barely walk down the street. There was a policeman or guardsman every five feet, and FBI agents roamed around, their eyes constantly scanning faces.

The ribbon cutting went on as planned. Cameras rolled and flash bulbs popped as Chip and Mayor Johnson held a pair of over-sized scissors and snipped the wide red ribbon. When the Mayor's speech started to get a little long, Myrtle Bauer gave him the cut-throat sign, and he abruptly ended.

As the ticket holders for the first showing started to line up, Chip gave his parents a quick tour of the theater. The first batch of popcorn was underway, this time without the burnt aroma. The hallway to the restrooms had a strong floral smell. No 'Out of Order' sign on the men's room door. All was right with the world so far.

"What do you think of the renovations?" asked Chip.

"Oh, darling, it's just like the theater where your father and I used to go when we were dating, isn't it, Doc? We saw *Lawrence of Arabia*. I had such a crush on Peter O'Toole. They don't make movies like that anymore."

"For once I have to agree with your mother, Son. The theater is quite an accomplishment. You should be very proud of yourself," his father said.

That morning over breakfast Chip had felt the beginnings of an alliance with his father, and now this. *Had the healing process Iver mentioned begun? Could he step-up and meet his father halfway?* For the first time, he wanted to try.

Maribelle was off on another tangent, as Chip led them out of the Bijou and down to the Bun.

Chip kept scanning the crowd, looking for Elizabeth Brown, but also looking for Jane. He hadn't seen her or talked with her for two days. He missed her. He needed her to help him get through this day. There was no place to sit down at the Bun, so he drove his parents back to his house, and took Runt for a walk.

* * *

SHORTLY AFTER 5:00 P.M. Chip dressed in his tuxedo and glanced in the mirror. Nothing like a custom-made tux to make a guy look classy, he thought. Chip and his parents headed back to town, he and his father in their tuxedos and Maribelle in her black gown. Her dress may have been understated, but her ruby and diamond jewelry reeked of wealth and sophistication.

Main Street had been closed to all traffic. The red carpet ran down the sidewalk in front of the theater and into the lobby. Photographs were already underway and reporters were testing their microphones. "Testing, one, two, three. Can you hear me yet?"

In the lobby he spotted Lance with Lucinda on one arm and Jane on the other, all smiling for the cameras. Both women looked gorgeous, Lucinda in her white, New York designer gown and Jane in a deep teal dress, designed and made by Mabel Ingrebretson of Turners Bend. In Chip's eyes, Jane took the prize. He stood back and gazed at her. She spied him, gave him a huge smile and a little wave of her gloved hand.

He felt a pleasant swelling in his chest, and he gave her a finger wave in return.

Sven, wearing a musty-looking tux and a beret, and a group of artsy-looking kids approached him. One boy sported what looked like an old smoking jacket, another a Grateful Dead t-shirt. The girl on Sven's arm was wearing a black bustier and a pink tutu.

"Chip, I want you to meet my friends from MCAD. Guys, this is the famous author, Charles Collingsworth, the guy who wrote *The Cranium Killer*, the book not the screenplay. He renovated this theater. Isn't it sick? Chip, do you think you could introduce us to Howard Glasser when he comes?"

Just then a stretch limo escorted by a State Patrol car pulled up in front of the theater, the door opened and out stepped Howard Glasser, a short, skinny man in his mid-fifties. He was dressed in black leather pants and bomber jacket, and he had the five o'clock shadow so popular with Hollywood types, but rarely seen in Turners Bend. He stopped mid-way to the door and posed for photographers in one direction, turned and posed again in another direction. There was a meteor shower of flashing cameras. Then the reporters lined up and he proceeded from one to the other for brief interviews. Lucinda finally came to rescue him and guide him into the lobby.

The reporters then interviewed Chip and his parents. "Mrs. Collingsworth, you must be so proud of your son," commented one reporter, as she stuck her microphone in Maribelle's face.

"Yes. Of course, we knew from the time he was a young boy that he was extremely talented. Men on his father's side of the family are all physicians, but Charles got his creative talents from my side of the family. In fact, I was a budding author in my early days, but I gave it up to raise my boys."

Chip was stunned. He whispered to his father, "Where does she come up with this crazy stuff?"

"I've lived with her for fifty years, and I still don't know." He smiled.

Sven approached them, this time without his friends. He had a worried look on his face. "Chip, could I talk to you, like alone, for a second?"

"Sure, let's slip into the theater office; it should be empty right now." Chip turned toward his father. "I'll meet up with you later. You better get Mom away from that reporter. There's no telling what else she might say." He shook his head, smiling.

Sven and Chip entered the small office off the lobby, and Chip shut the door. "What's up, Sven?"

"Do you think Dad is here someplace?"

"I wouldn't think Hal would be here, but why do you ask? Are you worried he might be?"

Sven hesitated, took a deep breath and continued. "Remember those two undercover DEA agents I told you about, the ones who questioned me about my dad and drugs? Well, I think they're here . . . not undercover as migrant workers . . . this time in black suits. Do you think they're looking for him?"

"I wouldn't worry, Sven. The FBI has brought in a lot of agents to cover this event. Those two guys are probably just part of the crew."

"There's one thing that's kind of weird though. I heard them whispering to each other in Spanish."

"Well, DEA agents often work along the Mexican border, so speaking Spanish with each other may not be that unusual. If they approach you again and you're uncomfortable, it's probably best to tell Special Agent Klein, he's the agent in charge today. Okay?"

Sven didn't respond. Chip sensed the boy had something else on his mind. He kept quiet and waited until Sven decided to speak.

"On one hand, I wish Dad were here. I'd love for him to see the theater and watch the movie with us. But, for his sake, I hope he's safe someplace else, far away from those two agents."

Chip put his arm around Sven's shoulders and gave him a brief hug. "I hear you, man. Go join your friends and try to put all of this out of your mind for tonight."

Lord, now I have to be on the lookout for Elizabeth Brown and Hal Swanson, too.

* * *

THE EVENTS OF THE EVENING proceeded just as planned. Howard Glasser gave a charming and witty introduction to the movie, praised the actors and thanked the town for the warm reception. He mentioned the theater renovation, "This place brings back wonderful childhood memories. It reminds me of watching *Star Wars* on Saturday afternoons and eating Dots and Junior Mints."

Glasser paced across the stage with a hand-held mike. "Ms. Patterson persuaded me to read *The Cranium Killer*, and I knew from the first chapter that it would make a blockbuster film. I'd like to announce that I was smart enough to snap up the movie rights to Mr. Collingsworth's next book, too. I hope to return to your lovely town for the premiere of *Brain Freeze* in about a year and a half."

After his speech, he was swiftly whisked away in his limo. One hour and thirty seven minutes later the movie ended, and the audience burst into applause. The crowd stood and shouts of "Bravo" echoed around the theater.

Jane was waiting in the lobby and she planted a kiss on his cheek and took his arm. "What's wrong, Chip? You look like you didn't like the film. I thought it was quite well done and the audience seemed enthralled."

"No one told me they were going to change the ending," he said. "I bet you anything Lucinda knew. How could they do that? I'm steamed. There was no way that Dr. Goodman would hook up with that detective; she just wasn't his type."

"Don't be. I think Hollywood does that a lot. Remember how they changed the ending to *The Horse Whisperer*, where Tom wasn't killed like in the book . . . that's Hollywood for you. Let's go to the gala. We can dance your troubles away. The dance band I booked is very good, and I asked them to play lots of slow numbers for us."

When they arrived at the high school, Chip was amazed at the transformation. He had to admit that Lance had outdone himself again. The 1930s theme was beautifully executed, Art Deco lamps on each table, Erte posters and antique mirrors on the walls, even a 1931 wooden Phillips radio on display. He and Jane danced in the gym, and ate shrimp toast and chicken wings. They played Black Jack in the lunchroom and drank champagne toasts everywhere. Jane stayed by his side all evening. He did not spend one second thinking about the killer until he saw Chief Fredrickson surveying the crowd

When Jane visited the bathroom, Chip sought out the chief. "Any sightings of our suspect?"

"Negative. Maybe the heavy police presence kept her away."

The two scanned the room. A woman Chip had never seen before caught his eye. Unlike the other women at the gala, she wasn't wearing a ball gown, just a simple black dress. She was tall and slender and had short-cropped brown hair. *My God, could that be her? Elizabeth Brown?* Chip's heart started to race. "Chief, that woman, the one over by the punch bowl. Check her out," he said in a shaky voice.

The chief laughed. "Yup, Ms. Stensrud. She's the middle school PE teacher. She's lived here in Turners Bend all her life, never coached up in Minnesota, I'm sure, if that's what you were thinking."

Chip watched as Tom Whittler, the high school coach approached her. They did not appear to be on friendly terms. The woman made a short remark, tossed her head and abruptly departed.

"That's Whittler isn't it? What's he like?" asked Chip.

"He's tough. Hard on the girls, but he gets results. He'd be a good match for Ms. Stensrud, but I hear the two are not on good terms, bitter enemies, in fact."

Jane returned to his side, and they watched the dancers. One of the biggest surprises of the evening was Chip's parents. They seemed to be completely enjoying themselves . . . even his father was laughing and dancing. They drew a lot of attention with their tango and foxtrot. The floor cleared for them as they executed the tricky two-step.

"Oh, it's just like *Dancing with the Stars*," said Flora Frederickson, who was no slouch on the dance floor herself.

Chip asked Ingrid to dance. She blushed but willingly followed him to the dance floor where he tried to execute his version of the lindy.

"No offense, Chip, but I don't think you inherited your parents' dancing skills," said Ingrid, trying unsuccessfully not to laugh at him.

"You're right there, but I do know how to pick the prettiest dance partners in the place. You look lovely tonight. With your tiara and blue gown, you look like a princess."

"Thank you, kind sir. You don't look too shabby yourself, Chip."

One of Sven's friends tapped him on the shoulder and cut in to finish the dance with Ingrid.

Jane glided into his arms. "That was so sweet of you to dance with Ingrid. She's lovely isn't she?"

"Yes, you've raised two great kids. You should be very proud of yourself." Chip danced her off toward the bar. "Now how about one last glass of the bubbly?"

At the end of the evening, Lance drew the name for the trip to Hollywood. Bernice shrieked and jumped up and down when her name was drawn. "Hollywood here I come. Universal City, Rodeo Drive, Disneyland, the Ellen Show."

Lance remained on the stage. "Friends, I have another announcement. Tonight I have asked Lucinda Patterson to marry me, and as luck would have it, she accepted."

Lucinda joined him on the stage and flashed a three-carat pink diamond ring to the crowd. Cheers went up from everyone except Chip, who stood still, not knowing exactly what to think or how to feel. He was relieved it was Lucinda, not Jane, who was the object of Lance's affection. He was happy for Lucinda, but wondered how her changed status might impact their working relationship. At this point, he just wanted to wrap up the two storylines in *Mind Games* and get her off his back.

He looked at Jane and saw that her eyes were glistening, and again he was somewhat puzzled as to what that could mean. Was Jane disappointed in Lance's choice or happy for the couple? Her behavior told him it was the latter, so he decided to be happy for Lance and Lucinda along with everyone else that evening.

CHAPTER THIRTY-SIX

Mind Games
Minneapolis, Minnesota
Early August

Frisco turned on the siren as they sped across the Hennepin Avenue Bridge, into the heart of a section of Minneapolis known by locals as "Nordeast". As they drove past Nye's Polonaise Room, Jo couldn't help but wish they were racing toward rescuing John, and immediately felt guilty for the thought. Kent Womack was obviously distraught over the disappearance of his wife. And with good reason.

Frisco parked on the street in front of the The Bean Counter. It was located in the row of shops and restaurants facing the Mississippi River a couple of blocks from the Stone Arch Bridge.

When they walked into the coffee shop, Jo's eyes quickly scanned the crowded room, but she did not spot Payne or Womack. She strode up to the barista, a young guy with a nose ring and dirty-blonde dreadlocks. His name tag read, Trent.

As she and Frisco pulled out their identification, Jo said, "We're trying to locate two women." She pulled out the photo of Sandra she had gotten from the pastor and a printout of Marjorie Payne's TV promo shot. "Did you see either of these people in here this morning?"

The barista wiped his hands on a towel and squinted at the pictures. He said, "Sure did. They were here for about twenty minutes or so." He pointed at the picture of Marjorie Payne. "She comes in here a lot. Always orders the Skinny Vanilla Latte."

Frisco said, "Never mind that. Did you see them leave?"

"Yeah, yeah, sure. I always watch her leave, 'cuz she's hot. Makes a great exit."

Jo rolled her eyes and said, "Look, this is important. Which way did they go?"

Trent came around the counter and walked to the open doorway at the rear of the coffee shop. When Jo and Frisco followed, he pointed to a red brick building across the parking lot. On the far side of the building, Jo could still make out the faded letters of the flour mill company that had once been housed in the rehabbed building. "They went into that entrance, over there. I see Skinny Vanilla Latte head that way almost every time she's in here. They left several hours ago."

"Do you know what's in that building?" Jo asked.

"Not sure what's in it now. Some rich dude bought it awhile back, thinking he'd renovate it and make a killing. Put in a music recording studio and some offices. Then I heard he failed epically during the recession. It's been empty over there until Skinny Latte showed up." He shrugged. "I figured she bought it and was picking up where the not-so-rich dude left off."

Trent paused, and then said, "Hey, I really probably should get back to work. People get crabby when they can't get their caffeine fix. You guys need anything else?"

"Nah, we're good. Thanks," Frisco said.

After the barista left, Frisco turned to Jo and said, "They might not still be in there, but you never know. We should probably put on our body armor before we head over, just in case. I'll go grab the gear and meet you out here."

When he returned a few moments later, they donned their Kevlar vests and dashed across the lot. They entered the building and looked around. The lobby was unfinished and scaffolding still lined the double-story walls. As they walked down a long hallway, offices were in various stages of construction; some areas were still delineated by studs, rather than drywall.

Frisco had his hand on his gun holster. "Got any ideas?"

"No. Guess we'd better search each floor, just to be . . ." Jo was interrupted by a crash on the floor above their heads.

Jo pulled out her Glock and they silently climbed the steps to the second floor. Moving quietly toward the area that was the source of the of crash, they swept their weapons back and forth to verify that there was no additional threat to them in the unfinished offices on either side.

They reached a closed door at the end of the hallway. There was a brass sign on the wall to the right that read, PDK MUSIC PRODUCTIONS. Jo pointed to a line of yellow light escaping from the bottom of the door.

Frisco nodded and carefully tried to turn the knob. It was locked.

A muffled scream came from the other side of the door.

Jo's hands felt clammy as she griped her gun. *It's got to be now. We wait any longer and Sandra Womack's going to die.* Jo took a deep breath and silently motioned to Frisco to break down the door. She stood aside, with her weapon raised.

This is the moment where everything can go sideways. She looked at Frisco and nodded. He counted silently to three with his fingers. As Jo yelled, "FBI", the detective drew back his leg and slammed his heavy shoe into the door, shattering it on impact.

Sandra Womack was tied to a chair at the far end of the room. Her frantic eyes located them and she shrieked, "Help me, please!"

Marjorie Payne whirled around as they rushed into the room with their guns drawn, stepping past the damaged door frame.

The TV reporter was almost unrecognizable. Her bright blonde hair that had always been beautifully styled for the cameras now hung in hanks around her face, lifeless and dull. A shiver went down Jo's spine when she saw the madness in Marjorie Payne's eyes.

Jo's eyes flew to the shotgun in Payne's hand and she aimed her Glock at the reporter. She shouted, "Put down the weapon!"

Payne ignored her command and pointed the weapon at Sandra Womack's head. The woman's eyes were wide and Jo noticed some bruising on her jaw. It reminded Jo of the marks on Annie McDonald's chin and neck and she briefly wondered if Payne had tried to force a note into Womack's mouth, just like the other victims.

Jo said in a firm voice, "Ms. Payne. We just want to talk. That's all. But you've got to put down the gun and let Mrs. Womack go. We don't want anyone to get hurt."

For the first time, Marjorie Payne spoke. "Go away! You can't have her. She has to pay for her sins."

"It doesn't have to be like this. We can help you, but you've got to help us in return," Frisco said.

Jo quickly assessed the situation. She briefly glanced around the room and saw dried blood spatter on the back wall. A spent shotgun shell lay next to the baseboard. *This has been her kill zone.*

With the weapon pointed at Sandra Womack, Jo had to calm the situation down quickly. She offered up a brief, silent prayer that she would take the right actions in the next few moments.

Jo spoke in a modulated voice, "Marjorie. Please. You don't want to do this." Never taking her eyes away from the reporter, she slowly crouched down and set her gun on the floor by her feet. She raised her hands in front of her, showing that she posed no threat.

For a fleeting moment, she was relieved when she saw Payne's eyes track Jo's gun to the floor and lowered her shotgun a fraction. Then Jo's mouth went dry when she saw that she was now the target. She fought to keep the panic out of her voice when she said, "Let me help you. I know . . . I know about your father. We know he abandoned you and your family."

Marjorie Payne sneered. "The bastard didn't just abandon us. He had my mother killed, did you know that? Put down, like a dog, just because he decided to go into politics. Wouldn't be proper to have a second family, would it?"

Jo took a wary step forward, her palms still up in the air. "We just found that out. I'm sorry no one figured it out, years ago."

"My brother tried to tell them. He was just a kid, but he saw. They wouldn't listen."

"I would have listened to him," Jo said.

Marjorie continued as if Jo had not spoken, "He heard every filthy thing. My father was on the phone, the day before the shooting. Bobby heard him say our mom 'deserved to die, because she was too stupid to take the cash.' So he used the money to have her killed instead."

She jammed the barrel of the shotgun against Sandra Womack's temple and continued, "The money that this bitch gave him."

Sandra trembled and sobbed out the words, "I didn't know! On my children's lives, I swear I didn't. We thought he was going to pay your mother for your care, so that she wouldn't tell his wife. Please . . ."

"Shut up! We had a family. Did you even think about that?" Payne shifted the gun barrel down to Sandra's cheek and said, "He was our father, until people like you poisoned him against us."

Just then, Jo thought she felt a small shift in Frisco behind her. Fighting to keep Payne's attention focused on her, she said, "You wanted him to pay for all that pain he caused, didn't you?"

"Yes. I met with him for months. He thought I was just another TV reporter, who found him fascinating enough to do a feature on his campaign. I just wanted to get to know my dear old dad," Marjorie said.

She barked out a laugh, "He flirted with me! Can you imagine? The sick son-of-a-bitch actually thought I was coming on to him.

"When I finally invited him here, he thought he was going to get laid. Couldn't get out of his two-thousand dollar suit fast enough. Of course, I stopped him, and told him who I really was."

Frisco, get ready.

"He was horrified. Not that he almost slept with his own daughter, but that another one of his children was threatening his precious career, his wealthy lifestyle. So I shot him in the mouth, the same way my mother was killed."

Jo caught a slight movement out of the corner of her eye. Frisco was slowly moving to the right as she kept Payne's focus away from him.

Jo held out her hands once more, palms up. She said, "Please, let us help you. No one else has to die here. Mrs. Womack didn't mean to hurt your mother. Your father paid for his sins with his life."

Jo was horrified to see that her words that were meant to calm Marjorie Payne had the opposite effect. Her eyes were wild when she screamed, "No! She has to pay, too!"

Frisco yelled, "Put down your weapon. Now, or I will shoot!"

Marjorie Payne turned to Frisco. The reporter reached into her pocket and there was a flash of white as she held two pieces of paper in her hand. She chose one, grabbed Sandra's jaw and shoved the paper into Sandra's mouth. Then she leveled the gun at the head of the pastor's wife.

Jo heard Frisco yell, "Stop!" even as he shot Marjorie Payne in the head.

There was a remarkable stillness after the loud boom of Frisco's gun and the collapse of the reporter's body.

Frisco put his weapon back into the holster at his hip as Jo kicked the gun away from Marjorie Payne's hand. She reached down to check the reporter's pulse.

Jo looked up at Frisco and shook her head. She stood up and rushed over to Sandra Womack, who had coughed out the note into her lap. Jo untied her and helped the woman to stand up.

Frisco called for an ambulance and the ME. While they waited for help to arrive, the three of them stood around Marjorie Payne's body as the blood pooled beneath her spread.

Pulling on a pair of latex gloves, Frisco plucked the note off the floor which had fallen from Sandra Womack's lap. He read it out loud, "If a man is discovered committing adultery, both he and the woman must die. In this way, you will purge Israel of such evil."

Sandra Womack sucked in a sharp breath. "That's from Deuteronomy. It's the opening quote to all our speeches about the sanctity of marriage. We meant the souls of adulterers will shrivel and die, not their human bodies. My God. She took it literally. "

Jo turned to the pastor's wife and said, "You are very lucky your husband mentioned the interview you had with her. He saved your life."

Mrs. Womack's face was ashen, as if the reality of what had almost happened hit her full force.

Jo crouched down next to the body and pulled the remaining piece of paper out of the TV reporter's hand. She said, "It's another one from Deuteronomy. It says: 'No one born of a forbidden union may enter the assembly of the Lord. Even to the tenth generation, none of his descendants may enter the assembly of the Lord.'"

Frisco looked puzzled. "Who do you think that one was for?"

Jo looked at the body of the reporter. "I think she meant it for herself. Even when she stopped being Michelle Bishop and re-invented herself as Marjorie Payne, I'll bet she still felt like there was no place for her with God. She was always going to be a child born of a forbidden union."

CHAPTER THIRTY-SEVEN

Turners Bend
Late March

ON THE NIGHT OF THE PREMIERE and gala, no suspicious women were sighted, no incidents had occurred, other than a couple of DUI tickets and a lost tiara. Authorities were stymied. Was the killer in town during the premiere? How could they have missed her? Was the last message possibly from a copycat killer? Or a prank?

The following week, Turners Bend went into hibernation. It was a period of decompression. The neighboring police, State Patrol and extra FBI agents were gone. The media crews that had filled the town and snarled the traffic, departed as quickly as they had appeared. Lucinda and Dr. and Maribelle Collingsworth left for home, Lucinda reluctantly but with stars in her eyes.

As Chip drove down Main Street, he was shocked at how desolate the town looked, sort of post-apocalyptic with heaping trashcans lined up along the curb. There were a few cars outside the Bend and the Bun, but no traffic moving on Main Street. The street's only stoplight was flashing yellow. He saw Agent Klein and another agent loading the FBI's van outside of Harriet's House of Hair, so he stopped in to see Masterson in her temporary office. She was packing a box.

"Mind if I interrupt? Looks like you are moving."

"Yes, I'm moving our office to Sioux City. Did you see the newspaper this morning?"

"No, I was going to pick one up from the newspaper box outside of the Bun. Care to join me for a cup of coffee and fill me in on the details?"

Chip was surprised she agreed to join him. It seemed a little out of character for her. They walked to the Bun, and when he spied the headlines through the glass front of the paper box, his curiosity was definitely aroused. It read: FBI CONFIRMS IOWA SERIAL KILLER BEING INVESTIGATED. The sub-headline read: IDENTITY OF PERSON OF INTEREST NOT REVEALED.

The only customer in the café was Chief Fredrickson, who was reading the newspaper.

"You might as well join us, Chief," said Masterson. "I'll fill you both in on what the press doesn't know yet, but probably will by to-morrow."

Bernice brought them coffee and cinnamon rolls. "On the house today, we've got lots of rolls and not enough customers." She returned to the counter and started filling ketchup bottles.

"We found two more bodies just where we expected based on the map, one in Ames in a deserted store and one in Council Bluffs in an old warehouse. We were able to ID the bodies and the next of kin are being contacted before we release their names. The only place left on the map is the Sioux City area. The remaining missing woman is the one that has been missing the shortest period of time. As you recall, the fabric samples were mailed from Sioux City. I'm moving my office there today. We're moving in on Elizabeth Brown. I have no concrete evidence that she is our killer, but I don't have any other suspects either. The Sioux City police got an anonymous tip. I think they will find her soon. If we can locate the last victim, I think we can find the evidence we need to tie her to the killings."

"I sure hope so," said the chief. "That message about looking for new recruits has still got me worried."

"We're pretty sure she didn't show up at the premiere last week. My people would have spotted her, if she had. I think Turners Bend can rest easy now. You're off the hook," said Masterson, pausing to wipe frosting off her fingers. "God, I'll sure miss these cinnamon rolls."

"It's still hard for me to think of a female as a serial killer, even though I wrote one into my next novel. It was the twist I needed. Now I just have my abducted doctor to rescue."

"I can't help you with your fictional abduction, but I know what you mean about a female serial killer. It doesn't fit the usual profile. Nevertheless, I'm 99% sure we have identified the right killer. By the way, I want to commend both of you. Your insights have been spot-on in this case. I underrated you both and I apologize. In fact, Chief, I've sent a commendation to the Iowa Bureau of Investigation."

The chief blushed and began to sputter. "Thanks, but it was just all in a day's work."

"And, Chip, I hope you understand that I have to be very careful about involving private citizens in investigations. I shared the info with you today, because I've grown to trust you and know you'll keep all this confidential until the case is resolved. For a hack crime writer, you're not too bad." The agent did something Chip rarely heard her do . . . she laughed.

"The van should be loaded by now. We're off to Sioux City to catch a serial killer. Wish me luck." Agent Masterson stood and shook their hands before leaving. Her shake was so firm it made Chip wince a bit.

He and the chief sat silently for a few minutes processing the new developments and taking in the agent's compliments.

"I don't know about you, Chief, but I feel kind of cheated. Wish we could be there to see this through to the end. I'd like to see how it all goes down. I'd like to see Masterson busting down doors and drawing her gun on the killer."

"I know what you mean. I guess we'll just have to be satisfied with the part we played, and it's nice to get back to our normal petty crimes and drunken brawls. It sure was quite the wild ride for a while, wasn't it?"

The café's door chime jangled and Lance strolled in, causing Bernice to perk up, flounce her hair and give him her version of a Hollywood starlet smile.

"I've never seen this place so dead," he said to the two men. "Mind if I join you?"

"I got police business to do, but you can keep Chip company. Bye boys. Thanks for the roll, Bernice." Chief Fredrickson departed and Lance took his chair.

"You're looking a little glum, buddy," said Chip. "Things going awry in Loveland?"

"It's the wedding. I thought it might be nice to get married here, since this is where we met. Lucinda is thinking destination wedding, she's considering everywhere from Aruba to some castle in Heidelberg. And that's not all. This coming weekend we are going to Chicago, so she can meet my parents. For some reason, my mother is under the assumption that we are going to be married in Evanston. She's already booked Northminster Presbyterian Church. I haven't dared to tell her

Lucinda is Catholic. And I thought this was going to be fun. I was sure mistaken."

Chip couldn't decide if he should be gleeful or sympathetic. He opted for the later. "Take it from a guy who's had three weddings. Keep a low profile and stay out of the planning. I do have to say, though, that I'm glad you tamed my agent and that she's too busy with wedding plans to ride me about my writing."

"Tamed her?" Lance shook his head.

"Yes, before you came on the scene, she was a hell cat. Now she's a pussy cat."

"Oh, I don't know, Chip. I think the hell cat may be returning. I'd sure hate to cross her on this wedding stuff. I had my head chewed off this morning over the phone."

"Better you than me, better you than me." Chip hesitated, and then continued. "To be honest, Lance, for a while I thought you were interested in Jane Swanson."

"I was, but Jane made it clear to me she wasn't interested. I get the impression that she has someone else in mind, and that someone is you."

"I thought so at one time. Even asked her to marry me. But I got shot down."

"Don't give up, pal. My guess is that she will come around."

Lance patted him on the shoulder, stood and said, "Got to go and put in a call to my mother. Wish me luck."

Chip's first impulse was to march over to the veterinary clinic, take Jane into his arms and sweep her away for a destination wedding. He thought better of it; best to go slow and let things percolate. Instead, he went home to write. Even with Lucinda off his back for the meantime, he still had to make a living, and Dr. Goodman was still being held by his captor.

CHAPTER THIRTY-EIGHT

Mind Games
Northeast Minnesota, Minneapolis & Brooklyn Center, Minnesota
Early August

IT WAS THE BUMPING BENEATH HIM that woke up Dr. John Goodman. His head snapped backwards and hit the wall behind him. When he tried to reach up to rub his aching head, he realized that his hands were restrained once again. The grim reminder that he had been abducted came rushing back to him like a tide. Slowly he opened his eyes. After they adjusted to the dim light, he saw he was alone and sitting upright. His hands and feet were strapped down to a seat that ran along the length of the back of a windowless van. He could feel the hum of the engine vibrating through the vehicle.

Not again! The last time he had been in the back of a van like this, the bad guys had been taking him to operate on Jo, trying to make her into one of their assassins. This time, he had no idea of where he was being taken, but it would have to be Jo's turn to rescue him. John felt a trickle of sweat run down his back.

He looked around and saw canvas bags of varying sizes and shapes scattered on the floor by his feet. Across from John was another long seat. He leaned as far forward as the restraints would allow and tilted his head to get a better view of a long, skinny wooden object underneath. He could swear that it looked like a canoe paddle. *What the hell . . . what kind of kidnapper carries a canoe paddle in the back of his van?*

John craned his neck, but he couldn't see out the front window to get an idea of where they were going. A panel divided the front cab from the cargo area in the back, with a small window between. Through the opening, he could see it had grown darker outside since he was last conscious. He also saw the back of a head in the front seat. As far as he could tell, there was no one in the passenger seat. John yelled out, "Hey! Where are you taking me?" He immediately regretted speaking so loudly when his head throbbed in protest.

The man in the front seat turned around. John could see his profile and recognized that his captor was driving. The man said, "Welcome back to the living, Dr. Goodman. You've been out for quite awhile. And let me tell you, I had a heck of a time getting you into that seat. You were nothing but dead weight."

He faced forward, focused once again on the road in front of them. John said, "You didn't answer my question. Where are we going?"

"Oh, I think you'll be pleasantly surprised. It's really quite beautiful." He chuckled and then said, "Of course, you may have a different opinion, since it will be the last place you will ever see." An involuntary shudder flowed through John.

The abductor continued, "We should be there in about another two hours, give or take."

John decided to keep the guy talking, hoping to get some vital piece of information that would help.

He tried another angle. "Well, maybe since we have so much time, you can explain to me how you know Agent Schwann."

John could hear the blast of a car horn somewhere off to the right and his captor was temporarily distracted. When the kidnapper finally spoke, he said, "People are always in such a hurry these days. Don't you think?"

The man turned his head again toward John and said, "Take you, for instance. Always in a hurry to have answers." He faced forward again and John thought he would not hear anymore from him.

A few moments later, however, he was rewarded with a response. "At first, I simply came to eliminate you. You see, you were directly responsible for the death of a very great man."

John's fuzzy brain sifted through his past case files, trying to recall this man's face in a sea of grief-wracked family members. "You said that I caused a death. Was he a patient of mine?"

The man chuckled, but it contained no mirth. "No, not a patient. He was part of a case that you were working on. You and the FBI."

John's head spun. He had lent his expertise to the Bureau on several cases over the years. However, he still couldn't place the man's face. "I don't understand. Maybe it's the whack on the head or the drugs you've been giving me . . ." John stopped abruptly and horror dawned on him. "You are talking about the NeuroDynamics case, aren't you? It's the only one I worked on with Jo. Is that what this is all about? It has to be. That's why you were bugging Jo's house, why you took me from there . . ."

"Now you're finally catching on."

"But you weren't a part of that case. All those people . . . they are all dead or in prison."

"Ah, but you are mistaken. As you can see, I'm a living testament to the brilliance of Dr. Candleworth."

John's eyes widened when the answer hit him. "You're Dennis Farley. The last of the test victims." He felt sick to his stomach. John realized he was in the hands of a man without a conscience. A man who had been molded to be the perfect assassin. *But why hasn't he killed Jo or me yet?*

Dennis Farley pulled to the side of the road and slammed on his brakes, coming to a halt. He turned in his seat once again, this time releasing the seatbelt. He poked his head through the window and spat out his next words. "Victim . . . you dare call me a victim? I am Dr. Candleworth's greatest triumph."

John tried to calm his galloping heart. He realized antagonizing this man would surely result in his death. *I need to stay alive. For as long as I can.* "I stand corrected. I read all of Candleworth's research. His strides in microchip and nanochip neurological usage were nothing short of groundbreaking."

Dennis rubbed his head and muttered, "Damn headaches." He put the van into drive. John heard the gravel spin beneath the tires as he pulled back out onto the road. Finally Farley responded, "I know when someone's blowing smoke up my ass, Dr. Goodman, although generally it's not so eloquently done. In this case, however, you are quite right."

John let out a silent puff of air. He was relieved Farley sounded much more reasonable again. The miles rolled beneath them as John's mind wandered from question to question. He wondered if Farley had already contacted Jo to set up a meeting place. *Why are we going so far away? Maybe he's headed somewhere remote; somewhere it would be easy to spot if Jo has back-up.*

John always circled back to the same question. *Why haven't we been killed already, if Farley only wants revenge? And, more importantly, what is he saving us for?*

* * *

THE SKY WAS SMUDGED GRAY and purple by the time Jo and Frisco walked out to his car in front of the coffee shop. Jo rubbed her burning, tired eyes. It seemed a lifetime ago they had first parked here. Before they had discovered so many of the answers that had eluded them until this point.

They climbed into the car and Frisco twisted in his seat to face Jo. "So, all those disguises we found: the hard hat, the construction overalls, and the cleaning crew equipment. That's what she used to get into secured areas without anyone noticing?"

"I presume so. We'll know for sure once the BCA techs compare the blood samples on the bins to the state rep. and the columnist."

Jo fastened her seat belt. "Pretty clever, really. Forensics proves she killed both victims here, in this old music studio. Another smart move. With all the sound insulation in that place, no one would have heard the gunshots."

Frisco rubbed his chin and Jo could hear the rasp of the stubble. "So, I guess she must've loaded the bodies in one of the bins and then took the service elevator down into the parking garage. Putting them into the van we found would have been easy with a ramp."

Jo nodded and said, "With all the remodeling going on at the State Capital building, who would notice the comings and goings of yet another construction worker hauling a cart full of equipment around? And as we know from my undercover work at NeuroDynamics' headquarters last winter, no one thinks twice about a cleaning person pushing around a garbage can. I'm guessing it will be Anne McDonald's blood in that one."

The detective was silent for a moment and then he said, "So, why do you think she bothered moving them at all?"

Jo shrugged. "Maybe she thought it was important to put them in the institutions that showcased their beliefs."

Frisco tugged on his own seatbelt and then started up the car. As they drove through the city streets, Jo thought again about John and wondered if he was still alive. She pulled out her cell phone, checking for missed messages. *Why hasn't the bastard who kidnapped him been in contact yet?*

The detective looked over at the phone in Jo's hand and said, "No word yet, huh?"

Jo stared out the windshield at the sky that had now turned nearly pitch black. "None."

Frisco cleared his throat and said, "You know, you should stay at our house tonight. We've got an extra bedroom that my in-laws use when they are in town."

Jo turned to Frisco and said, "That's very kind of you, Frisco. But I need to be home, in my own house. He's got to be able to contact me. That's the game."

The detective let out a puff of air. "I have to say, I'm not crazy about you being in that house alone. Not with a kidnapper-slash-stalker with his sights set on you." He paused, and then said, "But I guess you're right. Doesn't mean I like it."

Jo's lips curled upward. "I appreciate that, Frisco." She straightened out the wry smile a moment later. "Why hasn't he contacted me yet?"

Jo could see the frown between his brows in the glow of the dashboard lights. "Beats the hell out of me. But one thing we know about this guy is that he's a methodical son-of-a-bitch. Putting those cameras in place, the tracker on your car and taking John – all that took a lot of prep time. He's putting some crazy-assed scheme into motion."

* * *

JO ENTERED HER CUBICLE at the FBI headquarters and flicked on her desk lamp. She knew her night was far from over. Besides filling out the mountains of paperwork that came with wrapping up the Freemont/McDonald cases, she had to testify in court tomorrow for the wrongful death civil case brought against the Bureau by Charles Candleworth's widow.

She walked over to the break room and grabbed a bottle of juice from the refrigerator. She knew she should eat something, but the thought of eating anything made her throat close up.

Settling into her desk chair, Jo fired up her laptop. She retrieved the file she needed to fill out about Marjorie Payne's death, but all she could do was stare at the blank form. When she read the question of cause of death, the only phrase that came to mind was: "screwed-up family." She shook her head at her cynicism.

With a sigh, she set aside her laptop and reached for the files from the NeuroDynamics case. She needed to review them for court tomorrow, to make sure all the details were fresh in her memory.

The file on the bottom slipped from her hands. "I can't even hang onto a damned case file."

She crouched over to gather up all the loose papers that had slipped out. A photograph had slid across the carpet and when she flipped it over, she took a minute to study it. Something about the man in the photo looked very familiar, but she couldn't place him. She turned the photo over and read the label: *Dennis Farley, test victim. Current whereabouts unknown.*

As Jo stared at the photo again, she recalled all the hours they had put into finding this man. John was especially anxious to locate him, wanting to try to reverse the damage from the microchip and nanochips that had been implanted into him. When they finally closed the case, they had assumed he had gone off somewhere and died. That certainly had happened with all the other test cases.

But Jo couldn't shake off the feeling that she had seen these eyes more recently. She wracked her brain, searching through all the faces she had encountered over the last month.

Then it hit her. "Oh, my God . . . I've been so friggin' blind!" She stood up and grabbed her cell. She cursed when she saw her phone was dead. She had used it so much in the last twenty four hours that it had run out of battery power.

"Shit! He could have been trying to reach me, all this time." She plugged in her phone and saw that she had several voice mails, all from Agent Daniels' number. She swallowed her disappointment that none were from the kidnapper, but she entered her password and listened to the messages.

All the messages said the same thing, "Call me, I have some updates for you." But each message sounded more and more urgent. The last message included an additional comment, "Jo, where the hell are you?"

Jo quickly called Daniels. He answered on the first ring. Before Jo could say a word, he launched into his speech. "Where have you been? We've got all these new developments and I can't reach you when I need to. Where are you now?"

Jo rubbed her head. "I'm still at the office. My phone ran out of juice and I didn't realize it until just now."

"Don't go near your house."

"Whoa. Back up. Tell me what's going on . . . why shouldn't I go to my house?"

"We received a call from one of your neighbors tonight. I had left my calling card, just in case anyone saw Stephen Paulson return to his house. Well, she called and said that she hadn't seen Paulson per se, but his dog was barking like mad and howling. She called me thinking that meant he had returned," Daniels said.

Jo's heart began to pound. She was about to tell Daniels about the photo she had discovered when he continued. "We checked the house for any sign of Paulson, with no luck. So we went out back where the dog was fenced in. That damn dog was yowling and digging frantically. And Jo, he dug up a hand. A human hand."

Jo thought her heart would seize up. "Not . . . tell me it wasn't John's hand that the dog found?"

"No. Oh, sorry. Lord, no. The hand belongs to your elderly neighbor who lived in the house before Paulson. Further excavations revealed she had been buried in the garden with her son. Based on decomposition, the ME is thinking they've been there for quite some time."

"So you think Paulson killed the poor old woman and her son, just to get into the house?"

"Yes. But why *that* house?"

Jo's voice sounded dead to her when she replied. "Because Stephen Paulson is actually Dennis Farley and he is stalking me."

"Who is Dennis Farley?"

"He was the last missing victim of the NeuroDynamics mess." She filled him in on the photograph and the details of the case.

When she had finished, she heard Daniels' sharp intake of breath. "And he's tying up loose ends. Like you and John?"

"I'm afraid so."

"I'll track down any other properties that might be leased or owned in either name. We need to find the warehouse where John was filmed."

"Even if you find the warehouse, I think it's going to be empty. He's taking awhile to contact me for a reason. I think they are on the move," Jo said.

CHAPTER THIRTY-NINE

Turners Bend
Early April

CHIP SAT IN HIS KITCHEN, staring at his screen saver, unable to think of what to write next. Some call it "writer's block," but Chip knew it for what it was—lack of discipline, avoidance behavior, laziness. He just didn't feel like writing. Callie was no help. She jumped onto his lap and then walked across the keyboard, spelling out her own cryptic message.

"Okay, okay. I'll feed you."

He went into the kitchen and opened a can of tuna. Callie wound herself around his legs, weaving in and out. Chip had started out feeding her dry cat food. After a week, the cat had refused to eat it. He moved up to canned food, progressing from generic to a gourmet brand, until Callie had conditioned him to her preferred meals: tuna, cooked chicken and cheese and an occasional lick from a cereal or ice cream bowl. He was whipped and by a cat no less.

Out the kitchen window he saw a flashing red light and then the police cruiser driving up his road. Deputy Anderson was at the wheel and Fredrickson was riding shotgun. The chief stepped out of the car, rolled his eyes and shook his head as he approached Chip's back door. Chip opened the door to admit Turners Bend's finest and only police officers.

"Why the flashing lights? Is there an emergency?" asked Chip.

"Nah, Jim just likes to play with the lights and sirens."

"I haven't used them in a week," said Jim. "I think they should be tested every once in a while to make sure they're in good working order."

"To what do I owe this pleasure?" said Chip.

"You watched the news this morning?"

"No, I've been working, or trying to. What's up?"

The two policemen took the chairs Chip offered. The minute Jim sat down, Callie jumped in his lap, startling him. Jim pushed her down. Callie had a knack for knowing who didn't like cats, and she always chose to pester them.

"CNN announced this morning that the FBI detained a person of interest named Elizabeth Brown aka Karen Buttler in the Iowa serial killer case, and they are holding her for identity theft charges for now. I called Masterson in Sioux City to see what in the hell was going on," said the Chief.

"Karen Buttler? Was she using an assumed name?"

"She stole the identity of a deceased woman, got a fake Social Security card, driver's license, the whole bit. Here's the weird part. Brown is psycho, she really thinks she is Karen Buttler, denies any knowledge of Brown or her past life. They're scheduling her for a psych evaluation.

"They searched her house and car . . . nothing . . . no evidence to link her to the killings. Masterson is frustrated as hell."

"Have they found the fifth woman?"

"Negative," chimed in Jim.

"Is the suspect a milk truck driver?"

"No, she's a customer service rep in a call center, but that doesn't mean she couldn't have gotten a hold of some delivery forms," said Fredrickson.

"Does Masterson think we have been chasing the wrong killer this whole time? Who else could it be?" Chip asked.

"No, she's still convinced it's her. Said she is going to comb every square inch within ten miles of Sioux City. If she can find the body, she thinks she can link it to Brown. All she needs is a shred of evidence." The chief stood.

"Pretty quiet in Turners Bend today, so Jim and I thought we'd come out here and fill you in. Masterson said if we have any 'light bulb moments' to pass them along to her."

Chip saw them off and watched the cruiser barreling down his road, lights flashing and sirens blaring. He tried to return to his crime story, but his mind kept straying to the serial killer. Who else could it be? Maybe someone else on the team or maybe the dead women were also connected in some other way. Did they all date the same guy at some time? He wished he could talk through this enigma with Jane, but he couldn't. He was privy to more than he probably should be, as it was. He had to keep his mouth shut.

Jane was never far from his mind. Since the premiere she had been chummier with him, but chummy was not what he wanted. He decided to move things along a little. He called her.

"Hi, what's new in the world of Turners Bend's best looking vet?"

She laughed. "Not hard to be the best looking vet, when you're the only one in town, but to answer your questions, I'm fine. How about you? How's Turners Bend's best looking crime writer?"

Now it was his turn to laugh. "To tell you the truth, he's bored and needs a break from writing. The Bijou is showing *Turner and Hooch* tonight. It's an oldie but goodie. Would you care to join me?"

"I think I'd like that very much. I'll meet you at the Bijou for the 7:00 p.m. show. How's that?"

"Just what the doctor ordered."

His movie choice would be perfect. Turner is a police detective who falls for a vet. Hooch is the dog that changes his life. The only thing that could make it better would be if Turner were a crime writer.

His heart stayed with Jane, but his head returned to the final couple chapters of *Mind Game*.

CHAPTER FORTY

Mind Games
Brooklyn Center, Minnesota, & Northeast Counties of Minnesota
Early August

Agent Jo Schwann cut off the phone call to Agent Daniels and sat back. The only sound she could hear in her cubicle at the FBI headquarters was the whirring of the air conditioner kicking on. She swung her office chair around to face the window, and stared out into the night sky for a few minutes. With the heavy cloud cover, she could just barely make out the lights in nearby office buildings. *I brought all this violence into my quiet neighborhood, just by living there.* Logically, she knew it wasn't her fault, but she couldn't help seeing the face of the sweet elderly woman who had once lived two doors down from her.

She shook her head and turned the chair back around to dig into the NeuroDynamics file once again. This time she carefully sifted through the information about the Bureau's attempts to find Dennis Farley. The last time he had been in contact with any family member was the week before she had been called into the NeuroDynamics case.

Jo was reading through the notes for the third time when her cell phone buzzed atop her desk. She had to dig through some of the papers scattered across the surface before she located it. "Agent Schwann."

A deep voice said, "Special Agent Jo Schwann. Did you think I forgot about you? Not a chance. Just getting things ready for our next adventure together. Lots to do, lots to do."

Jo sat up straight in her chair and studied the face of Dennis Farley that stared up at her from the dated photo on her desk. He was heavier in the picture, and his hair had been grayer, but now that she knew who she was dealing with, she wondered how she could have ever missed the connection to her new "neighbor" before.

Holding the photo in her hand, she said, "Mr. Farley. Welcome back from the dead."

She heard a raspy chuckle on the other end of the line. "Gorgeous and a sense of humor. How did I ever get this lucky to fall in love with the perfect woman?"

Jo gritted her teeth and said, "Fall in love? My God, you really are a piece of work. This is how you show your love? By killing my elderly neighbor

200

and her son, just to move closer to me . . . by kidnapping my boyfriend?"

All humor disappeared from Dennis Farley's voice when he responded. "You think that this damned Boy Scout, this false hero, is your boyfriend? Well, that's why I took him. To show you the error in your thinking."

"What do you want from me? You obviously want something more than to kill us. You've had ample opportunity."

Farley spoke deliberately, as if explaining something to a slow, stubborn child. "I told you, you need to see that you are wrong about Dr. Goodman. And you are wrong about me."

"I seriously doubt that. Why don't we cut through the crap and you tell me where I can meet you, so we can end this."

"Fair enough. I have left a map for you in your house. It's been there since I put in the cameras."

That stopped Jo short. She bit her lower lip as she thought. *The answer to John's location had been in her house all this time? How the hell did we miss it?* The techies had been all through her house, from top to bottom. But then, the answer came to her. *We weren't looking for a map. We were looking for signs of John.*

Jo spoke, "All right, I'll bite. Where did you cleverly hide this map?"

He let out another laugh. "Oh, my love. I didn't have to hide the map at all. It's been on your wall in your home office all this time. It's the map of the Boundary Waters Canoe Area. The minute I saw the map on your wall, I knew we shared an affinity for the wilderness. And I knew that's where we had to meet."

Jo's mind wandered to the map at home. She had had it framed after she returned from a survivalist training program in the BWCA while on summer break from the University of Minnesota. It had been a life-altering experience, a turning point. It's where she finally made peace with her father's suicide and moved forward with her life. And now this bastard had turned it into something twisted.

She thought about the vast size of the area which bordered Canada. It would be the perfect place to dump a body . . . or two. And they would never, ever be found.

Jo swallowed and said, "The Boundary Waters covers over a million acres. How will I find you?"

"I marked the map on your wall. You will note it's slightly different from the trip you recorded on the chart from a previous trip. I would hate to make things too easy for you."

Jo stood up and began packing up the files into her briefcase. She wedged the phone between her shoulder and chin and said, "I am heading home now to get the map." She looked at the clock on her desktop. "It'll be several hours before I can get to where you are."

"Not a problem. I am a patient man. In the meantime, the good doctor and I will set up camp. The map I left you will put you in the general area only. Once you reach the spot indicated, you will receive the next set of instructions. Oh, and leave your cell phone at the office. I don't want it to be used to trace your whereabouts."

Jo shoved the file into her bag. "Put John on the phone. I am not going anywhere until you prove he is still alive."

"I had a feeling you would say that. Here he is."

Jo could hear some rustling in the background and then John's voice came on the other end of the line. His voice sounded brittle when he said, "Jo. Don't come . . . there's nowhere for you to get away from him here. Don't play his game."

Jo clutched the phone tight to her ear and closed her eyes. "You have to trust me . . ."

Jo was interrupted by Dennis Farley's voice. "That's enough. You have your proof. But I want you to listen very carefully. The cell phone number I am calling from is untraceable. You are familiar enough with this area to know that I can disappear with Dr. Goodman in a blink if I have any suspicions that you have brought assistance or anyone is tracking us. This is a private affair. Do I make myself clear?"

"Perfectly. I will be alone."

"We anxiously await your visit. I will be in touch."

Jo was about to ask how he would reach her, when she realized she was listening to a dial tone.

* * *

Jo approached Tofte, Minnesota, a small resort town on Lake Superior and pulled off to the side of the road. She clicked on the interior light and double-checked the map she had retrieved from her house. Before re-entering traffic, she waited for the pre-arranged signal from Agent Daniels. He had followed several car lengths behind in a non-descript sedan and had pulled into the restaurant parking lot just past where she sat idling.

When he flashed his lights at her, she turned left onto the road leading to Sawbill Lake, the destination point on her map. At this point, Jo knew Daniels would hang back several miles, since he would be easy to spot on such a narrow, gravel road.

Daniels had followed her every move via the tracker on her Bureau-issued vehicle. Before she had left her office, she called Agent Daniels and filled him in on the phone call from Farley. He wasn't happy when she insisted that if they came too close, they would put John in greater jeopardy. However, he was somewhat mollified by the use of her tracker.

Jo pulled up next to a rusted-out blue Chevy Tahoe in the gravel parking lot near the outfitters at the edge of the lake. She retrieved the cell phone Farley had left for her. She had found it earlier, taped to the back of the framed map. Quickly murmuring thanks to the recent addition of cell phone towers in the BWCA, she flipped to the number that had been programmed into the phone.

Farley answered after the first ring. "Agent Schwann. I assume you are now at Sawbill?"

"Yes. Where do I enter the lake?"

"Ah, not so fast. You still have more driving to do. Do you see the blue truck parked in the lot?"

With a sinking feeling, Jo looked out her passenger-side door and said, "Yeah . . ."

"That will be your mode of transportation for the remainder of the trip."

Jo's stomach lurched. *If I switch vehicles, there will be no way for Daniels to track me.* Her mind spun out a dozen alternatives, and she came up empty. "Why are you doing this?"

"You and I both know that FBI vehicles can be tracked. That piece-of-crap truck has no such device. It does, however, have a special feature that wasn't standard when it rolled off the assembly line. I installed a wireless camera, so I will know if you attempt to contact your co-workers in any way."

Jo muttered an oath under her breath. "So what's my next step?'

"I left the keys in the truck, under the floor mat. There is a portable GPS system on the dash, with the coordinates of the next stop programmed in. But just in case you get creative in keeping friends in the loop, I've set up a back-up plan. The minute you activate the navigation system, you also activate the camera, so I will be able to see everything you do from that point on. If you attempt to leave a note with the coordinates, I will know it and Dr. Goodman is dead."

Jo's mouth went dry. She was entirely on her own from now on. The best she could do is to leave a message in her SUV with the license plates of the replacement vehicle so that Daniels could put out an APB on her. But in the time it would take them to track down the truck, she would be deep into the north woods.

* * *

THE SKY WAS SHOWING the first streaks of daylight by the time she reached the picturesque town of Grand Marais near the northern tip of Minnesota. She turned west as the navigation system directed her a few minutes later. Jo traveled another sixty miles, bumping along the rustic, narrow road until she reached the entrance to Pine Lake.

When she ran out of road, even though the GPS urged her forward, she pulled the truck over and called Farley. Jo could hear the exhaustion in her voice when she said, "I can't find a parking lot. Where am I going?"

"We're by-passing the permits that are required to access the Boundary Waters. We don't want any nosey park ranger to know we're here, so you will have to hike the rest of the way in. Remove the GPS system from the truck and start walking."

Jo hung up and retrieved her backpack of gear from the passenger seat. The pack felt heavier than when she had placed it there hours before. She was clearly running out of steam.

Sighing, she hoisted the pack onto her back and climbed out of the truck. Stiff and sore from the long night of driving, she stretched and then retrieved some note paper and a pencil from her bag. Jo scribbled a note with the next set of coordinates from the Garmin navigation system and wedged it under the front tire of the truck.

Jo stowed the phone away and began walking. Checking the GPS system frequently, she was rewarded a half-hour later when she came upon a yellow canoe that was half-hidden in the brush. It was made of Kevlar, making it lightweight enough to portage over land. Jo saw there was a large green canvas bag in the bottom of the boat. Looking closer, she saw it was a Duluth Pack, the ubiquitous bag used by the majority of outdoorsman in the Boundary Waters. She bent over to retrieve the pack and unbuckled the canvas straps. Inside, she found a canteen, a water purifier and a few energy bars. She muttered, "How fucking thoughtful of him." She dug in a little farther and pulled out another handheld GPS device.

Stowing her own bag next to the Duluth Pack, she copied down the final coordinates on a piece of note paper and tacked it down with a rock, making sure that it could be seen from a distance. She climbed into the canoe and used an oar to push off from the shoreline. She paddled, following the directions on the new system.

She had been out for a few minutes when she heard a loon's lonely cry in the distance. The sky had lightened up quite a bit since she had first hiked into the brush and she could now see the pristine beauty of the wilderness around her. Her paddle strokes into the calm water were smooth and sure. It felt as if she had last been here two months ago instead of ten years.

Jo turned her head at a crashing sound on the shore to her right. She saw a large moose gamboling about, long legs awkward in the brush. It wasn't long before Jo realized she had relaxed a bit and was feeling refreshed. *I'm ready to take this bastard down,* she thought.

When she reached the far shore of the lake, she shoved her bag into the larger Duluth Pack and hoisted it onto her back. Pulling the boat up onto shore, she leaned over, grabbed the canoe by the yoke with both hands and heaved, until it was at waist level.

She took a deep breath, and then lifted the boat the rest of the way up, until the yoke straddled her shoulders. Jo adjusted her hands so that she could balance the canoe and began walking in the direction of the next lake. She was amazed she could still portage a canoe. Muscle memory had taken over.

Jo could smell the piney scent of the woods as she trekked along the narrow path that led to the next lake. She barely noticed the undergrowth that occasionally tugged at her pant legs, or the branch that scratched her arm.

She continued on this way for the better part of the morning, alternately paddling and portaging, frequently checking the directions. Every now and then, she pulled out the cell phone to check for a signal. Each time, she was disappointed to see "No Service." *Guess they haven't installed cell towers everywhere in the Boundary Waters yet. But of course, he knew that when he gave me the phone.*

Jo saw no sign of another human being, no motors, no voices. Nothing but the sounds of nature. It was as if she was the last person left on earth. What should have felt lonely, felt peaceful instead.

When at last she reached the final lake, her arms and legs began to shake from the strain and she rested a moment in the seat of the canoe. She closed her eyes and took a deep, cleansing breath.

And smelled smoke.

Her eyes snapped open and she began paddling. She saw the wisp of smoke in the distance and her back muscles strained as she increased the rhythm of her strokes.

CHAPTER FORTY-ONE

Turners Bend
Early April

CHIP WAS LOOKING IN HIS CLOSET, trying to decide what to wear to his movie date with Jane and selected a pair of designer jeans, now well-worn and outdated, and a blue sweater. His phone buzzed.

"Chip, I can't meet you at the Bijou. I don't know where Ingrid is."

Chip could hear the panic in Jane's voice. He had seen her in a number of crises and marveled at her cool, calm command of emergency situations, but he sensed none of that now. She seemed on the point of hysteria.

"What do you mean? You don't know where she is?"

"She always comes to the clinic after practice, and we go home together. When she didn't come today, I called around. Her friends say she left practice as usual. No one has seen her since. I've been trying her cell phone with no luck."

"Call Fredrickson, then hold tight. I'll be at your office as soon as I can."

"Hurry, Chip, something is terribly wrong."

Chip hesitated for a moment. "Jane . . ."

"Yes."

"What was she wearing?"

"I suppose she was in her Prairie Dogs warm-up suit. That's usually what she has on after practice. Why?"

He hesitated for a second. "Nothing. I'm out the door."

Chip grabbed a jacket and ran to his rental car. Gravel went flying as he tore down his road onto the highway. He could feel his heart pumping in his chest and his mind was racing. He replayed his earlier conversation with the chief and Jim. *Could Masterson be wrong about Brown being the serial killer? Was the real killer still out there? Or, could there be a copycat killer?*

He tried taking deep breaths to clear his mind. Ingrid could show up any minute. He wanted to convince himself she was probably just fine, but something deep in his gut told him she was in grave danger.

He lost his concentration and veered into a ditch alongside the road. He revved his engine and blasted out, back into the lane.

As he neared Jane's clinic, he saw the police cruiser and Iver's snow plow truck outside. He parked, jumped out and threw open the clinic door. Jane was standing in the middle of the waiting room sobbing in Mabel's arms. Iver was pacing around the room. He saw the chief on the phone in the treatment room, just out of earshot. Chip went to the treatment room and picked up on Fredrickson's phone conversation.

"Damn, we never identified and searched the vacant buildings around Turners Bend. Didn't think there was a need to since we had already found one body here," the chief was saying. Then he paused to listen, mouthing the name 'Masterson' to Chip.

"Right, right. Send as many people as you can. But in the meantime we don't have a second to lose. I'm going to call our firemen and first responders and as many others as I can quickly get ahold of, and we'll start the search. Yes, yes."

The Chief hung up the phone and blew out his breath. "Masterson is sending FBI agents and a SWAT team from the Des Moines office and police officers from neighboring towns. She's on her way from Sioux City. The FBI has had a detail on Brown, and we know she's there, so this is someone else. The first few hours after an abduction, if that's what this is, are critical. We can't send out an Amber Alert because we don't know for sure she's been abducted, and we don't have any perp or vehicle info, so we've got to rally as many people as we can and get out there. Let's move it."

They went back to the waiting room. Jane had composed herself momentarily, but fell into Chip's arms and began to cry softly. He could feel her trembling.

The chief took charge. "Jane, we're going to find her, I promise. You and Mabel stay here, she may show up. Check with all your relatives and Ingrid's friends. If you find out anything, phone Sharon at the station. Chip and Iver, go in Iver's truck. Iver, you know where there are vacant buildings on the outskirts of town, start checking by going west. Jim and I will head east. If you see anything suspicious, radio me with that old CB radio you have. Don't do anything foolhardy. I'll get firemen to start searching vacant houses and storefronts in town."

Chip took Jane's face in his hands, using his thumbs to wipe away tears. Her eyes were swollen and full of fear. He kissed her, held her close for a second and whispered in her ear, "I love you." Then he ran out to Iver's truck and jumped into the cab. They headed west on Main Street and then out to the highway heading away from Turners Bend.

It was dusk and light was quickly fading. Rural mailboxes and utility poles cast eerie shadows across the crusty snow piles that remained along the road. The temperature in the cab was falling, and Chip was wishing he had worn a warmer jacket. Iver had no jacket and didn't seem to feel the chill. The April evenings were still cold, and Iowa had recently had a late-season snowfall.

"This is what we'll do," said Iver. "When we come to a deserted place, I'll shine my spotlight on the road leading to the homestead. I don't plow those places, so if we see tracks in the snow, we'll go take a look. If not, we'll just go to the next place. Check the flashlights in the glove compartment and make sure the batteries are working, we may need them. The first stop is the old Mattson place, been empty for years."

They reached the road. Iver shone his spotlight on the road. The snow on the road cast a silvery glow. No vehicle tracks. Iver had not plowed the road during the past winter.

"The next farm is Lance's place. He's in New York with Bridezilla. Supposed to be back tomorrow. Guess we should take a look around."

They drove up to Lance's house. All was still. They both took a flashlight and roamed around the yard. All the buildings were locked. They looked in a few windows. Nothing looked out of the ordinary.

"What's the next place?"

"Half a mile down the road is the old Swanson place. When Hal's father passed away, the missus moved into town. But it's not vacant. Coach rents it from her."

"Coach?"

"Ya, Coach Whittler. He teaches PE at the high school and coaches basketball and track."

"What's your opinion of him?"

"Kind of a hothead. I saw a ref throw him out of a game recently. He's had winning teams, so I guess the school puts up with his bad behavior."

Like the final pieces of a jigsaw puzzle, snippets of information rapidly started to come together in Chip's head. "Let's check out his place, I've got a bad feeling about that guy. If nothing else, maybe he can give us some more information about Ingrid. Let's radio Fredrickson from the cab."

They sat in the truck. Iver radioed Sharon at the police station and asked her to patch him through to the squad car. He handed the CB to Chip.

"Hold this down to talk and let it up to listen."

Chip held down the button to speak to Fredrickson. "Chief, Iver and I are at Lance's farm. We're not far from Coach Whittler's. I think we should pay a visit. What do you think?" Chip was hoping that Fredrickson could read between the lines. "You know, girls' basketball coach, team with blue uniforms."

"Got ya. Jim and I will head over there. You and Iver wait for us, hear?"

"Roger. Over and out."

"You ain't fooling me," said Iver. "You think Coach has something to do with the murders or with Ingrid being missing, don't you?"

"Call it crime writer's intuition, but yes, I don't like what I've been told about Whittler. Ingrid once mentioned he sometimes goes 'postal'."

Iver reached under his seat and pulled out a revolver and checked the barrel.

Chip was astonished. "Why in the world do you have a gun?"

"Use it for killing snakes. Last fall I got a six- foot bull snake, and once in a while I see a timber rattler."

Iver stuck it in the waistband of his jeans. "Not waiting. You with me or not?"Adrenalin rushed through Chip's body as they drove down the road, slowing as they approached the Swanson farm. Iver parked on the highway and got out of the cab, flashlight in hand. Chip followed.

The house was dark, except for light that outlined the edges of the blinds in the side window. The moon came out from behind a cloud giving them enough light to see. They crouched down and slowly made their way up the road and slipped into the barn. Once inside they turned on their flashlights and looked around, checking stalls.

Chip whispered. "Did Hal's father have dairy cows?"

"Yes, he had a small herd. The milk parlor is over there."

Chip went into a small side room. It was filled with old tin buckets and wooden stools and what he guessed to be milking machines. On the counter was a ledger book. He opened it and saw something all too familiar. Then he heard a scream echoing through the still night air. It was coming from the house.

Iver drew his gun. "You go around the front. I'll go to the back. Here, take this shovel." Iver handed an old manure shovel to Chip, and both men ran from the barn toward the house.

Chip reached the front of the house and slid along with his back to the wall until he reached a window. The blind obscured his view, but he could hear a man's voice yelling. "Shut up or I'll kill you just like all the other girls. Stupid FBI wants to pin this on my Elizabeth. I can't let them do that. I did all of this for her."

That was enough for Chip. Rage overtook him. He wielded the shovel at the window; the glass shattered, making a tinkling sound. He caught a glimpse of Ingrid tied to a straight chair and a man standing with a gun in his hand. He moved to the front door and bashed it in, repeatedly striking it with more power and vengeance then he had ever felt in his life. He stumbled through the splintered door.

He heard a click and then a blast. A searing pain tore through his upper chest. As he fell backward he heard another shot. Then all went black.

* * *

CHIP COULD NOT MOVE, could not open his eyes. His sense of smell was the first to return. He could smell a strong disinfectant, reminding him of someplace, but he couldn't quite place it. A cloying perfume invaded him. Was it the Chanel No. 5 his mother lavished upon herself? It was replaced by a clean smell. Irish Spring soap. Then flowers, roses, maybe.

Time seemed to float. He tried to remember what day it was, but couldn't. Was it day or night? He couldn't tell.

Then he began to discern sounds. A beeper like an alarm sounded and then ceased. He heard squeaky wheels, they needed oil. Whispers and hushed sounds, words he could not make out, most of them soft and soothing. One voice loud and commanding. Was it his father? What would he be doing here? Where was "here"?

Someone was moving him and every part of his body hurt. Was that his voice crying out in pain? His mouth was dry, his tongue felt swollen and fuzzy. He finally got out one word, "Water." A cool sponge was run across his lips and inserted in his mouth. He sucked its wetness.

"Chip, it's me. Jane. Don't try to talk, darling. You've been shot, a through and through, in your right shoulder and out your back. You also have lots of cuts from broken glass. I know you're in lots of pain, but the doctors say you are going to be fine. It's just going to take some time to recover. Your father's here at Mercy Medical Center in Des Moines, seeing that you have the best care possible."

He opened his eyes, but could not focus. He saw two Janes, then one, than two again. He couldn't keep his eyelids open. She gave him more water.

"Ingrid," he managed to utter hoarsely.

"Ingrid is safe. She's had quite an ordeal. No physical harm, but emotionally she's very fragile right now. She's going to need lots of comfort and support from us. She been up on Pediatrics, but I'm taking her home today."

He wanted to stay with Jane, but he could feel himself fading off to a dark place. He always liked it when she said the word "us." He wanted to take care of Ingrid with Jane . . . us, together taking care of both a daughter and a son.

* * *

CHIP, THIS IS YOUR FATHER. They are reducing the sedation. You will feel some discomfort. Don't try to move; just open your eyes. Your mother is here, too."

He was able to open his eyes and focus on his father's face. He turned his head slowly and saw his mother sitting in a chair by his bed. She was holding his left hand.

"Charles, it's Mother. We're so proud of you. You saved Ingrid and helped catch the Iowa serial killer. You've been so brave. Your father says you are going to be better in a few days. Jane is taking care of Callie and Runt, so don't worry about them. Just try to rest now."

He fought to stay with them, but the pain took him away again. So like his father to call it "discomfort," he thought as he drifted off.

* * *

HE WAS FULLY AWAKE AND ALONE. He could see a hospital room. He turned his head and saw monitors with lights and a squiggly line moving across a tiny screen. There were two IV poles and tubes running into his arms. His mind started to clear and he remembered being in a barn with Iver. Iver had a gun. There had been gun shots. It was all starting to come back to him. He had so many questions; he was hungry for answers. A nurse came into his room.

"Good morning, Mr. Collingsworth. My name is Lisa. I'm your day nurse. I'm going to give you your painkiller. There's a control by your left hand. Try pressing it."

He did. "Good. Just press that if you need me for anything. There's an FBI agent here who has been waiting to talk with you. Are you up to seeing her?"

Chip nodded in agreement. Agent Masterson entered.

"Chip, I've been told I can only stay for five minutes and that I shouldn't expect you to talk. I wanted you to know what happened. Okay?"

He nodded, and she sat in the chair beside his bed.

"I was wrong. Brown is not the serial killer. She is just a person with severe mental problems.

"Whittler killed all the girls. He confessed and told us where the last body was stashed. It was located in an abandoned sawmill in Sioux Falls. All five women, Tracy Trent, Melissa McCloud, Emily Carlson, Sara Stewart and Anna Redmond, the starting five, are now at rest. The five locations are matching up with past coaching jobs he had. Seems he was the Athletic Director of Intramurals at the University of Minnesota and Elizabeth was under him."

Masterson paused and offered Chip a sip of water, placing the bendy straw between his parched lips.

"He was infatuated with her, and blames the team for sending her away. When he heard on the news that we had detained her, he wanted to shift the blame away from her, so he abducted Ingrid."

"How were they killed . . . the five women?" Chip asked between painful breaths.

"Our preliminary reports say they were first sexually assaulted and then beaten to death . . . pretty gruesome."

"And Ingrid . . . was she . . ." The thought was too horrifying to say aloud.

"No, Ingrid was not molested or physically harmed, although she certainly had a traumatic experience. Whittler was holding her just to deflect our attention away from Brown and try to clear her of murder charges."

The agent rose from the chair. "We found the milk delivery forms at the farm and remnants of the blue jerseys. He's a very sick man who will spend the rest of his life in prison. I know you probably have lots of questions and want to know more details, but for now you just need to heal. Call me when you are ready."

Masterson left her card on his bedside table. She put her hand on his arm for a moment and then quietly slipped out of the room
.

* * *

OVER THE NEXT FEW DAYS Chip improved. He was able to sit up in bed and began a diet of consommé and Jello cubes. His right arm was immobilized, so he was struggling to balance the Jello on a spoon using his left hand, when Chief Fredrickson arrived. The chief stood by Chip's bed and removed his hat.

"Chief, no one has told me about Iver. What happened? Is he okay? Was he shot, too?"

"Nah, he shot Whittler in the knee, busted it all to hell. He was untying Ingrid when Jim and I arrived. He's outside waiting to see you. Seems they only let one of us in at a time." The Chief started to laugh.

"What's so funny?"

"You two, you and Iver." He shook his head. "The minute you said 'Roger, over and out' on the radio, I knew you two were going to go Hollywood on me and do something stupid. Didn't I tell you not to do anything foolhardy?"

"Yes, Iver asked, 'Are you with me or not?' and I guess I flipped into crime fighter or cowboy mode. Did you know he carries a gun?"

"Sure, I issued the permit to him. It's for shooting snakes and other varmints. I didn't expect him to use it on a serial killer. Now he's a national hero. He was even on *Good Day USA* with Amy Chang. It's his turn next; I'll let him tell you all about it."

"Wait, why did Whittler send you those clues?"

"You and Jim were right, serial killers sometimes want to be stopped or want media and police attention. I think Whittler really wanted to be caught, even before he found out Masterson was detaining Brown."

The chief replaced his hat and gave Chip a little wave as he exited. Next Iver walked in looking uneasy; his usually ruddy face was pasty.

"I don't like hospitals. People are sick here."

"Yes, I remember when you had to take Mabel to Mayo. Fill me in, Iver, what happened at the Swanson place?"

"Shot that bastard. Sorry I didn't get my gun off before he shot you. Man, there was so much blood around that place, made me weak, almost lost my pork chops. Poor little Ingrid, she was hysterical. I don't want to play that scene again . . . ever."

"The milk delivery forms . . . Masterson said they found them in the barn," said Chip. "That's when I knew for sure Whittler was the killer."

"Ya, I guess that form was what you crime writers would call a red herring. The killer wasn't a milk truck driver, after all. Whittler just used the forms to throw off the authorities."

"But we did it, Iver, we got that bastard. You with a gun and me with a manure shovel."

"Yup, we sure did." They both grinned.

* * *

OVER THE FOLLOWING TWO WEEKS, there were lots of calls, cards and visitors, including TV reporters. There was also another round of surgery to remove bone fragments and lots of therapy, physical and occupational. Chip even had a few sessions with a shrink to emotionally process the trauma.

He had just returned from a walk to the nurses' desk and back, when Lance and Lucinda arrived. Lucinda was carrying a floral arrangement as big as a bushel basket.

"My God, Lucinda, I got shot. I didn't die. That looks like something for a coffin. How the heck are you two and where have you been?"

Lucinda stuck out her left hand. Next to the diamond engagement ring was a wide platinum band. Lance presented his left hand to reveal a matching wedding band.

"You did it, and I missed it."

"Don't feel bad, Chip. Everyone missed it, except for a New York Justice of the Peace and two witnesses that we didn't know," explained Lucinda. "The whole wedding thing was getting out of hand. I said 'just screw it, let's get married today,' and we did." The new bride was blushing and the groom was beaming.

"How did you resolve the New York-Turners Bend issue?"

"Lance came up with a wonderful solution. First, he is going to build us a new house in Turners Bend, then hire a caretaker to live in the old house and watch the farm when he's in New York with me. During the growing season I'm going to telecommute from Turners Bend. The agency went along with it because you're my biggest client. Then during the winter, we are going to split our time between my New York apartment and our new condo in St. Thomas. It was a little wedding present we bought for ourselves."

"Sounds idyllic, except for the times you'll be in my backyard to hound me about writing." Chip laughed, but truthfully it wasn't that funny to him.

"Now, what about you and Jane?" asked Lance.

Chip shook his head and sighed. "That's the million dollar question. I don't know about us. Love can be murder."

* * *

HE COULDN'T USE A KEYBOARD and he couldn't write with his left hand. With lots of time to think about finishing *Mind Games*, his creative juices began to flow, as did his frustration with not being able to capture his ideas. His mother came up with the solution.

"Why don't you use a digital recorder like your father uses for dictation? This hospital must have lots of people who can do transcription. I bet one of them might be eager to make some money on the side."

Before Maribelle left for home, she had purchased a digital recorder for Chip and found a woman to transcribe his recordings. Recording his punctuation was a challenge, but he quickly learned to say "quotes," "end quotes," "new paragraph," "next sentence in italics."

"Mom, you're brilliant. I may totally give up keyboarding and do this permanently," said Chip when his mother made her final visit.

"Thank you, dear. A mother needs to hear some praise from her children occasionally," said Maribelle. "I know you and your father think I am an air-head sometimes, but I'm more than capable of intelligent ideas. I'm happy the dictation is working out for you."

"I'm sorry I underestimated you. I think I've learned my lesson, and I hope you know how much I really love you."

She kissed him on the forehead before leaving. "See you soon. I think your father and I will come for the Fourth of July parade again this year. It was such fun."

Left alone, he re-read his last few chapters. Lucinda had printed them and brought them to him in the hospital, along with a few choice words to urge him to get back to work. One storyline had been resolved, now he would have to decide how to wrap-up the other. His experience at being shot gave him some ideas on how to up the tension . . . now to decide who was going to be brought down with a bullet.

CHAPTER FORTY-TWO

Mind Games
Boundary Waters Canoe Area, Minnesota
Early August

THE FIRELIGHT REFLECTED off the fresh blood seeping around the zip ties that dug into Dr. John Goodman's wrists. It seemed like every muscle in his body ached, but his shoulders and head bore the brunt of the pain. He directed his gaze to his captor sitting on the other side of the fire pit, seeing him through his good eye. His left eye was swollen shut, courtesy of Dennis Farley.

In order to keep him from escaping, Dennis had given John the task of carrying the two-person canoe whenever they were on land. Each time they reached shore, he would tie John's hands to the yoke, and force him to hoist the boat up onto his shoulders, at which point Farley would put the pack with their camping gear on his own back. As they reached the last lake front, John had patiently waited for Dennis to be distracted and then swung the canoe around, aiming to hit his captor in the head.

Unfortunately, Farley saw the boat come his way just in time and ducked, and John lost his balance. Dennis caught the canoe just as it was about to smash into the ground and steadied it. Once they were back in the boat, with John tied in place, Farley smacked John in the head with the paddle. "That'll teach you to be a hero, Goodman. If you try a stunt like that again, I'll shoot you and leave you for bear bait. Jo won't find a trace of you."

John's vision wavered for the rest of their journey across the lake. By the time they reached the shoreline, he couldn't see out of his left eye at all and his head felt like it would burst. Farley pulled John up to the clearing on shore and left him tied up while he went back to retrieve their gear.

John was wet and exhausted. It seemed like every square inch of skin was either scraped or inflamed with mosquito bites. He just wanted to lie down and sleep forever. The only thing that kept him awake was the knowledge that Jo was on her way.

So, as he sat by the fire, he kept his good eye on Farley and watched, waiting for his chance.

Unfortunately, his wrecked body had other plans and John had just about dozed off when he heard Farley moan. He saw his captor wince and reach up to massage his temples. Dennis dug into his pack for a bottle of ibuprofen and shook out a few in his hand, swallowing them without the benefit of a drink of water to wash them down. John tilted his head. It was the fourth time since they had set up camp that the man had taken pain meds. *Could the NeuroDynamics' microchip be causing the head pain?* If so, it might provide him an opportunity to escape.

John knew from working on the NeuroDynamics case the microchips had been implanted on the victims' Circle of Willis, the ring of arteries in the brain where aneurisms generally occurred at weak spots. Farley was the only survivor of the microchip technology; all the others had died of burst vessels in their heads. If John could somehow increase the blood pressure in Farley's head, he might be able to incapacitate him. He had to figure out a way to increase his stress level.

John lay down on the cold ground, stretching out as much as possible given that his hands and feet were bound. He finally drifted off to sleep, schemes rolling around in his head like a lullaby.

He had no idea how long he slept, but woke up to the screech of a bald eagle overhead. From the position of the sun in the sky, he guessed it was mid-morning. He jerked his head up and looked around in time to see Farley walking toward him.

"She's here," Dennis said.

John sat up with a grunt. His body was sore and every muscle protested. But his mind alternated between horror and happiness that Jo was here. At last.

* * *

JO STEPPED ONTO THE SHORELINE and pulled the canoe up on land. When she saw the bright blue tent through the stand of evergreens, she reached into her pack and pulled out her Glock. She crept along the narrow trail leading to the site. The first thing she saw was John sitting by the fire pit, looking battered. In spite of all his injuries, he was the best-looking sight she had seen in a very long time and she felt the smile spread across her face.

Jo wanted to run to him, to check every bone, every bruise, but she knew she had to be wary. Dennis Farley couldn't be far away. She had to think about what trap he would have set for her. She swept her gun, back and forth, looking for John's captor.

She stopped on the other side of the fire from John. He stared at her, as if she were an apparition. Finally, his face broke out into a wide grin. After a moment, though, the smile faded and he turned his head slightly.

A movement behind him caught her eye. Farley stepped out of the brush and had a gun pointed at John. "Welcome to our adventure, my love. I trust you had a safe journey?"

The bile rose in the back of her throat at the term of endearment, but she ignored it. She aimed her gun at John's captor, and said, "Now that I am here, what do you have planned?"

Dennis Farley shook his head and chuckled, "I've always admired your spunk and candor. You certainly don't beat around the bush."

He lowered his gun to the back of John's head and said, "Before we get started, though, I think perhaps you should throw away that gun of yours. Behind you."

Jo tried to keep the disappointment out of her face. With the weapon trained on John, she dared not disobey. She turned and tossed the Glock into the woods.

Dennis said, "Very good. Now I will answer your original question. I intend to prove to you once and for all that you belong with me and that this . . ." He walked over to stand next to John and pointed his gun at him. "This man doesn't deserve you."

Not taking her eyes off Farley, she cleared her throat which had suddenly threatened to close and said, "And I suppose you think you do?"

Farley shrugged and said, "But of course. Now, since you are so curious, I will explain just what I have in mind for the rest of our time here."

Dennis flipped off the safety of his gun and pointed it at John's leg and pulled the trigger. Before Jo could yell "stop", John was writhing on the ground in front of the fire, screaming in agony.

Jo was about to run over to where John lay on the ground, but Farley stopped her by saying, "Don't come any closer or I will shoot a more vital organ of his body." He waited patiently as Jo halted. Her instinct was to leap across the fire and tackle Farley, but she knew by the time she could get close enough to him, he would fire another bullet into John. She clenched her teeth, waiting for his next words.

She didn't have to wait long. "As I was saying, here's what we're going to do. We're going to load your boyfriend into the canoe and shove it out onto the lake. I will leave him with a day's supply of water and food. If you agree to the rest of my plan, then I will contact the local authorities to come to his rescue."

Jo found she couldn't take her eyes off of the gun pointed at John's head. "And, just what is the rest of your plan?"

"You and I will take the other canoe and make our way to the Canadian border. Once we are there, we will move to a country of our choosing and live out the rest of our lives as man and wife."

Jo's eyes widened at the lunacy of his plan. "What makes you think I wouldn't kill you the first chance I get?"

"Well, at first I'll just have to be extra cautious, won't I? You will be tied up or locked up while you remain a threat to me. But, given enough time together, I'm sure you will come to see we are meant to be together and none of that ugliness will be necessary."

"You are insane, you know that?"

Farley's face turned stony. "Show a little more respect to your future husband."

As if I would ever marry a bat-shit crazy man like you. Jo stopped herself from saying the words out loud, when she saw the gun waver closer to John's temple. *Easy, Schwann, easy.*

Jo looked around quickly, desperate to find something she could use as a weapon. Her eyes landed on a narrow log, about the length of her arm, smoldering in the fire pit.

Averting her eyes, she forced a subservient tone into her voice, and said, "Can I least bind his wound before we leave? At least give me that."

Farley rubbed at his temple with his hand still gripping the gun. He was silent for a moment and, in spite of the tightness in her chest as she glanced down at the blood soaking John's pant leg, she waited for his response.

When he spoke, his voice was flat. "There's an extra shirt in the bag at my feet. You can use that to slow the bleeding. But don't mistake this for empathy. I wouldn't want him to bleed out before he's served his purpose in motivating you. And don't forget I have a gun pointed at him."

"Thank you." Jo skirted the fire pit and knelt next to John. She considered reaching for the narrow log, but decided she needed to attend to John's injury first. Pulling out the shirt, she quickly wrapped it as tight as she could around the wound. She heard John's sharp intake of breath when she tied off a knot and felt his eyes on her. She stole a brief glance at his face and gave him a small smile.

John's face was ashen and he was sweating profusely. For the first time since she had first stepped into the camp, John spoke. His words were halting and she could tell he was struggling not to pass out, but he said, "Farley, you seem to be having a lot of problems with headaches. Not feeling too much . . . too much stress, I hope."

Jo started. John was obviously trying to tell her something. He wouldn't purposely taunt Farley this way. *Think. What is he trying to tell me?*

And then, it hit her. Farley was the last test victim of NeuroDynamics to survive. He was showing signs of severe headaches, which meant he could be headed for an aneurism. *Stress . . . John said stress. He's trying to tell me that if we can raise Farley's stress level, he might be stopped.*

She thought quickly. Her plan was a terrible risk, but they were out of options. She stood up. "I'm not going anywhere with you. You are a piece of shit, not even a real man. You think you could ever satisfy me?"

Farley's face turned beet red. "Wha . . . ? Don't fuck with me."

Jo thought about grabbing the gun out of his hands, but even with his recent weight loss, he still had a good seventy pounds on her at least. She got into his face, and doing her best to ignore the gun in his hand, she poked him in the chest. "You aren't half the man John is. Take a look at him. He's strong, handsome. And smart. Everything you could never be."

Dennis Farley's face transformed into a mask of fury. His normally pallid skin was splotchy and his eyes blazed with hatred. He spat out the words, "I will kill . . . I will kill him slowly and make you watch. Then I will take you with me."

"I'd like to see you fucking try, you coward."

Farley roared. He aimed a vicious kick at John's wounded leg, causing John to scream in pain. Farley pointed at John, who was now huddled on the ground. He said, "You think that's bad? I can make him suffer in ways you can only imagine. You WILL come with me."

Jo's knees threatened to buckle as she watched John writhing in pain. *I might as well be the one kicking him. I can't keep this up much longer . . . I can't keep watching him suffer.*

Jo was about to give up when she saw Dennis grimace and clutch his head. *It's working. His head must be killing him. I have to try again. God help us if this backfires.* "You and I are not going to happen. Ever!" Jo exclaimed.

Jo's heart stopped when she saw Farley raising the gun to John's head once more. She realized her gamble had backfired. She had provoked him into killing John. Jo would never forgive herself.

At that moment, Dennis squeezed his eyes shut, as if in unbearable pain. Out of desperation, Jo seized the opportuniity to reach down to grip the charred log with both hands. The embers along the wood seared her palms and she let out a startled yelp, but managed to hang on to it in spite of the pain. She swung the piece of firewood like a Louisville Slugger and it connected with Farley's chin.

The kidnapper roared in pain and staggered back with the blow, trying to regain his footing. For one fearful moment, Jo thought she had failed.

Just as she reared back to take another swing, she saw Farley's face collapse upon itself and he dropped like a stone at her feet. His eyes rolled up into the back of his head and he was still.

John said, "Is he really dead? I think that hit of yours must have finally caused the aneurysm to burst."

Jo kicked his weapon out of Farley's hand and checked for a pulse. Even when she couldn't detect a heartbeat, she kept picturing him springing up to shoot John. In Jo's mind, Dennis Farley had become the boogeyman and could never truly die. Finally, she felt John's hand at her elbow and she turned to him.

Being careful of his wound, she knelt next to him and removed his restraints. She wrapped her arms around him. He murmured words of love and comfort into her ear, but it took a few minutes more before she actually heard them. And then she was crying into his chest.

CHAPTER FORTY-THREE

Des Moines, Iowa
April

CHIP SAT IN A WHEELCHAIR in his hospital room waiting for the hospitalist to discharge him. He didn't need the chair, but it was hospital policy—all patients were taken to patient pick-up in a wheelchair, whether they could walk or not. Out the window of his room he could see a flower bed with yellow tulips. Spring had finally come to Iowa. It was late by Eastern standards. Back in Baltimore flowers and trees would be in full bloom, and it was Cherry Blossom Festival time in DC. He missed those early springs, but not much else about his former life. What he had missed in the past two weeks was Turners Bend. He missed Callie and Runt and his friends. Most of all he missed Jane. She was coming to retrieve him from Mercy Memorial and drive him home. The doctor arrived with papers in hand.

"Morning, Mr. Collingsworth. Here are your discharge orders and your prescriptions. I've faxed your PT plan to the clinic in Ames. You'll need rehab twice a week until you have better mobility in your right arm. I'm sorry to tell you your dreams of becoming a major league baseball pitcher are over, but you should eventually be able to do most things. You shouldn't have any trouble keyboarding." He handed the papers to Chip. "By the way, my wife read *The Cranium Killer* and *Brain Freeze*. She wanted me to tell you I'm not unlike Dr. Goodman. Those were her words, not unlike."

"And in my dreams I'm not unlike Ernest Hemingway," said Chip. Both men laughed.

A pert candy striper with a name tag that read EMILY wheeled Chip down to the door. She couldn't have been more than sixteen, and she reminded him of Ingrid. He said a silent prayer than her innocence wouldn't be marred like Ingrid's had been. He recalled Jane had used that "us" word again when talking about Ingrid's need for emotional healing. He wanted to help Ingrid. She was beginning to feel like a daughter to him.

"Could we wait outside? I haven't had any fresh air for two weeks."

Emily pushed the wheelchair outside and locked the brake. He sat basking in the mid-afternoon sun, letting its heat warm his face. He closed his eyes and inhaled the scents of spring. He heard a vehicle approach and opened his eyes expecting to see Jane's truck. Instead it was Jim in Turners Bend's squad car. His heart sank as Jim hopped out and opened the back door on the passenger side of the police car.

"Jane called and asked me to fetch you home. She had an emergency call, something about a breach calf out at Hjalmer Gustafson's place."

"Thanks, Jim, seems like Hjalmer has a lot of calving problems." He got into the car and felt like a caged criminal as he looked through the barrier between the front and back seats.

"Sorry about that, Chip. Police regulation, you know, no one can ride up front with an officer. I'll have you home in no time."

As soon as they cleared the Des Moines city limits and headed north on I-35, Jim turned on the lights and sped toward Ames. He exited the freeway and headed west to Turners Bend. When he turned off the highway and approached the town, he switched on the sirens. Instead of continuing through town and out to Chip's farm, he pulled into a spot outside the Bun.

"Bet you haven't had a decent cup of coffee and a cinnamon roll in weeks. Let's make a quick stop before I take you home," Jim said.

"Look at all these vehicles; the café must be really busy today."

Jim held the Bun's door open for Chip, and as he entered, the patrons stood and clapped. Chip saw a banner running above the counter. It read: THANKS TO IVER AND CHIP, TURNERS BEND'S OWN SUPER HEROES. Chip could tell Bernice had gone all out in decorating the Bun. He had never seen tablecloths on the tables before, and real daffodils, not artificial ones, were in bud vases on every table.

He was overcome, the back of his throat filled up and his eyes stung as person after person shook his hand or patted him on the back. Ingrid wove her way through the crowd and gave him a long hug, tears sliding down her cheeks.

"Cinnamon rolls on the house," said Bernice, as she passed through the tables with a huge tray of hot rolls.

"Hey, where's Iver?" Chip had just noticed his crime-fighting partner was missing from the festivities.

"He and Chief Fredrickson were both here before you arrived, but they had to leave for an emergency. Seems a truck on the way from Perry to the poultry processing plant in Ames overturned out on State Highway 17. Lots of chickens broke out of jail, and it's a real mess with feathers flying all over the place," said Bernice.

"Wish I was there to see the two of them running around like chickens with their heads cut off," said Chip.

Suddenly he was very tired and felt weak. He sat for a while, drank a cup of coffee and ate a roll, then asked Jim to take him home. As they drove up his long driveway, he saw Jane's truck and his weariness floated away.

Jim opened the car door for him. "Looks like you have company," he said. "So I'll just get back to my public safety duties. Nice to have you home, Chip."

The back door of his house opened and Runt came barreling out. The dog barked and raced around him. Chip knelt down and Runt gave him a thorough face washing. Jane stood on the step, holding Callie and laughing, as Runt plowed Chip over onto the damp grass.

"What a welcome home, first all the people at the Bun, then Runt and best of all you," he said, as Jane took his hand and eased him off the ground, being careful of his injuries. "I thought you were off delivering a calf."

"I was, but I finished in time to stage a little surprise for you. Come into the house."

As he passed through the door, Chip heard the strains of Gershwin and spied the bottle of sparkling cider on the table, along with a bag of microwave popcorn. He also noticed her hair was down and she was wearing a close-fitting shirt, the one he remembered so well from the first time they made love.

"I tried to re-create our first night together, darling. It was magical. I had to replace the Chardonnay with cider, wine and pain killers are not a good mix. If you're up to it, I'd like to revisit that evening. She put her arms around him, and he felt her heat, as his began to rise.

He pulled away for a moment and gazed into her eyes. "And if I propose, will you say 'no' again?"

She moved back into his arms and whispered into his ear, "Try me."

* * *

OVER THE NEXT FEW WEEKS Chip's road to healing and his road to romance were smooth sailing. With the wind at his back he breezed through his physical therapy. Jane resolved her indecision about marriage and accepted his ring. He finished *Mind Games*. Lucinda and Lance had their first newlywed's spat. She was on Chip's back like fleas on a dog. She wanted him to blog and do interviews with the media and resume his book signings, all the things he hated about being an author. Lance was in the dog house, but somehow Chip felt like he was getting the worst of it. Some things never change.

CHAPTER FORTY-FOUR

Mind Games
Epilogue
Grand Marais, Minnesota
Early August

Dr. John Goodman woke up to the sounds of light snoring. Confused, he pried open his good eye and sat up in the bed. He looked across the room to see Jo sprawled out in the hospital room chair, sound asleep. He winced when he saw her hands bound in bandages, a result of the burns she received when she snatched the burning log out of the fire. The sunlight filtered in through the blinds and lit up strands of her red curls like flames. His heart felt lighter just being able to see her again. He grinned at her decidedly unlady-like snoring. Jo had had a rough couple of days and he was glad to see her rest at last.

He thought about all she had done, all she had sacrificed to rescue him. After Dennis Farley had died of the aneurism, she had re-dressed his gunshot wound and stoked the fire, making it easier to be located by air. Jo had told him about the trail she had left for the Bureau to find. An hour later, they were rewarded with the sighting of a sea plane which belonged to the BWCA ranger station. After the plane sidled up to the shoreline, Agent Daniels was the first to step out of the plane and helped load John aboard.

Jo finally fell into an exhausted sleep when they were on their way out of the Boundary Waters. During their flight, Daniels filled John in on all they had discovered about Farley and the extraordinary steps Jo had taken to save him.

"Knock, knock."

John looked toward the hall and smiled at Detective Frisco, who hovered in the doorway. "Frisco! What the hell are you doing here?"

The detective stepped into the room and pulled up a chair next to John's bed. When he sat down, he turned his head at the sound of Jo's snores and laughed. "Wow. She's really out, isn't she? Well, guess she earned it." He turned back toward John and said, "Just making sure the two of you are safe and sound. I heard some rumor that you managed to find some trouble, again."

John felt good being able to laugh along with Frisco. "Yeah, well. All in the day of the life a neurosurgeon, you know. How about you? In between naps, Jo filled me in on the case the two of you solved just before she had to come and rescue me." John shook his head. "What a shame. For everyone."

"You can say that again." Frisco shoved his hands in his pocket, and looking down at his feet, he said, "So, I really should be staying out of this, but . . ." The detective turned red.

While Frisco struggled with his thoughts, John said, "Mike. I think I know what you are going to say. You want to know what my intentions are toward Jo, right?"

Frisco grinned sheepishly and said, "Am I that obvious? She had a real rough time when you guys called it quits. Jeez, you would think I was her father or something . . ."

"I think you earned that right. You've been a terrific friend to Jo and I'm glad to know that you've got her back. But, here's the deal. I fully intend—" John said.

It was John's turn to be interrupted. "Yes, just what are your intentions, John? I'd be interested to know myself." Both men turned toward Jo. They had failed to notice she had woken up while they were talking and John wondered just how much of their conversation she had overheard.

John cleared his throat, his chest suddenly tight. Frisco stood up and said, "Um . . . now that I know you guys are still alive and kicking, I really should be going. I promised the wife that I'd stop in and check on her mother while I was up here. I'll be seeing you guys."

Jo got up from her chair and gave him a hug before he headed out the door. "Thanks for everything, Frisco. Don't know what I would have done without you these last couple of weeks," Jo said.

"Right back atcha."

Jo sat down in the chair Frisco had vacated. She carefully clasped John's hand and pulled it to her lips. "Glad to see you smiling again, John. I've missed you."

"Couldn't compare to how much I've missed you."

He looked at the bandages on her hands and said, "Do they hurt very much?"

Jo shook her head and said, "Not so much now. Leave it to you to ask me about a minor burn when you are the one who is in the hospital."

John said, "So, what's the latest verdict from the doctors in here? Seems like there's been quite a few, coming and going."

"The surgeon who removed the bullet from your leg said you should regain total use of your leg again. You might have a slight limp for a while, and physical therapy is going to be a bear, but he's pleased."

John pointed to his bandaged eye. "And what about this?"

"Your eye is healing nicely, and the swelling should be gone in another day or two, although you're going to have a heck of a shiner for awhile.

"The only thing keeping you here right now is that slight concussion you got when Farley whacked you in the head."

John smirked and said, "Good thing I have such a hard head, then."

Jo smiled back. "You can say that again."

He looked around the room. "So, when am I supposed to get out of here?"

Jo tilted her head, and then continued in a quiet voice, "Why, do you have someplace to go?" Her eyes were deep green and he knew what she was really asking from him.

John studied her and said, "Yeah. I do. I gotta get back to Baltimore, because I have a lot of packing to do. Caddy and I need to get settled here before the snow starts flying. I have a feeling I'll have to learn how to shovel snow."

Jo pulled back and her eyes grew wide. "You mean . . . you mean you are going to move here?"

"Yup. You got a problem with that?"

Jo shook her head, making her curls dance. A smile lit up her face. "And just when did you come to this conclusion?" Her smile faded a bit and her eyes narrowed. "It didn't have anything to do with your trip to the Boundary Waters, did it?"

"No, not at all. The minute Sally handed me that plane ticket to Minneapolis, I made up my mind. I realized what a total ass I'd been when things got complicated. Jo, I can do my job here as well as anywhere else. Hopefully, Minneapolis has room for another neurosurgeon. If not, maybe I can take up snow plowing."

Jo's laughter sounded wonderful to his ears. She swooped down and gave him a long, deep kiss. And all he could think about was waking up to her every morning for the rest of their lives.

EPILOGUE

Turners Bend
April

Hal Swanson slipped out of the bright sunshine into the dimly lit bar. He waited as his eyes adjusted and then scanned the interior of the Bend. It had been a while, but his old stomping grounds remained unchanged. Still the scarred tables, the scuffed floor, the tattered beer posters and the malty, smoky aroma reminded him of the days and nights when he moved from beer to the hard stuff.

It had been hours since his last drink and he felt edgy, his skin itching for alcohol. "A little hair of the dog would calm the nerves," he said to himself.

His physical appearance had changed in the past year. He had lost twenty pounds and grown a beard and mustache. His facial hair was darker than the hair on this head had been. That hair was gone and his shaved head was smooth and shiny.

The place was empty, except for the bartender. He was thankful it wasn't Joe, who would probably recognize him despite his changed appearance. The guy behind the bar was not someone he remembered.

"What'll you have?"

"Bourbon on the rocks. Make it a double."

"Sure thing."

The bartender put the drink in front of Hal, and studied his face. "You new in town?"

"Just passing through. Place is empty. Where is everyone?"

"Big doings over at the café. The owner of this place is over there. It's a celebration for two local guys . . . one of them just got home from the hospital. Maybe you heard about them. They captured the Iowa serial killer. Made the national news."

"You don't say." Hal lifted his empty glass. "I could use another double before I hit the road."

Hal downed the second drink, paid the tab and walked down to the Bun. He stood outside and looked through the window. The café was full of familiar faces. All seemed to be having a good time. He did not see his ex-wife or son, but he secretly watched as his daughter approached the crime writer and hugged him.

Hal knew the story, had followed it on the news. That guy may have helped Iver save his daughter, but that didn't change how he felt about him. The little creep screwed him and was probably screwing his wife. His gut began to boil. He vowed to be patient and wait for just the right moment. He stuck his hand in his jacket pocket and wrapped his fingers around the cold metal.

He glanced up and down the street, the same street that had been a bustling business center when he was a boy. The Bijou had been brought back to life, but there were still abandoned and boarded-up shops on both sides of Main Street. His eyes glimpsed a shadow in the window above the old butcher's shop, the apartment where Hans Mueller had once lived with his wife, Greta. He shook it off. Get a grip, Hal. You ditched those two hombres who were tailing you way back in Florida, there's no way anyone could have followed you to Turners Bend. Relax and keep focused on your target.

Book Group Discussion Guide

1. The Hunter is a stalker. Have you or anyone you know been stalked? What happened? How did it make you feel? Is tracing someone's whereabouts and activities on social media a form of stalking or not?

2. Both Lucinda and Lance and Jo and John are attempting long-distance romances. What are the challenges involved in a long-distance relationship? How successful do you think they can be?

3. Revenge is fueling the murders in both stories. How do you feel about "getting even" when you feel you have been wronged? Is it healthy or destructive?

4. Detective Frisco has made a job change for his wife's career. What makes a successful dual-career household? What are the pitfalls that can lead to failed relationships?

5. Maribelle Collingsworth finds it difficult to be the wife of a prominent husband and the mother of two successful sons. What advice would you give her?

6. In both Turners Bend and the Twin Cities, the characters have favorite eating places and foods. Where would you go for the best pizza? The best hamburger? The best hot roast beef/turkey sandwich?

7. The series titles, *Headaches Can Be Murder* and *Love Can Be Murder*, each have a bit of whimsy. If you were one of the authors, what fun name would you give to the third book?

Invitation to Book Clubs and Reading/Writing Groups:

We love meeting with groups, sharing our books and the story of how we became authors and a writing duo. If you would like us to attend one of your meeting in person, via speakerphone or skype, please contact us on our website, www.rauschanddonlonauthors.com